Her Pirate Heart

Lisa Ann Verge

About **HER PIRATE HEART**

A rousing swashbuckler . . . a wonderful read!"
--*RT Book Reviews*

"Sweaty, gritty and suspenseful. Don't miss it!"
--*Rendezvous*

"Verge is a tale-teller whose writing is stunningly real."
--*Affaire de Coeur*

WINNER "Best Swashbuckler of the Year"
--*RT Book Reviews*

Don't miss Lisa Ann Verge's other sexy, adventurous, historical romances!

The Celtic Legends Series: Boxed Set
TWICE UPON A TIME: Book One
THE FAERY BRIDE: Book Two
WILD HIGHLAND MAGIC: Book Three
THE O'MADDEN: A Novella

Romantic Journeys Collection: Boxed Set
HEAVEN IN HIS ARMS
HER PIRATE HEART
SING ME HOME
THE CAPTIVE KNIGHT

The Cabin Fever Series
ALONE WITH YOU: Book One
LOST WITH YOU: Book Two
TAKEN WITH YOU: Book Three

Also available--the Novels of Lisa Verge Higgins

THE PROPER CARE AND MAINTENANCE OF
FRIENDSHIP
ONE GOOD FRIEND DESERVES ANOTHER
FRIENDSHIP MAKES THE HEART GROW
FONDER
RANDOM ACTS OF KINDNESS
SENSELESS ACTS OF BEAUTY

CHAPTER ONE

Saint-Malo, France, 1693

Silence is the worst part of battle, Roarke thought, as he stared at the black expanse of the sea.

Standing on the stone ramparts of the old city, he listened to the lap of the tide rising. The wind whistled through the narrow streets behind him. The English had already destroyed a fort on one of the rocky outer islets, but they had halted their bombardment this evening. The moon had not yet risen so he could see nothing in the darkness, but he sensed with a growing restlessness that some other plan was afoot.

He prowled the northwest ramparts until by torchlight he spied a sentry hunched over the wall.

"At ease," Roarke said as the sentry startled.

"Have you seen—"

The sentry lunged. Roarke saw the flash of a dagger just as he felt the cold slice of steel in the fleshy part of his palm. He swerved to one side to avoid the next strike, and then swung out an arm to grab him. But this sentry was no brawny soldier—he was small, slight, and quick. Roarke caught nothing but air as the boy dashed in the direction of the next sentinel.

Damn it.

Roarke shot off after the boy, who was fast but shoeless. Soon he had a handful of the urchin's collar in his uninjured hand. He disarmed the fighter of his flashing dagger before the boy could inflict any more damage.

"Idiot." Roarke retrieved the offending weapon from the stones upon which he'd knocked it. "You'll alert the city for nothing."

"I know an English accent when I hear one." The boy struggled like a wild thing, landing sharp blows on Roarke's shins. "And I know my enemies are English!"

"Your commander is, too."

Roarke squeezed his fist to stop the bleeding. This was the second time today he had been mistaken for the enemy. The folks of Saint-Malo were a suspicious tribe in the best of times, and not every soldier knew that an Englishman had recently been elevated to commander.

Nobody trusted a traitor.

But the mention of his rank had the intended effect, for the boy finally went still. Roarke sensed the urchin's terror as the boy dropped his gaze. He supposed it was better to have an overanxious sentry than one who let the enemy slip by. But it galled him that despite his fluency in French, remnants of the Devon accent kept slipping through.

His mother was rolling in her grave.

He shook out his hand and gave the boy a good look-over. "How old are you, boy? Twelve? Thirteen?"

"What does it matter?"

"Answer me."

The boy's sharp jaw hardened. "I'm fifteen."

Roarke knew a bald-faced lie when he heard one. The urchin barely reached his chest in height. By the ease with which he'd lifted the imp by the scruff, the boy could weigh no more than a hundred pounds.

"If the English knew how badly this city was guarded," he muttered, "they'd have launched a full assault."

"I'm not green." The imp rubbed his upturned nose with the back of his sleeve. "I've been working on the sea all my life."

"A few years tarring hemp doesn't make you a soldier."

"Pirates don't waste their time tarring hemp," the boy countered. "They spend all their time shooting cannon and fighting."

The mention of cannon teased a fragment of

memory. He'd been observing the performance of each soldier during the earlier bombardment of the city. When and if he ever received his privateering papers from the French, he'd have to hire sailors for his new ship. There was no better opportunity to gauge a man's fighting skill than in the thick of a fray.

Now he remembered that he'd seen this boy loading cannon on the northern ramparts. Though the skinny boy had struggled with the sixteen-pound cannonballs, he could sight along it like a seasoned veteran.

He said, "You're far too young to be taking up a pirate's life."

"I'm a son of Saint-Malo, Englishman."

Roarke conceded the point. He'd traveled half the world to get to this city on the English Channel just for the Malouin sailors, who were bred, like this boy, for the sea. Still, this sentry was as scrawny as a feral cat. It dismayed him that the defense of an entire city depended on barefoot sailors and ragamuffins.

"Go home, boy." He flipped the boy's dagger and offered it up, handle first. "I'll take your watch tonight. I can't allow a bedraggled child guard the most vulnerable side of the fortifications."

"I can fight." The boy seized his dagger and raised the blade to the torchlight. "My knife sports a commander's blood."

A smarter brat would have left that truth unsaid, but Roarke understood where his brass came from. A young boy on a pirate ship would learn to be a scrappy fighter, sharp of teeth and nails, for someone this small would be the whipping boy of any crew. Some pirate crews treated their weakest no better than many captains of the British Navy.

He set that dark thought aside.

"That dagger-needle did nothing but scrape my skin. And I could have you whipped for using it against your commander."

"You should have identified yourself."

"You shouldn't have been as skittish as a woman."

"I'm not skittish, I'm *careful.* And I can't leave my post." The boy thrust his hands into the pockets of his loose breeches. The wind pressed his shirt against his bony shoulders. "The sentry paid me to take his place. I won't get the other half of what he owes me until he relieves me in the morning."

"You'll never see that coin. He's drinking it away in some tavern."

"I'll see that coin," he insisted. "I've got two bellies to feed."

Other street children, he thought. This pip was probably in one of the many gangs of youths that ran through the city. Roarke suppressed a sigh and reached into his pocket to pay the boy to return to safety.

Then a dog bayed. Its bark was high and thin, carried raggedly by the wind. Roarke went still and he felt the boy stiffen, too. The guard dogs of Saint-Malo were vicious beasts. Nights were usually cursed with the animals' barking, but the bombardment had cowed them into silence.

This dog sensed something coming.

He scanned the ocean, trying to discern the rocky shapes of the islets and their small forts, or the reefed sails of the English fleet, but the cloudy, still-moonless night obscured all form and color.

Then the wash of the sea on the sand changed rhythm and became choppy and short.

Beside him, the boy whispered, "Something's approaching."

"A ship," Roarke said, as a shape loomed into view, "and it's coming straight for—"

Then the world exploded.

Adriana felt her feet leave the ground as the blast hurled her into the air. A turret of flame thrust toward the sky, blinding her as she sailed backwards until she hit the opposite side of the ramparts. Stunned, she slumped onto the flagstones as explosion after explosion lit up the sky and the rank smell of sulfur singed her nose.

A hand slapped on her wrist. She was dragged bodily across the flagstones to the protection of the outer ramparts. She felt red-hot nails, bits of flaming cordage, splintered pieces of wood, and the shells of bombs bounce all around her, a fiery rain pelting her back and legs. The hem of her linen shirt sizzled then burst into flame. The same hand that had dragged her across the ground released her long enough to slap out the fire.

She shoved away those hands before they could get any closer to what no man must ever touch. The commander's head shot up in irritation. By the blaze of the flames, she finally saw his face clearly. He was younger than his voice had led her to believe. Black hair swept off his brow. He had a bend in the slope of his nose, and a light-eyed gaze that seemed to pierce through all her secrets.

Then, though her ears were numb from the sound of the explosions, she heard the undeniable roar of the ocean rising. He heard it, too, for he slung his arm over the ramparts, ducked his head down, and pinned her against the stone wall with his body.

"Hold your breath," he shouted. "The sea's com—"

The first wave crashed over the wall with a force that made her head judder against the stones. She gasped with the frigidity of it. She dug her fingers into the commander's shoulders as the torrent of water pulled on her body, trying to yank her into the current that sluiced down the rampart walkway. She could hear it making a roaring cataract down the stairs to the streets of the old city, but the current had no effect on the man. It was as if his big body was a stone in the midst of a raging river.

Her breasts pressed against his chest. She could feel her nipples, tugged free from their bindings when he dragged her across the flagstones, needling him.

I can't be caught.

She shoved her hands between them and pushed, even as a second wave washed over the ramparts.

"Damn it," he sputtered, seizing one of her flailing hands, "stop squirming."

"You're suffocating me!"

"Better than being drowned."

"I'll make it down the street before the next wave—"

"And be dragged through the glass and gravel."

"I can swim!"

"This isn't a tidal pool, boy."

Boy

He didn't know. He hadn't noticed. She seized a measure of relief for that as another wave washed over them. When it was done, he loosened his grip on her and hazarded a glance over the ramparts in the blinding light of the rising flames. She tried to skitter out from under him but he stopped her with the pressure of his knee. She clawed to lift her bindings over her chest. Debris still fell. Sections of burning sail drifted upon the chimneys of Saint-Malo, igniting flames on the rooftops. Windows of the houses lay gaping and open. A babble of panicked voices rose from the alley below.

"A fire ship." He barked a laugh and shot to his feet. "They couldn't destroy the walls with cannon. So they sent a ship full of explosives."

Her head ached and her body shuddered from the cold and she felt the pain of burns on the backs of her hands. She didn't really care what the English had sent against them. She just had to get away from this man.

She'd rather be killed in battle than discovered as a woman.

Another wave crashed against the walls but this time only spittle and sea-spray splattered over the edge. She took the opportunity to scramble to her feet and dart toward the stairs. She slapped a hand on the wall to stop her headlong skid on the seawater-slick stones.

"Yes, run home, boy," the commander shouted above the crackle of flames and the crash of waves against the ramparts. "Go home and tell everyone that the English have failed."

Then she looked back at the commander, haloed by golden fire, and remembered something her mother had once told her.

Beware the devil, she said, because he's not what you think.

The devil is beautiful.

CHAPTER TWO

Long ago, Adriana and her mother had lived in a modest merchant's house on the west side of Saint-Malo, a house of airy, high roofs and bright, golden light. Adriana remembered the sound of a soft, lilting voice reciting Psalms. She remembered the gleam of the furniture and the warmth of a crackling hearth. She remembered the brush of fine wool and linen against her skin, the way her mother's skirts whirled as she danced, and the weight of her own long hair brushing against her back.

She remembered soft kisses and tight hugs.

But these were less like remembrances than impressions, gentle feelings she had to scramble to invoke, and they were overwhelmed by two distinct memories.

The first was the day the news came of her

father's death at sea. Creditors had burst into their home, swarming through, stepping on her toys. In loud voices they had demanded their due, descending like vultures to devour a widow and orphan's peaceful existence. They scoured drawers for money, sent in rough men to seize the furniture, and then threw her and her mother out of their own home. Suddenly, she and her mother were forced to abide in a series of dark, cold hovels.

The second memory was on a day not long after her mother started inviting men into those dark hovels. The men did strange, noisy things to her mother that caused her to cry. After one of those sessions, her mother came out of that terrible room and took the dolls Adriana had saved from the old house. She seized her skirts, her ribbons, and the little child-sized corset Adriana had been so proud to wear. She tossed everything into the hearth fire and then came at Adriana with a razor.

A woman with no husband, no means, and no vocation had only one choice, her mother told her. But a boy had options.

Now, standing in the cold air in front of the smoking, ashy remnants of the last hovel she and her mother had shared—on the other side of town from that first lovely home—Adriana felt nothing but a sinking relief that her mother's worries and cares and troubles were finally over, and the hollow-eyed, rum-stinking woman her mother had become was now nothing but warm ashes, whirling up in the wind.

A ball of fur leapt onto Adriana's shoulder. She tumbled back to the harsh present, to the cold sunrise, to the smoky streets of Saint-Malo, and the feel of her pet on her back.

She raised her hand to scratch him. At least Chou-Chou had survived the chaos. She hadn't lost everyone she loved.

"Much good you were to me last night," she murmured, running his striped tail through her fingers, "when I was attacked by an Englishman on the ramparts."

Chou-Chou made a chirring noise as he dug his little claws into her scalp. She'd bought the lemur from a street thief in St. Mary's, Madagascar, when she was just a powder boy on her first voyage. He'd been with her ever since.

"Looks like we'd best get back to sea," she said, tilting her head so she could look into his eyes, as round and shiny as little gold coins. "I wager you won't mind returning to warmer climes, eh, Chou-Chou?"

Holding in tears, she turned away from the ruins and headed in the direction of the harbor. From what chatter she'd overheard, the battle of Saint-Malo was over. Unable to breach the walls, the English had retreated. That also meant that the uneasy amnesty she and all the other street urchins of Saint-Malo had enjoyed during the fighting would soon be over. The sooner she signed onto a ship, the safer she'd be from a prison cell.

At least stealing supper would be easy today. The streets of Saint-Malo were littered with slate, burned pieces of masts, cordage, and bobbing fruit and vegetables. Chou-Chou tumbled off her shoulder to seize an apple rolling about unclaimed, while she collected iron nails and other tidbits she might be able to sell in the square for a tidy profit.

In the higher city, the lingering odor of charred wood and sulfur permeated the air as she passed through the main entrance to the shoreline. Sail-makers, carpenters, and cordiers were conducting a brisk business with traders who sought to fix the damage to their ships anchored in the bay. Ships of all sizes were sailing in now that the English warships had retreated. Sailors worked small boats, unloading cargo. Bags of grain, bolts of Indian calico, unmarked barrels, crates of fish, and boxes of spices littered the beach. Everyone who worked the port knew the hour when it would rise to lap against the rampart walls.

Adriana squinted to try to identify the ships. Because the tide was low, they were anchored too far out for her to read their names on the bows. She counted a few wide-bellied merchant ships, with false cannon holes painted on their hulls. A few light frigates, several two-masted corvettes, and a number of large ships were hidden behind them. Glancing down the beach, she noticed cannon being loaded onto rowboats and several large groups of sailors gathered in clusters near the blackened city ramparts. The hilts of daggers gleamed dully against the knees of their jackboots, and they had skin of every hue.

Pirates.

Excellent.

Adriana strode in their direction and then nudged her way to the inner circle of one of the crowds. Chou-Chou yelped, leapt from her shoulder, and then scurried away to find a safe retreat until her business was done. Adriana listened to the men talking about which ships were looking for sailors. The names of the captains were impressive—Duguay-Trouin, Danycan, Boscher—all successful Saint-Malo privateers. She'd be happy to get a berth on any one of those ships.

Then she heard one other name. *Le Loup de Mer.*

Captain Wolfe.

Possibilities prickled through her. In the years before she'd returned to Saint-Malo to see her mother, she'd sailed the waters of the Indian Ocean where the Sea Wolf's name was spoken in whispers. This pirate's prizes included the head ship of the Great Mogul's fleet. While her last pirate ship had been careened in St. Mary's in Madagascar, Adriana had met some sailors of the Sea Wolf's ships. Some had lived off their booty for months.

What she wouldn't do to finally grasp that kind of security.

She strode to the group of men gathered around the Sea Wolf's foppish lieutenant. "Get out of my way, landsman." She pushed her way past a burly man and wedged herself in front of him. "Make way for a real sailor."

"Why you little whelp."

Her feet left the ground. She kicked back. Though her heel hit him hard, the man didn't flinch.

"Do you think you can worm your way in front of *me*," the man said in a too-familiar voice, "you stinking little rascal—"

"Gwynn?"

The man stopped shaking her. She twisted to glance over her shoulder and found herself eye to eye with a Welshman.

"Why if it isn't that little pip from *The King's Arse*— Ow!"

A well-placed kick opened Gwynn's fist. Adriana tumbled to the sand. Chou-Chou leapt on Gwynn's back and started to sink his teeth in his shoulder.

"Chou-Chou, stop!"

"Still got your sea-rat, I see." Gwynn clutched his shoulder as the lemur raced to her side. "I should have fed that creature to the sharks long ago."

"He served you well enough once," she said, "outside that alehouse in St. Mary's."

Gwynn's heavy beard split in a grin. "Aye, he did that—and me having a night of ale for not a *sou*. But look at you, lad. It's been a year and you've not grown an inch! We'll be calling you a dwarf before long and you know how suspicious we seamen are."

She knocked him in the belly. The blow had no more effect than to smudge his tarred leather jerkin.

"What are you doing here?" he asked. "I thought

you'd still be on *The King's Arse.*"

"I found a better ship—one that brought me here." She didn't tell him that she'd been gone for over three years and had a yearning to see her mother. "But you deserted that floating wreck a month before me. I thought you'd still be spending your booty on some piece of—"

"Booty!" He scowled. "That whoreson of a captain gave me a mouse's share of the takings. It lasted no more than a month. I boarded a corsair out of La Rochelle and made my way up the coast. I've been working these waters for months. It's wartime, so they're as rich as everyone said they would be."

"Looking to work for the Wolf?"

"You know damned well he's the richest. But steer clear, he ain't the kind for the likes of you."

She rolled her eyes. Gwynn warned her away from every pirate captain.

"Lad, think twice. In a rage, the Sea Wolf once killed half his crew, and then as a warning to the rest—"

"—cut the dead sailors' bodies to pieces to use as fish bait?" She rolled her eyes. "That's a tale told in the darkness to idiots."

"The dead sailors are sure wishing they believed it before they signed on."

"I'm no brainless sailor, nor a legless landsman. And there's not a man in Saint-Malo who can climb rigging faster than I can."

Laughter erupted around her and she realized

that everyone was listening. She scratched the white fur beneath Chou-Chou's chin and ignored them.

"This isn't a pirate ship," Gwynn warned. "It's a privateer—"

"No difference at all."

"A privateer captain can hire royal soldiers to keep us all in line. You're not too young to kiss the whipping post."

"You're just afraid that he'll hire *me* and not *you*."

He barked a laugh. "I'll worry about that when you finally grow into your breeches." His gaze fell upon the Breton horn protruding from Adriana's rope belt. "If you want a berth, at least show us your real talent. Play that horn of yours."

She didn't hesitate. She was welcomed onto *The King's Arse* because of her skill with the Breton horn. A sailor who knew music had an advantage. Being so small meant she needed every advantage she could get.

She pulled the thin wooden horn from her waistband. The horn used to be smooth and well-oiled, a sleek piece of workmanship given to her by her mother in better days. Now it was bleached and pocked from wear, but none the worse for playing. At the sight of it, Chou-Chou sat at Adriana's feet with his striped tail wrapped around his neck, watching the horn in fascination.

The high, reedy sound quieted the tumult around them. Soon all the sailors were tapping their feet, and not much long after, two men began to step lively and dance. Another one twirled into the crowd and pretended to be a woman. Fluttering his eyes and pressing his chest together to form a sort of cleavage, he pursed his lips and danced with his legs tightly closed, making everyone roar with laughter.

Then she thought of her mother, teaching her this song in the quiet warmth of their sunroom so long ago, and a sudden sadness swelled in her breast.

The music died in her heart, and on her lips.

She shoved the horn under her rope belt, only noticing vaguely that the men had stopped dancing and tapping their feet long before she'd stopped playing. In the growing silence you could hear the wind moaning over the ramparts.

"I was playing a jig, not a funeral march," she snapped, glaring at them. "You're acting as if you'd seen the devil himself."

Only then did she feel a prickling at the back of her neck and realize someone new had arrived.

She took a deep breath and faced him.

The commander did not look nearly as dangerous in the bright of day as he had by torchlight. The southeast wind blew his hair away from his sun-bitten face, revealing eyes the color of the sea. She felt that breeze flattening her shirt against the linen bindings underneath. It had to be her imagination that his gaze seemed to pierce her as easily as the wind. To the men behind her she knew they saw nothing but a rag of a boy, but in front of this man she felt, oddly, like a woman.

"Ah, an Englishman," she said, not liking the feeling. "Scum seems to settle here at low tide."

The silence thickened. She expected Gwynn, at least, to laugh at her quip. Certainly these sailors didn't fear this land-loving soldier. Certainly this man was nothing but some young, rebellious English aristocrat who happened to be in Saint-Malo during the bombardment. He was commander no more, since the battle was over. Her gaze traveled over his rich attire: well-polished boots, thin-legged culottes, and a finely-fitted burgundy coat. He was dressed like one of the rich bourgeois that the sailors scorned so much.

Why did they stand behind her, paralyzed and mute?

The answer came to her as swiftly as the blood that rushed to her wind-stung cheeks.

"Perhaps you have the courage of a man," the Sea Wolf said in a low voice. "Or maybe it's the brashness of a foolish boy."

There was no backing off now. "A bit of both, I'd wager."

"I don't allow the spineless on my ship." His eyes glittered. "But I will hire mouthy boys who can shoot cannon and play music—provided they learn to temper their tongues."

Her mind tumbled over itself. Did the notorious Captain Wolfe just ask her to sign onto his ship?

His gaze fell to the lemur now curled around her leg. "I suppose you'll want to bring that creature aboard?"

"I won't leave without him."

A strange half-smile curved his lips. "How easily you risk my offer."

"Chou-Chou is all I have." She wished she could bite back the words the moment they left her mouth. "That," she added swiftly, "and my Breton horn."

One dark brow lifted. "Chou-Chou?"

Hesitant laughter gurgled among the sailors.

"I didn't name him," she lied, for her mother had called her that endearment in better days. "And it's too late to change it for that's all he'll answer to."

In the silence that stretched, once again she had the strange feeling that those gray-green eyes could see through the linen of her shirt and bindings to what she'd hidden from the world since the summer of her sixth year.

"Be here before the drums beat at sunrise." Captain Wolf raised one brow. "The first thing you'll have to do on board, boy, is prove that you can climb the rigging faster than any other of my crew."

The captain's ship, *L'Aventure,* nosed its way out of Saint-Malo the next day. With only the mainsail billowing above him, the pilot steered past the islets and hidden rocks that littered the shallow water just beyond the city. Adriana watched the color of the sea turn from blue-green, to a darker, opaque blue-gray. Then, reaching the open channel, she joined the crew in unfurling all the snowy white sails of the three-masted frigate until the wind caught them and propelled the ship over the waves.

Though the sun shone bright on the water, the wind was cold. Wrapped in the coarse woolen coat she had bartered for during her last moments in Saint-Malo, Adriana could hardly believe her good fortune. The frigate held twenty-six guns and weighed well over 250 tons. It was one of the finest fighting vessels she'd ever been on. As she pulled the rigging according to the bosun's orders, she took stock of the other sailors. The crew was a motley mix of French, Irish, and dark-skinned Africans. She could tell that they were the most experienced of pirates by the way they set effortlessly to the bosun's commands.

Chou-Chou pressed close to Adriana's legs for warmth. She had fashioned a new harness for the lemur out of pieces of cordage found in the Saint-Malo streets. In the harsh northern seas, Chou-Chou could easily be swept off deck by a wave in a storm. To prevent this, she had attached a leash to the harness and tied it beneath her cloak at her waist. This allowed the animal some freedom but kept him safe.

The ship surged forward as the wind billowed its sails. They had escaped the land and now felt the full force of the northeasterly winds.

"Pretty, isn't she?" Gwynn came up behind her and squinted at the sails. "It's like looking up a harlot's skirts."

"More sail than ship," she said. "She'll be easy to

maneuver."

"Especially around all those heavy-laden merchantmen."

"Laden with pounds sterling, I hope. The sooner we get our portion the better."

"Don't expect anything soon. The English are still out there. They'll probably guard any ships coming in or out of the Channel for the next few weeks."

"Soon enough, the Channel will be open again. A few days won't matter."

"Aye, but I hear the Sea Wolf doesn't have patience, lad."

"Isn't that a good thing?"

She didn't hear Gwynn's answer above the shouted orders to twist the sails to port. Adriana pulled on the rigging for the main yardarm, the rough hemp dug into her cold hands. She glanced up at the forecastle and saw the captain—Captain Wolfe. He hadn't said another word to her since he'd taken her on. That was a blessing, for his eyes were unnervingly sharp. She'd hoped to be treated like any common sailor, far below his notice.

As if he sensed her stare, the captain suddenly turned toward her.

"Joubert!"

She startled, released hold of the hemp, and ran over the planking to the base of the forecastle with Chou-Chou at her heels. From this angle she couldn't help but notice the captain's powerful legs and the width of his chest stretching above his waist.

Silly things to notice on a man who had the power to lay bloody stripes on her back.

She stopped at the base of the stairs. "Yes, sir!"

"You climb rigging faster than anyone on this ship, eh?"

"Better than anyone," she said, gesturing to her pet, "except him."

"Not shy, are you?"

"Modesty doesn't put food in my belly."

"Or wool on your back, yes?"

She stayed silent as she contemplated his remark. He must have seen her on the shore bartering with a ragman for this coat. She'd driven a hard bargain, but in the end, the ragman had relented. A boy needed to show some nerve to be respected by a man.

"Look at this boy, Drake," the captain said to the lieutenant standing by his side. "He's got the mouth of a street thief and the eyes of an orphaned child."

"Scrawny little creature." The lieutenant wrinkled his patrician nose. "His bones would crack with one hit of the lash. How are you to discipline him? Spank him?"

"I suspect," she interrupted, "that you'll discipline me like any other sailor on board, sir. I am being paid like any one of them."

"Then prove yourself." The captain gestured to the top of the mainmast. "Hie up to the crow's nest, and keep your eyes open for sails."

"Aye, aye, sir."

She tied Chou-Chou's harness more tightly around her waist. She stopped at a barrel of pitch, dipped her fingers into it and rubbed the sticky black tar over her hands. Then, taking a deep breath, she leaped onto the main rigging. Chou-Chou jumped off her shoulder and landed on the webbing just above her. She followed his quick, agile steps up the first stretch of rigging until they reached the midpoint of the mast.

Her heart beat furtively in her breast, but she did not rest. Clutching the thick hemp of the rigging leading to the crow's nest, she quelled the queasiness of her stomach and wedged her feet in the webbing. Mimicking the lemur's confident, unerring steps, foot over foot, hand over hand, half-suspended in the wind, she ran ever upward. As the rigging narrowed, her steps became smaller and quicker until she clutched the floor of the crow's nest. Pulling herself inside, she wrapped her legs around the main topgallant mast. She wished she could see the captain on the forecastle, but the ship's fore-end was hidden by the square foresails. So instead she waved at the sailors watching below. Through the whistling of wind she heard cheers of approval.

A few more moments like this, she thought, and the suspicion that I'm a girl will never pass their minds.

Chou-Chou clung to the tip of the mast just above her. She reached up and scratched his chin. He crawled into the space between her belly and the mast, and she folded him inside her cloak. "That wasn't so bad, Chou-Chou," she whispered. "It couldn't be any worse than the trees you used to climb in Madagascar."

The lemur shivered in response.

Clouds had already obscured the morning sun and the north-northeast wind howled in the timbers of the ship. The three masts, loaded with sails, bent precariously leeward. If Adriana were to fall, she knew she would miss all the sails and rigging and drop directly into the churning gray sea. She scanned the foggy gray horizon. The yardarms creaked below her as the master ordered them adjusted according to changes in the wind. The sea grew rougher and the frigate began to sway up and down with the motion of the water.

An hour passed before she saw a sail.

At first it was only a shadow on the horizon, easily mistaken for a cloud, but as the ship moved closer, she discerned the distinctive pattern of sails for a three-masted frigate. Rising to her knees on the platform, she yelled down to the deck.

"Sail! Sail! Off the starboard side."

She heard a burble of voices below. She squinted toward the sails until she had no doubt of what she saw, then, ignoring the lean of the mast and the wind that buffeted the rigging, she released Chou-Chou and scuttled down the rigging until she landed upon the solid wood of the upper deck.

"Where's that sail?" The lieutenant named Drake

stared with impatience off the starboard side.

"Two o'clock." She rushed to the gunwale and pointed toward the shadow. "It's a frigate, low in the water."

Drake barked orders so the bow of the ship turned. Filled with wind, the sails soon made *L'Aventure* cut a frothy wake.

"It's a frigate, all right."

Captain Wolfe came up close behind her. With a start, she realized she had been gazing at the frigate instead of manning her post at the mainmast rigging. She started toward her post but the captain slapped a hand on her shoulder to stop her.

"You have sharp eyes." His long woolen cape flapped in the breeze. It mocked the elements, for it exposed his entire body from neck to toe. "Keep an eye out for any other ships that might be guarding."

She focused her gaze on the horizon though her mind was focused on him, tall and steady, standing just at her side.

"The frigate has a fractured foremast," she stuttered.

"Which is why it is trailing behind," the captain murmured.

"Trailing behind what?"

"The rest of the English fleet."

Her blood ran colder than the sea-spray that splattered over the bow of the ship. Her mind balked at what he had said. He couldn't possibly be considering engaging the English fleet, even if the ship they could see was hobbled.

Then Adriana saw another shadow on the horizon. "There's a second ship."

"The boy is right." The lieutenant strode up to join them, raising a glass to his eye. "It's moving faster than the first."

Captain Wolfe swiveled on one boot and headed back up the stairs to the forecastle and the lieutenant followed, talking in low tones.

She returned, summarily dismissed, to her post.

"Didn't I say as much?" Gwynn said. "The Sea Wolf is not a patient man. He'll attack the first prize he sees."

"Gwynn," she whispered, "this ship isn't a merchantman."

She closed her mouth, unwilling to voice the full of her suspicions. Captain Wolfe was English, even if he did speak French well. She wondered if he intended to deliver this ship, one of the finest ships in the French privateering fleet, into the hands of the British. Her head said no—he'd fought for the French at Saint-Malo—yet if he continued toward multiple war ships, he was either asking to be captured or giving himself up.

No single privateering vessel could capture two British warships without expecting defeat or, at the least, irreparable damage.

She noticed the moment that the first frigate sighted them. Without the use of its foremast, it maneuvered awkwardly in the water, trying to turn its bow toward them. As it twisted, she counted the cannon ports along the side—thirty-two.

Already *L'Aventure* was outgunned.

And the second frigate was on a path to aid the first.

"Prepare the ship for battle, men," Captain Wolfe bellowed. "There's an English warship for the taking."

CHAPTER THREE

"You heard the captain!" the lieutenant shouted. "Clear the ship!"

Adriana snapped to the orders of the bosun and helped secure the sail-yards to the masts. Other sailors ran below decks to remove the hammocks and stow them in the quarter deck. She heard the gunners' mates yell for more charges, fuses, and balls. The master barked in fury as the edges of the sails shivered, and she helped trim them until they grew taut with wind. She realized that they would have to engage the first disabled ship before the second frigate came within range, if they were to have any chance of a prize—or survival.

The captain stood stony on the forecastle. Lieutenant Drake called all hands to quarters. She scrambled to her post to help supply the gunners with powder. Through the cannon port, Adriana and the gunners watched as they drew near the damaged ship.

"She may be hurt but she's still got over thirty guns," one of the gunners whispered. "If the captain doesn't watch his sails we could catch a broadside."

"She's not much damaged," another added. "Only her foremast is cracked. She's got enough sail to maneuver, and her rudder is all right."

"That second frigate is running free with the wind on the port quarter. She'll be upon us soon."

"We'll be facing sixty guns."

"If I wanted to be fighting warships," another piped up, "I would've signed on in the royal navy."

The men mumbled their agreement and the whispering spread in earnest.

Adriana's heart pounded as they closed within cannon distance. On the other ship's upper deck, the English sailors raced to maneuver. Adriana heard Captain Wolfe order the showing of the colors. A moment later, cannon barrels protruded from the side of the enemy frigate and smoke burst from every barrel.

The oncoming cannonballs whined through the air. Adriana braced herself. As always before battle, her mind burst with random thoughts and images— her mother sewing before a fire, an alehouse in St. Mary's that stank of rum, the fire ship explosion, the captain pressing against her body, Chou-Chou curled against her—*Chou-Chou.* She glanced down and realized she'd never put him back in the harness after coming down from the crow's nest. She hoped her pet had found a safe place to hide.

The series of ocean splashes proved that the cannonballs had fallen just short of target. *L'Aventure* lurched hard about, and she saw the English ship trying to keep pace. But her ship had the wind and maneuverability. Within minutes, they approached the gilded end of the frigate's stern and then propelled fast to just within cannon range.

Adriana could see the men on the wounded frigate struggling with rigging, just as her master gunner paced down the row to prepare every other cannon with his priming iron. Then he lit the slow fuses.

On deck, the captain shouted *Fire!*

She stayed clear as the cannon recoiled. The weapon strained against the bolts that held it to the wooden floor. The cannon deck filled with dense gray smoke and the stench of brimstone. With her sleeve held against her mouth and nose, Adriana rushed to the stores to resupply the gunners with charges of powder while they cleaned out the hot barrels. Hearing the cheers of the men on the upper deck, she paused, waved away the dense smoke from a cannon hole, and peered out to see what had happened.

The English frigate's rudder was smashed, its mainmast held aloft only by rigging. Perfect aim—the ship was dead in the water. And by the torque of the boards beneath her, she knew that Captain Wolfe had his mind now on the second frigate.

The master gunner slapped her on the back of

the head. "No time for gawking. Get me powder."

She stumbled off to the stores. Chou-Chou leapt out of nowhere to clamber onto her shoulder. The lemur's nervous, shifting weight and digging claws were an annoyance, but she knew she couldn't tether the animal anywhere on the ship, not during the madness of a fight.

Footsteps pounded across the deck above her. Officers barked orders as they neared the second British ship. The enemy had the advantage of the wind, Adriana realized, as she ran back to her post with charges of the black powder. *L'Aventure* had lured the British frigate away from the dead ship, forcing it to chase them southwest.

Still, the enemy ship was gaining on their stern.

Back at the cannons, the lieutenant soon gave the order to fire. She clamped her hands over her ears as the fuses were lit. In uneven staccato the cannons burst, shaking the floor and spewing their smoke into the room. With Chou-Chou shouting in her ear, she rushed to the stores to bring more powder just as the timbers around her shook with the force of a hit.

The sickening crack of wood reverberated through the hull. A man screamed on deck. The ship lurched to starboard and the flutter of a flaming sail hung just outside the aft cannon ports. As the floor tilted, she slapped a hand on a hot cannon and then hissed as she took it off. The ship twisted to an uneasy halt.

"Man your post, boy!" one gunner yelled, his face

black with soot. "Bring more powder!"

On deck, the lieutenant gave the order to fire at will. The floorboards protested against the weapons' powerful recoil. Another hit vibrated through the ship and she heard the faint rush of water through wood below decks. She coughed at the thickness of the smoke as she reached for a bucket of seawater to cool the heat of the iron barrels. She emptied the water over the nearest cannon. Steam rose from the black surface.

The haze was so thick that she could see nothing through the ports. In a moment of reloading she heard the crack of muskets from the upper deck and realized that the enemy ship was nearly abreast. A cannon fired and the force of recoil tore it from the floorboards. A pinned gunner screamed. Two men ran to his aid and struggled with the scorching, heavy cannon.

Adriana startled when she heard the terrifying, rhythmic sound of grapnels being thrown over the edge of the ship. She heard the captain cry, "All men to deck!" She dropped the powder charges on the floor. The gunners reached for the swords and pistols piled beside the stairs and climbed up. Adriana waited until they all had climbed and then climbed herself. On deck, through the haze of musket and cannon smoke, she made out the rigging and masts of the enemy ship, directly abreast.

"Prepare to fight, men!"

She followed the voice to where the captain

stood, feet braced, his sword gripped in his hand. He'd torn off his cloak. Sweat plastered his linen shirt to his skin. He barked orders to the sailors as he paced, waiting for soldiers to emerge from the smoke.

"You!"

She started. He was pointing right at her.

"You, boy, you stay out of the fighting." With the tip of his sword he pointed to the huge anchor cables coiled near the stern. "Stay behind those and watch for fire."

She ran to the huge anchor cables, rounding the mizzenmast which lay shattered on the poop deck. Its tangle of rigging littered the aft-end of the ship. Many of the sails that only hours ago billowed with snowy whiteness now hung in dirty tatters from splintered yardarms.

As she crouched behind the coils, Chou-Chou peeled himself from her shoulder to huddle by her feet. She pulled the harness from her pocket, slipped it around him, and attached it to the anchor cables. Through the thick smoke, English soldiers climbed onto the rail of *L'Aventure*. They lunged at the pirates with vigor. She sensed in their focus a determination to avenge the humiliating defeat they had suffered at Saint-Malo. The privateers waved their cutlasses and attacked.

As she watched, many died.

There was a time, long ago, when her stomach would have heaved at the sight of so much blood. There was a time when she would have wept to the heavens as friends fell in battle. She'd learned to suppress those feelings, to act like she was a man even though she wasn't even a boy. Adriana did not show tears or weakness. She'd been working on ships since she was nine years old. She'd trained herself to imagine these fights as if they were macabre dances where one of the partners must die. Only the strongest, the quickest, the smartest, and the best-armed would survive.

Death came for all of us. When she'd returned to Saint-Malo from the Indian Ocean several months ago, and laid eyes on her mother for the first time in years, she knew this to be true. All the hoarded booty she'd saved to present to her mother couldn't doctor her mother's once-joyous spirit back into that worn-out, diseased body.

A quick death was far better.

A flare of light brought her attention to a pile of splintered timbers. She jumped from her hiding place to suffocate the flicker before it became flame. As she ran back to the protection of the cables she saw the captain near the gunwale. The man he fought wore the uniform of an English officer. Captain Wolfe's breeches were torn in a bloody slash at the thigh, yet he fought as if he had no wounds at all. Sweat pasted his shirt to the indentation of his back. With unyielding determination, he drove the English officer against the wall of the quarterdeck. Another English soldier, noticing his beleaguered captain, rushed to his aid. Without missing a stroke of his sword, Captain

Wolfe raised his good leg and pushed the second officer away. Reaching for the pistol lodged in his belt, Wolfe aimed at another uniformed enemy heading in his direction.

The English captain shouted, *"No."*

"Surrender," Captain Wolfe shouted, his voice rising above the clatter of swords, "and no more will die."

Hearing these words, another English soldier lunged to aid his captain. She grabbed a piece of splintered mizzenmast that lay on the deck and rushed to intercede. She swung the wood with all her might at the back of the soldier's knees before he could reach the captain. The soldier crumbled to the deck, cursing.

She staggered back as the English sailor recovered from the blow. He rose to his feet and turned toward her.

"Quarter!" The English captain shouted. "I surrender!"

A shuddering silence spread through the ship as the clang of sword hitting sword ceased. The English soldier eyed her and then, in frustration, tossed his sword on the deck. The moans of the wounded rose in the silence.

Adriana stood, mute and trembling, as the ritual of reparations began. With clipped efficiency the captain ordered his lieutenants to board the English ship. His officers rounded up the English soldiers. The surgeon clambered on board and surveyed the scattered bodies to assess the wounded with the best chance of survival. The sailors who still had strength carried the wounded down to the orlop deck, where the surgeon plied his trade. A carpenter rushed down the stairs, his arms laden with shot plugs and nails, to caulk the hull where a cannonball had penetrated. The French bureaucrat whose job it was to catalogue the prizes poked his head up from below decks, and then skittered across to board the captured ship. Captain Wolfe stared up at the masts, rigging, and sails, assessing the damage.

Gwynn Sayer, bloody but grinning, approached her. "We won, lad. You can stop shaking in your boots."

"Aye, we won." How could he grin while standing in a pool of blood?

"It was a bold move to capture two British warships."

"Many paid for his boldness."

He paused a moment, eyeing the carnage. "Their people will be compensated well, as by custom."

"Will they?" She had to stop shaking or Gwynn and the other men would think her weak. "This is no Mogul treasure to be parsed out in the evening. We'll have to ransom the officers. It could take months before we see our shares."

"Keep your voice down." His gaze skittered around the deck. "Others are saying the same, but you don't want to be the one caught with the words in your mouth."

Gwynn stepped away to help another sailor carry a wounded man. Stirring herself into action, Adriana followed the men carrying the wounded until she reached the fore-part of the lowest deck. The surgeon, stained from beard to boots, worked over a makeshift table. The ship's priest groaned the last rites in a Latin that was barely audible above the noise of misery.

"Boy!" The surgeon saw her figure in the dimness. "Fetch me linens."

She had to step over the wounded to reach the surgeon's extra supplies. Tearing the chest open, she grabbed a handful of linens and returned to his side.

"Hold his leg, there, boy—hard."

Adriana put pressure on the leg and braced herself as she looked into the sailor's terrified face.

No shaking.

No crying.

For hours she stayed in the dim, stifling lower deck, fetching camphor and needles and ammonia and holding down patients as the surgeon worked. After the most seriously wounded were tended, the less wounded men made their way down. Any sailor worth his salt could sew, so Adriana agreed to sew the less serious gashes as the weary surgeon and his mates plied their quicker needles. Between patients she played her horn for the men. It seemed to give them some comfort. Other than reading from the Bible, it was all the kindness she could offer.

"Have time for one more patient?"

She glanced up to find Captain Wolfe standing before her.

The surgeon hurried over. "Of course, Captain—"

"I was speaking to this ship's mouse. I wasn't aware that the lad knew surgery."

"A strong constitution, that boy." The surgeon leaned over to get a look at the captain's bloody leg. "But it'll take him ten minutes to stitch that and it'll only take me two—"

"He'll do."

The surgeon glanced up in mild surprise and then shrugged. "See you do your best, boy."

Her stomach dipped as she closed the Bible she'd been reading to the sailor now asleep on the pallet beside her. As she stood up, Chou-Chou squealed his annoyance as his bed unfolded beneath him.

"The light is better over there," she said, gesturing to the surgeon's table.

The captain turned around and tore off his bloodied shirt. His back, craggy with muscles, flexed.

"Come now, lad." He glanced over his shoulder. "Surely you've seen the work of the British Navy before?"

It wasn't the whipping scars she'd been noticing, and that realization made her strangely mute.

"Even I had to work as a ship's mouse once." He worked the buttons of his breeches. "I was about as mouthy as you."

"They did that to you when you were young?"

"Not much older than yourself." In the darkness

his face took on sharp, harsh angles that the sunlight made soft. "I had a tongue as quick as yours, but I was big enough to pose a threat. Not all captains are as lenient as I am to irreverent urchins."

A retort flew to her lips, but it died in her throat as he eased his legs out of his breeches. His bloodstained linens followed.

Adriana had seen more naked men than she'd like to admit. It was unavoidable on long sea-voyages, especially through the tropics where the sailors preferred to work in the briefest of loincloths. Bony, barrel-chested, brawny and slight, men came in all sizes and she'd long lost any curiosity. But she could say with all honesty that she'd never seen a man so magnificently proportioned as Captain Wolfe, now standing before her in all his fleshy glory.

He climbed on the table. The red-gold glow of the lanterns tinted his skin bronze. The muscles of his arms and chest swelled from exertion. His abdomen folded in on itself. When her gaze roamed lower, hot blood rushed to her cheeks.

Fine proportions, indeed.

"Stop standing there like a mute," he said, "and stitch this up."

She forced her gaze to his injured thigh. The slash was ragged, bloody, and stretched from just above his knee to halfway to his hip.

"I can't do this," she said, breathless. "It's too long."

"Women have been telling me that for *years*."

Scattered in pallets around them, the sailors barked in laughter. She hoped the dim light concealed the heat of her cheeks.

She said, "I'll get the surgeon—"

"He's already in his hammock." He braced the butt of his palms on the table and leaned into her. "Stitch it up. That's an order."

Left with no choice, she approached the table and reached for clean linens. Dipping one in fresh water, she washed the dried blood from the gash. A light spray of hair covered his thighs. He smelled of pitch and sweat...and *man*, but not in the smelly way men got when they were too long without a bath.

Chou-Chou chose that moment to surprise her by crawling on the bloodstained table. The lemur was usually wary of strangers, except for about two weeks every spring when he became weird, smearing the musky scent that oozed out of his wrists on every piece of available wood. During those days, he stayed alert all night, his tiny heart beating fast in his chest, prowling the decks and releasing plaintive cries, peering at any living creature that passed.

The captain reached toward her pet. "Don't," she said, splattering some bloody water over him. "He doesn't like to be touched by anyone but me."

The captain ignored her and scratched the lemur under his chin. The lemur stilled, but, after a minute, he released a quiet, satisfied chirr.

Damn it. "He must be tired from the battle."

"I'd like to think it's my charm."

"It's a he, captain."

"What a pity. We could use a few women on this ship, even hairy ones."

The sailors laughed again and she realized that he was pitching his voice so all the wounded could hear him. She also realized that he chose to sit naked on a table in the middle of the orlop deck and let a ship's mouse stitch his wounds so that every sailor in the ship would know that he was just like one of them.

Maybe he'd already heard the grumbling amid the ranks.

"So, ship's boy," he said, speaking above her head, "where did you learn to read?"

So he'd been watching her. "My mother taught me."

"It's odd enough to find a man who reads, much less a boy." He winced as she made the first stitch. "How old are you?"

Not much younger than you. "Fifteen."

"You look smaller."

"I've been working ships since I was nine." It took all her will to concentrate on the gash beneath her fingers. "Pirate ships, of course."

"So that's where you learned to speak your mind at every opportunity."

"I'm not strong enough to fight with my fists," she said, "so I fight with words."

"I heard you doing just that when you stole that coat."

"I didn't steal it," she said, wondering where he

was amid the crowd while she was working the ragman. "It's full of holes and hardly worth the plucked goose I traded for it."

"A rotting goose, by the smell." He swiped her forehead and held up his dirty finger. "If soot were gold, you'd be a rich urchin."

She noticed his clean-shaven face and her eyes narrowed. "You're a captain fond of bathing, I wager."

"I ought to scrub you pink just so I can see what you look like."

Her heart did a summersault. "It's not healthy to scrub the skin off a lad's back."

"You'll do it if I order it."

She tilted her chin. In this, above all things, she would risk everything—including a flogging—to win.

"Your face speaks insolence. Careful, boy. Lieutenant Drake thinks I ought to whip you until you know your place."

"Drake's an overdressed fop. He's prettier than a woman and I'm surprised you listen to him at all." She thought she saw a twitch at the corner of his lips, but it was gone before it was truly there.

"You just insulted my first lieutenant and one of my best men."

"Am I to be punished for the truth?"

"Truth is a valuable quality," he said, "but often dangerous. You remind me of someone I once knew."

She plunged the needle through his skin again,

hoping the whole bath idea was forgotten.

"You intrigue me, Joubert. Speak your mind. I want to hear what thoughts run through the head of a fifteen-year-old ship's mouse."

She could no more stop the words rushing to her lips than she could stop the rush of water through a breach in the ship's hull. "Twenty-seven sailors died this afternoon," she said. "Was the prize of a British warship worth the fight for those who still live?"

The room went silent but for the rustling sound of men shifting under their bedclothes. Her throat tightened as she felt his gaze grow hot on her head.

"Those English warships," he said, "had just finished bombarding your native city."

"We're not soldiers. We signed on board to capture rich English merchantmen, not fight their navy."

"This is a privateer, boy. We fight against the English—whether they are merchantmen or warships. Everyone in this room knows the difference."

The silence grew tense. She had an inkling that he'd prompted her to speak her mind just so she would say those words aloud. He had pitched his voice so everyone could hear again, and the message could not be denied. Still, this was the notorious Captain Wolfe before her, frightening even in his nakedness. She could see each angry muscle tense in his long, lean body. And she was a fool to think just because he'd prodded her that he'd hold back from giving her a set of stripes.

"You gave me leave to speak my mind," she said with a whiff of defiance. "And so I did."

"And only a fifteen-year-old boy would be mad enough to take me by my word." He pointed to his wound. "Finish the stitching."

With nervous, fumbling fingers she stitched the last of the gash. She secured the wound by wrapping a clean linen binder around the bulk of his thigh. When she finished, she stepped away from the captain and awaited the inevitable punishment.

"Look at me, boy."

Chou-Chou whined as he leapt from the table. He clambered to her shoulder and then grasped her head.

"Another captain," he said, "might strap you to what's left of the mizzenmast and whip your hide red. But I am a lenient man."

She couldn't seem to draw in enough air. Her head swam and the deck began to roll under her feet.

"There's something else." He eased off the table and reached for his linen undergarments. "You disobeyed orders this afternoon when you came out to fight."

She startled. "I was putting out a fire when I saw——"

"I told you to stay hidden."

She tightened her jaw.

"In the process," he added, "you saved my life."

More bedclothes rustled in the silence. She felt the attention of the entire crew upon her, an uncomfortable scrutiny.

She shuffled, wishing she could leave. "It was all part of my duty."

"No it wasn't." He reached for his breeches. "I'm in your debt now, Joubert. Use that chit wisely."

CHAPTER FOUR

Roarke stepped out of his cabin into the chilly air. Before him, the harbor's edge of the Breton city of Roscoff glimmered. For a full week his ship had been anchored here. He grew restless at the forced inactivity, especially knowing that the rest of the British fleet was already racing across the Atlantic Ocean.

If only the delay were due to repairs, he thought, as the tip of his rolled tobacco glowed. The mizzenmast had been replaced and new sails had already been attached to the yardarms. The cordiers of Roscoff had completed their work on the rigging. The entire hull had been fixed and then made fast with tallow, soap, and brimstone. The cause of the delay lay with the small-minded, paperbound bureaucrats of the French Admiralty.

After days of a formal inquest, where a stiffly

dressed idiot asked question after question about the seizure and contents of the ships, Roarke still waited for word from the Vice Admiral about whether the *Princess* and the *Dartmouth* were legitimate prizes. Today, he visited the offices only to find that an answer had not yet arrived. With his drawn sword, he had ripped the wig off the man's balding head and told him to have an answer tomorrow.

He needed to hunt down the rest of the British Warships. Captain Samuel Leighton of the British Navy was on route to the Caribbean in one of those ships. Roarke had seen the man with his own eyes through the long telescope of his glass. Roarke had stood on the forecastle amid two smoking prizes and waved to the murderous bastard until he was sure Leighton knew who'd inflicted the damage. Roarke liked the idea that the naval captain now felt the hot breath of retribution on the back of his neck.

But every day he spent delayed in this port was one more day he'd have to make up to catch the captain who'd killed his brother.

He tossed the glowing tobacco into the sea and listened to the sizzle as it extinguished. He *could* threaten the authorities that he would leave with his prizes. That would force the Vice Admiralty to either make a decision or relinquish all possibilities for profit. The thought of that bourgeois' face reddening in anger when he discovered Roarke's audacity almost made the risk worth taking. Unfortunately, in order for his threat to be valid he had to be fully prepared to carry through with it.

He didn't have enough men to sail three ships across the ocean. So any threats he made would be idle.

He never made idle threats.

Roarke suddenly heard an odd sound on the ship. He stilled. The ship lay low and heavy in the water due to the weight of the extra provisions. The slow undulations of the tide slapped against her hull. The wind whistled in the rigging, and the loose edge of a sail on the mainmast flapped against the yardarm. But the sound he heard was higher and more melodious. He followed the noise until he reached the forecastle and saw that the man on watch was the little mouse of Saint-Malo.

The boy was singing in a high, thin voice. As he watched, the urchin put the lemur on the railing and held the animal's paws as the creature danced on his hind legs. When the boy finished singing, the lemur jumped into his arms and the boy buried his face in its fur.

A weakness pierced him. This boy was too young and too soft for this life, just as his own brother had been.

Roarke considered turning away and leaving the imp to his privacy, but curiosity kept him still. The boy had a tongue as sharp as a knife and he wasn't afraid to use it on men three times his size, yet when the boy played his Breton horn, the music often turned melancholy. When Roarke saw him reading the Bible to a dying sailor, the boy's voice had cracked, and Roarke knew that it wasn't solely from growing pains. And yet this boy was so quick to respond to a shift in winds that it seemed seawater flowed in his veins.

The urchin belonged on a ship and yet he didn't belong at all. He was a puzzle Roarke couldn't solve.

"Captain?"

The boy clutched a dagger in his hand as he braced himself atop the forecastle stairs.

"Don't wave that thing at me," Roarke said. "I know your aim is true."

The figure relaxed. Roarke climbed the steps to join him.

The boy stepped back. "You're still limping. That should be healed by now."

"A certain surgical novice sewed it tight."

"*You* made me do it."

"So I got what I deserved." Roarke glanced around and said, "You are the only one on watch tonight?"

The boy shrugged, a movement of his whole upper torso. "I told the other sailor to go in town. I can take care of everything."

"You've had the night watch every night since we've anchored in Roscoff."

"The sailors like to drink. Wine makes men stupid. I don't want to be stupid. I'd rather be paid to sit and do nothing."

"Bartering again."

The boy just shrugged. Roarke wondered where the kid was keeping his stash of coins. This one was as wily in business as any portside peddler.

"There are women in port, too." Roarke didn't need a lantern to know the boy's shoulders had stiffened. "Fourteen isn't too young to have a woman, lad."

"*You* aren't with one."

"We've been in this particular port too long." He remembered, with a tightening in his loins, the evenings he'd just spent in a discreet little house with a lusty, russet-haired butcher's wife. "I find that if I linger, a woman gets to thinking about rings and swaddling clothes."

The boy crossed his arms. "You've only been with strumpets."

"On the contrary. Strumpets tell you up front how much they cost."

"You don't think very highly of women."

"And what would you know of them, lad?"

"I had a mother."

Past tense, Roarke noted, and clearly a sensitive subject. The boy's pet sensed the sudden tension, for he leaped from the rail to the deck and then the lemur sprung to the nearest stretch of rigging.

"You really can't blame a woman," the urchin said, "for trying to marry."

"I'd like to meet a woman who could enjoy a bedding without sinking her teeth into a man like a shark on flesh."

"But what can a woman do without a man? She can't work on a ship. She can't work as a shoemaker or a *cordier* or a blacksmith. Oh, there are some things she can do—in Saint-Malo some women weave sails—but a woman makes less than half of what a man makes for the same work." The boy did that whole-body shrug again. "Unless a woman is born into money, she has three choices: she must marry, become a whore, or starve."

Roarke raised his brows. He had never bothered to think too deeply about the women who came willingly to his bed. He enjoyed their bodies and made sure they received pleasure from his touch, but considering his tumultuous career, there was no possibility of any relationship beyond that. Yet with a few words from this young sailor he suddenly had an inkling that some women were as firmly trapped in the confines of a ruthless society as he had been in the British Navy, all those years ago.

It was a disturbing thought.

He let it pass.

"Quite a comment from somebody so young," Roarke said. "You've crushed my suspicions that you were a bourgeois' son who ran off for a life on the sea."

"If I were born rich I'd not be so fool-headed as to leave a warm house and a well-stocked kitchen."

"Not even for the opportunity to see new worlds, new peoples?"

"To risk whippings, to eat rancid meat and

moldy bread? Give me a good leg of mutton and I'd give up all this adventure in a moment."

His gaze rested on Joubert's tangled thatch of dark hair. A well-read, deep-thinking urchin, too wise for his youth.

Strange, strange creature.

"My mother once had to make a choice." The boy spoke while plucking at splinters on the gunwale. "My father died in a shipwreck, leaving my mother and me with nothing but debts. We were thrown out of our home. My mother had no skills, no family. No one would marry her because she was penniless and not young and pretty any more. So she…"

"She sent you to work on a ship," he finished, so the boy wouldn't have to speak the obvious. "When you were barely off the breast."

"Pretty much."

"You're not the first boy who's been sent to sea young. My brother Adam," he said, rushing over the unexpected hitch in his throat, "was barely twelve when he signed onto a naval ship."

"Was he a bourgeois' son who ran off for a life on the sea?"

"Yes, in fact." Why did he bring this up? He didn't talk about Adam to anyone. "In any case, your mother should be proud. She made a fine sailor out of you."

He tousled the boy's hair. The boy ducked out from under his touch. Roarke didn't know why he felt compelled to do that, but he suspected it was because he had his brother on the mind.

Adam died because of his mouthy impulsiveness.

And because of Captain Samuel Leighton.

"Captain?"

Roarke shook off his darkening thoughts. "What is it?"

"Will there be lots of riches in the Caribbean?"

The boy's lips stumbled over the unfamiliar word. Roarke knew that the new orders had caused some grumbling among the sailors. From interrogating the English officers on his ship, he'd found out that the English fleet that had attacked Saint-Malo had been commissioned to go to the colony of Jamaica in the Caribbean Sea. Because Leighton was on one of those ships, Roarke was determined to follow.

So he said, "The Caribbean is swarming with Spanish ships loaded with gold and silver and jewels from the mines on the mainland." That much was true. "There'll be ships with holds full of sugar and molasses and rum, tobacco, and rice from the islands. We'll be riding the same trade routes that the English and Spanish ships take back from their colonies. This time of year, they may not even be guarded." Roarke noticed that the boy shifted to his side to gape. "Are you counting the legs of mutton in your head already?"

The boy reached for Chou-Chou as the lemur jumped to the deck. "So it's riches we're after?"

"There'll be greater riches crossing this ocean

than sitting about waiting at the mouth of the English Channel."

"I'm asking," the boy continued, "because there are rumors, Captain."

He shook his head. "Pirates are always complaining."

"They say you're chasing the British ships not for profit, but for revenge."

His jaw tightened. He supposed it was no secret. Many of the men he'd signed onto the ship had spent years in the Indian Ocean, and probably knew what had happened with him and his brother all those years ago. And if anyone of those sailors had heard him interrogating the English prisoners before they reached shore, they might have heard a mention of Captain Samuel Leighton.

"When they signed up," the boy ventured into the stretching silence, "the men expected to be on a privateer that would sail through the Channel and catch English prizes. They didn't expect to be sent halfway across the world."

"Two days ago, I gave them a choice to take an advance for the sale of the two English frigates and leave."

"It's the dead of winter, Captain."

He didn't want to hear that truth. Surely there were still a few ships around who'd sign up new sailors despite the bad weather.

"Mind, I'll go to Jamaica or Timbuktu," the boy said, "so long as there's a profit in it. But if I were captain—"

"If *you* were captain?"

"—I would tell the crew that tale of Spanish gold, and I'd do it real quick."

CHAPTER FIVE

Roarke sat in his cabin calculating latitude from the measurements he had made the previous evening. A month had passed since they had left the harbor at Roscoff. He expected to reach the Americas, if nothing went wrong, in six to eight weeks. He leaned back in his wooden chair and stared out the wide stern windows at the rolling sea.

The sound of edgy laughter filtered through the walls, followed by the high, angry voice of the boy. The inhuman scream of the lemur rose above it all.

He sighed. He had tried over the past week to keep the sailors so busy that they had no time to think of mischief, especially mischief against the ship's mouse. It had started at the baptism ceremony as they passed the *Raz de Fonteneau*. The boy's objections that he had already sailed past this end of Brittany twice had been ignored. While the ship churned in the swift currents, the master's mate dressed in a ragged cloak and knighted the boy with a wooden sword. Then, each of five score and ten sailors doused the boy with buckets of seawater. The tarred leather jerkin that hung from the boy's neck to his knees was useless against the frigid waterfall.

Roarke caught a whiff of vengeance in all this. After the drums had beat for the departure of this ship from Roscoff last month, thirteen sailors still had not reported on deck. So Roarke delayed departure in order to scour the waterfront for his delinquent seamen. He found them cowering in sundry taverns and inns. Dragging them through the bustling streets, he forced them onto the ship and imprisoned them in the dank hold of the ship until they were too far to swim to shore. Roarke suspected they blamed the boy for their discovery, since ship's mouse had been the only one on the ship the night before.

Now the urchin's voice rose to a pitch he didn't think any boy could reach. He supposed he should go on deck and see what the fuss was about. The storms of the North Atlantic had kept the sailors busy, but they were far behind them now. Caught by the balmy trade winds that would sweep them to the Caribbean, the sailors had too much time on their hands.

Hauling himself out of his seat, he walked out of the cabin, through the separate officer's dining room, and onto the upper deck. He squinted against the blinding noonday sun.

Suspended in midair by the Welsh sailor, Joubert

struggled like a sailor possessed by bad rum.

"Sayer," Roarke barked. "What's going on here?"

"Just having some fun, Captain."

Roarke glanced at the lemur tied up by the mainmast, baring his teeth and breathing hard. "I thought someone was being tortured."

Sayer dropped the struggling boy to the deck and Roarke heard the breath whoosh out of him.

"Torture, it was." The imp struggled to his feet. "They were going to throw me into the sea."

"We were talking about it, sir," the Welshman admitted, "but we wouldn't have done it."

"You held me over the side, you round-bellied whor—"

"We just wanted to give the stinking whelp a bath, Captain." The Welshman gripped the boy and held him at arm's length. "He stinks like the devil."

Roarke couldn't deny the obvious. The boy's only concession to the heat this week was to remove his tarred leather jerkin. He still wore his full-bottomed breeches and an oversized linen shirt. Roarke could smell the boy from where he was standing, several paces away.

With the mood among the sailors so black since they left Roscoff, he was of a mind to let them have this fun, if only for the boy's unwitting benefit.

"Lieutenant." Roarke squinted up at Drake watching the drama from the quarterdeck. "Any words?"

"A scrubbing," Drake said, with a twinkle in his

eye, "never did anyone any harm."

Perhaps Drake was the wrong man to ask. During the Atlantic storms, the terrified lemur had bit and torn through anything he could get his teeth into—including several sailors and one of Drake's best waistcoats.

Roarke said, "Come here, Joubert."

"No."

Stupidly defiant, as always. The boy still struggled under Gwynn's meaty grip. The urchin should know that it'd go easier if he just submitted to the inevitable. But the boy's pert, impish face crumpled in frustration and something else. Roarke couldn't be sure, but it looked a lot like panic.

Well, he knew this urchin wouldn't be the first sailor to be terrified of drowning.

"Give him a scrubbing," he ordered the Welshman. "But don't throw him into the sea. Am I understood?"

He didn't wait for an answer. As he headed up the forecastle stairs, he heard a rush of footsteps and the Welshman's triumphant laughter. As the first pail of water crashed against the footboards, the boy cried out.

"Captain!"

His voice was so desperate that it made him pause. He turned to find the boy racing toward him with the crew in pursuit.

"Captain, please—"

His words were lost in a gurgle as a second and

then a third pail was emptied over his head. The seawater sprayed on Roarke's legs. Undaunted by the proximity of the captain, the crew gathered in a clump behind the boy and lifted their pails in the air. They baptized him, one pail after another, until the boy was driven to his knees at the bottom of the forecastle steps. The urchin struggled to lift his head, sputtering *captain, captain.*

Roarke frowned. He had battled men with knife and cutlass and saw the terror in their faces when they knew they were outmanned. He'd stood on the deck of a ship under attack among sailors who knew that at any moment a cannonball or a sliver of broken wood could put an end to their lives. It disappointed him to see that terror on the boy's face now. He'd thought the boy had more courage.

And yet the urchin's fear was so palpable that he felt an unwitting sympathy.

The pails of water kept coming. The urchin's filthy clothes sagged on his body. His linen shirt slipped off one narrow shoulder. The boy crossed his arms in front of him and bowed low, but not so low that Roarke did not suddenly notice the way the linen clung, showing pale skin beneath and two dark, peaked areolas.

Realization was a bright light exploding in his mind.

CHAPTER SIX

"*E*nough."

Through the gurgling cataract of seawater washing over her, Adriana heard the captain's shout. The flow suddenly ebbed and she saw the captain approach, a blur through a curtain of dripping water. He seized a handful of her shirt and dragged her up the stairs despite the frenzied cries of dismay from the crew.

"Enough," the captain shouted, his grip on her shirt tightening. "You've had your fun. Back to your duties!"

She stuttered, "Captain—"

"*Shut up.*"

He dragged her through the officer's mess and toward a door at the far end. He pushed it open and hauled her in, slamming it behind him. He turned back to her and, with one hand, ripped her shirt open from neck to waist.

Panic squeezed her. He stared wide-eyed at her exposed breasts, now gleaming with seawater.

She tried to cover herself, but her bindings were a twisted tangle around her waist. The torn edges of her shirt kept slipping through her numb fingers. Her nipples had gone tight in the cold, scraping against her palms as she finally used her hands to cover what she could.

Endless seconds ticked away. She wanted to scream—*Stop! Stop looking!*—but already it was too late. The captain stood as still as stone, his attention riveted. Her naked breasts became prickly, goose-pimply, under that gaze.

Never in her life had they felt so damn full.

"Damn it," she blurted, hardly recognizing her own strained voice. "Look *away.*"

To her surprise, he swiveled on one heel and showed her his broad back. His shirt stretched across that back as he ran both hands down the length of his face. No longer under the intensity of his scrutiny, she scrambled to seize the torn ends of her shirt and drag them across her body. The fabric did nothing to hide her secret, for the wet fibers snagged on her nipples and then tumbled off.

He spoke in a low, furious voice. "How long?"

She blinked at the question, not understanding.

"How long," he repeated, "did you expect to play this game?"

Game.

Like this was a joke. Like she'd just been playing at being a sailor. Like she was some idiot on a dangerous lark. Like she hadn't spent her *entire life* as a boy, surviving in the only way she knew how.

"If you hadn't noticed," she snapped, "I was *born* this way. If you hadn't succumbed to the whims of that pack of dogs you call a crew," she said, "this *game* would have continued indefinitely."

"Who knows about this?"

"You. Obviously."

"Who *else*." Spoken through his teeth.

"Not a soul."

"Don't lie to me, boy—" he caught himself on the word. He half-turned. She saw a muscle move in his cheek. "Someone is watching out for you. Not the idiot Welshman. He wouldn't have risked the bath."

"I trust no man. I'm not a fool."

"You are the biggest of fools."

"Fool enough to trick you for over a month."

"But no longer."

The consequences of that truth shivered over her, chilling her skin though the room was closed and hot and humid.

He turned and that gaze didn't rest on her face, but roamed again, in astonishing leisure, down her throat, her breasts, and still lower, to linger where her bellybutton lay, a deep indentation in the stretch of her stomach.

"A girl," he muttered, "with no protector, sailing on a privateer in the middle of the ocean. Do you have any idea what would happen if—"

"I've sailed with pirates since I was nine years old."

"Do you understand what a man would do to you," he said, stepping closer, "when he hasn't seen a woman for months?"

She didn't want to fall into that stormy gray gaze or notice the pale lines that fanned out from either side of his eyes. She didn't want to see the throbbing pulse in his throat, or the way his mouth parted as his breath came fast. She didn't want to notice the crescent scar right above one eye, or how his gaze fell unwittingly to her lips.

An uneasy look crossed his face. "This isn't possible." His jaw tightened, a shifting of bone. "You fought in battle. You stitched my wound. You loaded sixteen-pound cannonballs and—"

"You said I was a good sailor."

"Who is your protector?"

"The only person who ever protected me," she retorted, "died in Saint-Malo weeks ago."

"Your lover?"

"My mother."

Something flickered in his eyes. He took a step back and paced away, plunging his fingers through his dark hair. She wondered if he remembered the conversation they'd had on the ship outside Roscoff, when he'd tousled her hair. She thought he'd grown fond of her. She thought he felt some sympathy for her plight.

She could use that sympathy now.

"My mother made me into what I am," she began, thinking of the razor, her burnt dolls, her mother's hollow eyes. "When my father died we lost everything we owned—"

"A story told a thousand times. A story that never ends with a woman becoming a sailor on a privateer."

"My mother showed me that there's no hope for a woman in the world. She brought me breeches and told me I'd live better as a boy."

"Is this better?"

Yes.

For her own sake, she swallowed the word. He wouldn't understand. Consumed by their own troubles, men rarely spared a glance at a woman's.

He snarled, "What's your name?"

"Adrian—Adriana." Her tongue stumbled over the extra syllable. "No one has called me that since I was a child. I *am* a boy, Captain–"

"You most definitely are *not.*" He tore the fabric out of her hands and spread the edges so he could see her breasts again. "You're full grown, and long past the time for charades."

"So," she sputtered, not bothering to cover herself anymore, "will you steal what I will not willingly give?"

He raised one slashing brow. "So you do understand the danger."

"Better than you ever will."

"But you're unwilling to pay the consequences."

"Avoiding those *consequences* is exactly why I chose to live as a boy."

How defenseless she felt, standing here so exposed. Without the dagger that Gwynn had knocked out of her hand, without Chou-Chou who she could hear scraping at the door, the only weapons she had were her words, her wits, and the will to be left untouched. Never before did she understand how right her mother had been to shield her from men.

The silence stretched and her thoughts tumbled over one another. Would he strip off the rest of her clothes? Would he put his rough hands on her breasts? Would he spread her legs wide and force her to take him inside her? With a tremor she remembered his privates.

Captain Wolfe was not a small man.

Her heart started to skitter. She forced herself to stay calm and clear-headed. She had very little to bargain with. Maybe she could convince him to keep her secret if she offered herself to him alone.

No.

Yet wouldn't it be safer to service one man than be at the mercy of a hundred?

"You seem to have lost your wits, *Miss* Joubert."

"I haven't lost my wits," she stuttered, her heart and mind racing, "any more than I've lost the ability to work as a sailor on this ship."

"Out of the question."

"I've proven my worth—"

"Whether you were a good sailor is irrelevant. You're a woman, and a woman is nothing but trouble."

"Yes, I remember," she said, thinking about their last conversation. "We always want something from men."

His jaw flexed. "Do you deny you want my protection?"

"No." A thought came to her like a flaming arrow. "In fact, I'm going to demand it."

"You aren't in a position to demand anything."

"But I am," she said, in a triumphant rush. "You owe me a debt, Captain Wolfe. I'm calling it in."

His jaw tightened. He looked at her like he very much wanted to tie her hands around the mizzenmast and set Drake on her with the cat-o'-nine-tails. Or at least tie her hands around the mizzenmast.

"Very well," he said, in a voice so calm it unnerved her. "I'll protect your secret. At least until we reach land."

She let out a breath she hadn't known she was holding. If he kept to his word—if he kept her safe until landfall—then she could get off this ship and hire on as a mouse on another ship and sail away to new places.

"I'll need a new shirt." She tugged on the tangled linen of her bindings. "I can't work on the deck like this."

"You're not working the deck." He turned her around and nudged her toward the alcove she noticed earlier. "You're now my cabin boy."

She stumbled toward the alcove, full of light pouring in from the stern window. An empty tub filled the space, but there was enough room to push it to one side and hang a hammock from the roof beams.

The thought passed through her mind that these would be better ship's lodgings than she'd ever had.

"Cabin boy?" she said, diverting the discussion from what remained unspoken. "At half wages?"

"Still bargaining?"

"Always."

His nostrils flared. He ran his gaze over her, from head to foot.

"I'll get a full day's wages from you, Adriana," he said. "You can be sure of that."

CHAPTER SEVEN

The captain personally fetched two pails filled to the brim with seawater and gave Adriana a look that brooked no argument just before he left the cabin.

So she bathed, because she could.

She poured the water into the hip bath and sank into it. It was cool and it would leave dry white traces of salt on her skin, but, oh, what luxury! Finally she could scrub away all the sweat and grime and stink. It wasn't easy to keep clean on the ship, especially when her courses were upon her. They used to come every few months but now that she had steady food, they came more often. She was growing a reputation for being careless with her dagger because of the gashes she had to make as an excuse for all the bloody linens.

She scrubbed herself pink and tried not to think too hard as to why Captain Wolfe was insisting she take a bath. She figured he preferred his women clean and smelling sweet. Smelling of lavender and roses, no doubt, all of those women soft of foot and hand and lips. Well, simple perfume could make her smell like lavender and roses, but her feet and hands would never be soft.

In the middle of the sea a man can't be choosy about his bedmates.

Then that rumbling began, that quivering low in her belly, a lush, full feeling that unnerved her. She supposed if coupling was going to happen, she could do worse than lie with the captain of a privateer. At least he was man enough to bide his time until after she was clean. She could only hope that coupling with him wouldn't be as brutal as some of the couplings she'd witnessed over the years, with the sailors pounding into standing strumpets with such force that the poor girls' heads banged against the walls.

She poured some water over her head and rubbed a bar of lye through her short hair and wished she could wash out some of the fleshy thoughts sweeping through her mind, not all of them unbidden.

She stilled as the door to the main cabin opened and slammed shut. She heard a patter of paws before Chou-Chou charged into the alcove and sprung onto the edge of the metal tub. He shivered, skinny and wet.

"Oh, Chou-Chou." She leaned into him to burrow her face in his damp fur. "They didn't hurt you, did they?"

"Your fears are misplaced."

Her heart stopped.

"Your pet took his pound of flesh," he said, stepping into the alcove. "You should check his teeth for remnants of my lieutenant."

She shifted Chou-Chou to her chest as the captain tossed a sack of clothing into a dry corner of the room.

Chou-Chou kept moving around, trying to climb on her head while she struggled to keep him against her chest. The captain's gaze burned over her, taking in everything she couldn't hide and her pet refused to. His gaze smoldered with a strange gray-green light.

No man had ever seen her naked. The experience was strangely unnerving. He made no move to leave. He leaned against the doorjamb, looking his fill. Chou-Chou finally gave up fighting. His paw fell on the curve of her breast.

"Lucky lemur," he murmured, "to touch you like that."

She didn't bother to remove her pet's paw. The ship dipped into a swell, causing the water to swirl around her, causing disturbing eddies and currents around her privates. She felt a sudden urge to invite him to touch her. Perhaps if she stood up and revealed everything to him, she could at least take control of a situation that was swiftly becoming uncontrollable.

She might have the courage to do so, if her legs

weren't trembling so much.

He asked, "How old are you?"

She was tempted to tell him she was fifteen again, but she didn't think he'd believe that now that he'd seen her body. "Coming up on twenty, I think."

His breath hissed through his teeth. She ran her fingers through Chou-Chou's wet pelt and pretended it didn't matter.

"You're small," he said. "Even for a woman."

"My mother was tiny." She remembered watching her mother being laced into a corset, her waist so small it seemed she'd break in half. "I never reached her height."

"Your mother," he said, "who earned her keep with her body."

She met his eye to show that his cruelty didn't hurt, though hearing those words spoken aloud cut deep.

"Tell me, did you try your mother's vocation first, before you turned to the sea?"

"She saved me from that by shaving my head." Her jaw tightened. "That was the point."

"But you aren't a boy. Did you take a lover in some distant port? A Madagascan native who took your fancy—"

"And risk being discovered by my shipmates? Do you think I'm daft?"

"Then you've never had a lover."

She felt her cheeks grow warm. She knew, without the soot to hide her reaction, that he saw her blushing as well. The humorless half-smile faded from his face. He dropped his gaze from her body to focus on the floorboards with an attention the battered old wood didn't deserve.

In the stretching silence, the water gurgled around her knees with the gentle rise and dip of the ship. A storm must be coming, she thought. She heard footsteps above as the men trimmed the sails. She wished she were there, where the world was more familiar, rather than sitting naked in this alcove with this tall, muscle-bound man.

Suddenly he pushed away from the doorjamb. "Keep dressed around me, Adriana. I've been at sea for too long."

Then he retreated into the main cabin. She clutched Chou-Chou so tightly that her pet squealed and wiggled out of her grip. What had just happened? She'd expected him to pick her up, drag her to the bed, and do what men are wont to do. That was their unspoken deal, wasn't it?

She felt vaguely...disappointed.

She shook herself mentally and stood up out of the bath to do exactly what the Captain advised: Get dry and get dressed. Chou-Chou perched by the stern window and licked the seawater from his fur. With unsteady hands, she pulled a pair of culottes out of the sack. She tied a clean linen binder around her breasts and covered it with a voluminous shirt. She pushed the hip bath aside and strung her hammock from the ceiling. She'd need buckets to drain this bath, but that would have to wait until later. When she finished doing everything and anything she could possibly think of in the alcove, she peered around the open doorway.

The captain stood staring out at the sea. He must have heard her, for he turned and riveted her with his clear gaze. He stubbed out his tobacco on the nearby desk.

"Your new duties as cabin boy consist—"

"Do you mean to cut my portion?"

His pause was pregnant with impatience. "Your duties will consist of this," he continued. "You shall serve meals to me and my officers at dinner and at supper. You shall be responsible for the care of this room." He gestured to the clutter around him. "You shall be responsible for my clothes—"

"I shall be your valet." She walked deeper into the room. Chou-Chou followed at her heels, sniffing the air. "Do I dress you, too?"

He lifted his brows. "A wiser woman wouldn't make such a suggestion."

She cast her lashes down. She'd been thinking as a boy, just ticking off her duties. But as a woman, she had to be careful. Simple words were so frequently misconstrued.

"Look at you," he said. "No wonder you kept yourself as dirty as a street urchin. Your skin turns pink on the slightest provocation." He glanced down at the ashes of his tobacco, scooped them up in one hand and came at her.

"So you'll dirty me up, after I went to all that trouble to get four weeks of filth off my skin."

"If it will hide your sex, then yes."

He seized her jaw with his big hand. His fingers felt as rough as Chou-Chou's tongue on her skin. She knew it was useless to struggle so she suffered his touch until, suddenly, he stopped brushing ash on her face.

She met his gaze. His eyes were the clear, gray-green color of the harbor outside of Saint-Malo. The air in the room grew thin and hot, and she wondered if he, too, was suddenly having difficulty breathing.

He released her chin and returned to the window, slapping his hands free of soot. "You'll have some outside duties. The gilding on the stern of this ship needs to be polished before we reach the Caribbean. You're small enough to be hung from the side to do it. I want the forecastle scrubbed—"

"You're treating me differently than before," she said. "You can't do that."

"You're very glib for someone in a vulnerable position."

"The crew will notice if you take me off the crow's nest."

His face tightened. "The crow's nest I'll approve, so long as it keeps you out of the way of the men."

"Yes, Captain."

"Dinner is served at sunset." His eyes rested on her in warning. "Start swabbing the forecastle now, and make it look like a punishment. Send Drake in as you leave."

She startled. "You're not going to tell him?"

"Indeed I am."

She felt the old panic. "But—"

"Drake looks like a fop but he's got the heart of a warrior and the loyalty of a mastiff. He'll hold his tongue."

His tone left no room for questions. Closing the door behind her, she crossed the narrow hall that served as a dining room for the officers and stepped out into the sunshine of the upper deck.

Drake stood on the forecastle, leaning in the shade of the foremast. His usually stiff, snow-white shirt hung in limp folds. He wiped his forehead with a lace-edged pocket handkerchief. She thought that he was far too fair to be under the tropical sun. Vanity prevented him from protecting his skin with tar and soot.

"Ah, if it isn't our wayward urchin." Drake made loud, dramatic sounds of sniffing as she approached the forecastle steps. "It seems that our captain saw fit to give you a bath."

"A pity he ruined your fun."

"I was looking forward to drenching you, but..." His lips stretched over his teeth. "I got your pet instead."

Chou-Chou, still soaked, rushed past Drake and climbed to the first yardarm. He settled on his wet haunches and opened his arms to the sun.

"The captain wants to see you," she said sullenly.

"Now?"

"Yes." Conscious of the act she must play, she rubbed her behind as she walked toward the cleaning supplies. "In his cabin."

"You had it coming, boy." He walked off the forecastle deck and playfully slapped the back of her head. "You survived."

She glared at his back. Picking up a brush, a pail of water, and some soap, she sat down in front of the forecastle railings.

Gwynn soon appeared below her, a sheepish look on his face. "The cap'n didn't hide you too badly, did he?"

"It's your fault."

"Your face is still dirty as hell." A light of mischief entered his eyes. "At least you don't stink like a rotting carcass."

She couldn't help herself. All of this was Gwynn's fault. So she tipped the pail of soapy water over the rail and soaked him. Laughter burst among the crew as Gwynn roared in annoyance.

"Now you won't stink like a rotting carcass," she mimicked, shaking the last drops of soapy water on his head.

Furious, Gwynn whirled up the stairs. She sprang from her post and rushed to the other end of the forecastle. He seized a slippery bar of lye where she'd dropped it and headed straight for her.

"Sayer!"

At the sound of the captain's voice, Gwynn

stopped in his tracks. She skidded to a stop on the wet deck. The captain stood just outside the quarterdeck with Drake a step behind him. The captain's glare was pure ice, and it was focused on her.

"How quickly you forget your orders, Joubert."

"It wasn't the boy," Gwynn confessed. "I was just having a bit o' fun—"

"This is a privateering ship, Sayer, not a nursery." The captain's eyes narrowed to slits. "Drake, tie him to the mizzenmast. Give him a bone to bite for a few hours and maybe he'll remember his duties."

Gwynn's ruddy face whitened. The blaze of the midday sun could bake a man to a crisp in a matter of hours. She heard the crew shuffling in disapproval, for Gwynn's punishment far outweighed his crime.

Drake took Gwynn by the arm and dragged him toward the mizzenmast. On the main deck, the sailors watched in a dead silence.

"And you, Joubert," the captain warned. "You know very well what consequences you will suffer if I catch you away from your post again."

The captain returned to his quarters. She turned back to her post.

But all she could see, as she scrubbed the deck, was Gwynn tied to the mizzenmast and the crew's sullen, angry faces.

CHAPTER EIGHT

The weather turned stormy and rough. For five days, the rains fell and the sea rolled beneath the ship. Though she'd battled the storms of the northern Atlantic and more tropical cyclones than she could count, the captain ordered her to stay in the cabin. Not even her leather jerkin, he argued, could hide her sex if a wave soaked her upon the deck.

Now Adriana lay restless in her hammock and listened to the boom of waves. The storm was ebbing, but the yardarms still creaked and the sailors ran frantically across the decks. Above the moaning of the ship's timbers, she heard the captain's commands as he ordered repairs as the wind abated.

Chou-Chou leapt out of her hammock, long tired of the wild swinging. Even the charms of her Breton horn had worn thin. He raced into the captain's cabin but was pulled short by his rope harness.

"Don't give me that look," she said, as the lemur pinned her with his wide gold gaze. "After what you did to the captain's shirt yesterday, you're barred from his cabin."

The captain was bad-tempered enough without Chou-Chou exacerbating the situation. She'd blame the captain's fury on the storm, but she sensed there was more to his mood than constant work and a lack of sleep. Her very presence irritated him. She was the same person she'd been days ago, but now he treated her like a plague of fleas.

The leash suddenly slackened in her hand. She sat up on her elbows to see the empty harness at the other end.

Damn!

She struggled out of the hammock and clutched the door frame as the ship bucked under a wave. She scanned the cabin and saw her pet batting the feather quills on the captain's desk.

"Chou-Chou, *ici!*"

Startled, the lemur cried out and sprung off the desk, upsetting an inkpot in the process. She stumbled across the swaying floor to tip it back into the hole, but a small puddle of inky liquid stained the papers. She searched the desk surface for a rag, then, not finding one, she yanked open one of the drawers.

Papers, papers, papers. An inventory of the two British warships. Official-looking dispatches tied up in twine. A privateering *lettre de marque,* made out to Captain Wolfe and made regal with the raised yellow seal of King Louis XIV. She was about to shut the drawer and search elsewhere for a rag when a flash of red ribbon caught her eye.

She hesitated, glancing at the door. She could still hear the captain's voice coming from above, shouting orders to the men.

She pulled out the letters tied with ribbon. The paper was old, yellowed, but made of fine stuff that crackled when she unfolded the first. The letter was addressed to Roarke Lee Cameron and written in French.

My darling son Roarke,

I am writing this note to you alone, because you brother would not appreciate the sentiments I wish to convey before you both set off on your adventure. Adam is a fine young man of great intellect who will do great things in this world, but with his gentle constitution and his insistence in speaking his own mind, I fear that he may not fare well at first under the rigid discipline of the royal navy.

And so I must ask you to watch over him during the trials, to guide him as I would in your place, to stifle his brilliant impudence even if it requires a gentle cuff or two, so that he may soon grow in wisdom as well as in strength. I hope you will bear this last request of mine with good humor, and forgive a mother for wanting to reach across the miles to protect her two most precious children.

I look forward to the day when I see you walking up the road in your fine red uniforms, for that will be the day we are reunited.

Your loving mother,

Marguerite Cameron

Her lips stumbled over the English surname. She repeated it under her breath. It was a fine name, a strong name. This Marguerite was the mother of Adam. She remembered that the captain said he had a brother by the name of Adam, when they spoke on the deck of the ship outside Roscoff.

Roarke Lee Cameron.

She rolled the name over her tongue, wondering why his privateering papers were registered instead under Captain Wolfe.

She startled as Chou-Chou sprang onto the captain's bed to bounce about, and she suddenly remembered the spilled ink. She re-folded the letter, slipped it under the red ribbon, and returned it to the bottom of the drawer.

When the door to the main cabin burst open, she was soaking up the spilled ink with a corner of her shirt.

"What the hell are you doing?"

"Cleaning up," she said, as the name *Roarke Lee Cameron* rang in her head. "The inkwell overturned when the ship bucked."

She tried not to shoot a dirty look at her pet, who'd settled by the alcove, where he cleaned his fur.

"Come pull off my boots." He paced to the bed and sat on the edge. "They're filled with water."

She knew that the captain—*Roarke*—preferred being barefoot on deck during a storm, so since he was wearing boots he must have gone below decks to check the level of water in the hold.

"Is there much damage?"

"Some."

She gripped the boot and pulled. "Anything serious?"

"Some tangled rigging, one torn sail, a bilge full of water."

The boot came off with a sucking sound, splattering seawater all over the floor. "I could go below decks," she said, as she tossed the boot aside, "and help pump out the water—"

"The water is deeper than you are tall." He held out his other booted foot. "You'd be soaked and your charade would be undone."

"It's as dark as midnight in the hold." He seemed to forget she'd been doing this for years. "No one will notice—"

"I will notice."

"Because you already know." His other boot came off in her hands and she fell on her behind.

"You argue like a serving wench."

"I argued like this when you thought I was a boy, and never did you say anything stupid like that."

His jaw shifted in that way she'd come to know too well. He was holding his tongue and didn't much like it.

Someone knocked at the door. He barked an impatient *come in*. A sailor slipped a bowl of stew and a hunk of dark bread on the table near the portal, and then closed the door tight.

The captain—*Roarke*—reached over his shoulder to grasp a fistful of shirt to peel it off his back. "Why this sudden anxiety to get out of here?" he asked. "You've been in storms. You know what it's like to stand on a slippery deck—"

"I'm bored to death."

"Then fetch me a dry shirt."

He wadded his sodden shirt and tossed it in a corner. At the thud, Chou-Chou rushed into the main cabin and burrowed his head in the wad of wet linen. She made no effort to remove the lemur from his new plaything, despite the annoyance on the captain's face.

"He's been locked up for days." She lifted the lid of the sea chest, pulled out a shirt, and tossed it at him. "You are keeping us prisoners in here, Chou-

Chou and me."

"You aren't a prisoner." He ran the clean shirt over his wet, naked chest. "You can stay below decks."

"And do what? The cook doesn't want me around lest I set the ship afire."

"Then," he said, gesturing to the room, "do your work here."

"I'm not a housemaid."

"You'll make a horrible wife to some unfortunate sot."

"Yes, I would, since I'm a sailor, not a wife."

Although as she watched him stand up, shirtless, muscular, and gleaming, she found herself thinking of wifely sorts of things.

Even more so when he began to unlace his breeches.

"Look at you," he said, tugging the ties free. "Blushing like a bride."

Anger rose but she put a cork in it. Every day she saw men pull their members out to relieve themselves over the rail, and she'd never blinked twice. Yet in front of this half-dressed man she found herself acting and feeling like a flighty young girl. She didn't trust these feelings she was having, cooped up so long in this room with a man who knew the truth.

"Come, come," he said, in a deep-throated, teasing voice, "it's not as if you haven't seen me before. Would you like to check the wound?"

She turned on one heel, unnerved by the timbre

in his voice. "I'll wait in my room until you need me."

"That may be sooner than you think."

Once in the alcove, she sat on the little ledge of the window, gripping the sill as the sea still rolled, but not as fiercely as the rolling within her own body. She pretended to be absorbed in the view but her senses prickled. From the other room, she heard the clink of crystal against crystal and knew he'd opened one of the few remaining bottles of brandy. Chou-Chou was jumping around in the main cabin but she didn't care. Let the captain toss him out—no, let Roarke Lee Cameron toss him out.

"Get out here, Joubert," he said, after she'd heard the clink of crystal against crystal a few more times. "Hang up these wet clothes to dry."

She entered the cabin with some caution. He leaned back in the chair. He had changed to a dry pair of thin-legged breeches and hiked his bare feet on the desk. He'd combed his hair back off his brow and it glowed with a blue-black sheen in the gray light of the room. As she gathered the clothes, she felt his gaze drifting up and down her body with disturbing intensity.

"There are times," he said, "when your femininity overcomes this disguise, Joubert. I admit, I find it intriguing."

She bundled his wet breeches close to her chest, wondering what to make of his soft voice, this strange mood.

"I don't know what you are," he continued. "I

look at you every day and wonder how I could ever think that backside of yours had anything but a woman's curves. It's like stripping a ship and finding a dozen hidden compartments—"

"You've been drinking."

He raised his glass. "Your perceptions are impeccable."

"You're not yourself."

"Indeed, I'm not. I'm not the kind of man to bring a woman on a ship, or let one stay with me in my cabin."

"You're raving, so you must be famished."

She turned to bring him the food the sailor had left on the table and saw, instead, Chou-Chou standing on the tray.

"Chou-Chou!"

The lemur shot up. His catlike face was smeared with the drippings of the stew. She heard the captain's chair scrape against the floorboards just before he came around the desk and lunged for the lemur, just missing his ringed tail as he darted, screaming, into the alcove.

"Don't!" She rushed to stand in the doorway of the alcove, between the two. "He was just hungry, you can't blame him—"

"He's the best-fed soul on this ship."

She couldn't deny it. The lemur had a bad habit of leaping on the officers' dinner table and sampling the dishes before a furious lieutenant could bat him away. But still she didn't move from her position even though the captain loomed over her, his breath smelling like brandy.

"Bring me another bowl," he snapped, stepping away. "And make sure that pet of yours stays away from it—and me."

In the alcove, she seized her pet and wrapped him in his harness more tightly than usual. "It's all right, Chou-Chou. I won't let the captain hurt you." He thrust his muzzle in her neck and she buried her face in his amber fur. "But don't go wriggling out of this again or else both our hides will be tanned."

She snatched the dirty bowl and headed out of the room. In the brick-floored galley, the cook was tending several contained fires, cooking furiously now that the worst of the storm was over. She dunked the bowl in salt water and then held it out. "Captain's plate. He wants seconds."

"He does, does he?" The cook scowled. "He'll be food for fish if he's not careful."

Adriana frowned. She knew the crew was dissatisfied, especially after Gwynn's punishment, but this was dangerously bold, even for a pirate. She wondered what else had happened on deck while she was closed up in the captain's quarters.

She climbed atop one of the unopened barrels of salted meat and searched for a less dangerous topic of conversation. "The storm is stopping, it seems."

"Oh, it's just beginning, boy. And it's been brewing since we left Roscoff—"

"What's this?" Lieutenant Drake approached

through the dimness. "The captain's mouse, out of hiding?"

Drake's gaze was intense, baffled, and probing, as it had been since Roarke had tipped him off to her true identity.

"I'm not hiding," she said, her throat tight.

"I haven't seen you on the upper deck, lad, fighting the storm like the rest of us."

"That's no fault of mine."

"You should be grateful to the good captain—one big wave and you'd be swept over."

"I've battled worse storms."

"And now," Drake said, "you'll live to battle more."

The lieutenant took the bowl that the cook offered with an averted face. Rather than bring his food to the officers' dining area, Drake settled on his haunches and rested his back against one of the tubs. He ate with methodic, polite rhythm. Gwynn had told her that Drake was the third son of an English viscount. He looked every bit the aristocrat, eating his rancid stew with a silver spoon he had fished out of his ruined satin culottes.

"It won't be long now," Drake said, "before we sight land. There'll be fleets of merchant ships just off the coast of America."

"America?" She frowned. "Have we been thrown off course that much? I thought we were headed to the Caribbean."

"We were. But the captain always has the welfare

of his crew in mind." Drake pulled a handkerchief out of a pocket and patted his lips. "He wants to capture a few well-laden merchant ships before heading after the British fleet."

There was no question—Drake had heard some kind of grumbling. He'd have no other reason to bring this up.

She met the cook's wary eye as the cook held out the captain's now-filled bowl. "Well," she said, hopping off the barrel she'd been sitting on, "here's to easy gold and quick glory."

She took the bowl and headed to the stern of the ship to take the stairs to the quarterdeck. When she got to his quarters, the captain was sitting at his desk absorbed in his charts and calculations. His hair was no longer neatly slicked back. It looked like he'd spent the time she was away raking through with his fingers.

"Just leave it there," he said, not even looking at her.

She left the bowl by his elbow and returned to the alcove. Chou-Chou lay motionless on her hammock, dead asleep. Absently she reached out and scratched his fur, and her pet made a strange, gurgling moan. Curious, she leaned closer. He was panting as if he was hot. He smelled bad. His white underfur was stained and he was as limp as if someone had beaten him. She noticed a dark spot on the floor beneath the hammock.

Anger flaring, she strode into the main cabin. "What did you do?"

The captain lifted his gaze from his papers. "Do?"

"If you hurt him—"

"Lower your voice."

"—if you even *touched* him—"

"Joubert."

Her name was a barked order. Instinct made her go quiet though anger tightened her hands into fists.

He said in a lower voice, "What's wrong?"

"Chou-Chou." Her throat tightened. "He's hurt."

"Not by my hand." The captain straightened up, his brows drawing in concern. "He didn't leave the alcove."

She did not know why, but looking at Roarke's face she knew he spoke the truth.

He rounded the desk. "Let me see."

"No." She headed into the alcove ahead of him. "He doesn't like to be touched by anyone but me."

She entered the dim room, loosed the harness, and slipped her arms under Chou-Chou's small body.

"Maybe he's just sick." She hefted her pet to her chest.

"He threw up my dinner." Roarke was a tall warmth behind her. "Bring him into the light. Hold him while I look him over."

Her heart began to pound. The captain stood close and searched the pet's splattered fur, slipping his fingers over the froth at her pet's mouth and lifting those fingers to his nose. Chou-Chou's eyes had fluttered closed.

Something was terribly, terribly wrong.

"Maybe," she said, "I should get the surgeon." At least Chou-Chou's whimpering had stopped. "Maybe he can give him something—"

"Adriana."

Her name on the captain's lips was husky and foreign and she almost didn't hear it. She didn't *want* to hear it, not now, not while Chou-Chou lay sick in her arms. But the captain had straightened up from his examination and now stood looking at her with an odd expression on his face.

"The surgeon," he said softly, "can no longer help."

CHAPTER NINE

So it has come to this.

Roarke had once prided himself in knowing with uncanny accuracy when sailors became sullen and disgruntled. He'd captained enough pirate ships. He understood the anger that grew during the long stretch between prizes, or when bad weather and incessant work embittered the sailors. He cast back over the last weeks and wondered when everything had turned. Was it when he dragged those thirteen sailors out of the taverns of Roscoff? Was it Gwynn Sayer's punishment? He didn't really know. His alertness had slipped since the dirty urchin now living in his cabin had turned into a sylph of a woman.

That woman now stood before him, hugging her dead pet.

"You're wrong," she said, in a voice that was as soft and feminine as any dulcet young bride. "Chou-Chou is warm, he's just sleeping."

"Adriana."

She didn't look at him. She scratched the dirty fur beneath the animal's chin and then pressed his head back and forth with one finger and whispered for him to wake up. He wanted to pull the body out of her arms so she would stop poking at the dead. He didn't want to witness the way her breath grew shorter as she struggled with the truth.

He recalled the night on deck in Roscoff when she'd played her Breton horn to make the creature dance. He remembered the way the animal had clung to her shoulder, the way she had fought to protect him from the cruelty of the other sailors, the way the creature curled up on her chest when she slept.

Now she stared up at him with eyes as dark as midnight, breathing as if she'd run a thousand miles, with a look as if she expected an explanation for what she already knew. She didn't seem to notice when a single tear slipped down her cheek and dripped onto the lemur's fur, but the sight unhinged him.

He felt as ungainly as a boy. He didn't know what to say or how to move. He felt the urge to give her a pat on the shoulder—like he'd do to a child who'd lost a toy—or, alternatively, bark an order to wrap the creature up for his funeral and send her off so he could turn his mind to the greater danger. Should he turn his back to save her from the shame of her grief, or should he bundle her into his arms?

The former seemed wiser, the latter too dangerous.

This would be so much easier if she were still the sharp-tongued urchin that he had brought on board in Saint-Malo.

"Just a little while ago," she said, taking tiny sips of air between words, "he was jumping around."

"It happened fast, Adriana. He did not suffer."

"Did he...choke on something?"

She glanced around the room, searching, but in the end her gaze rested upon the newly-replaced bowl of stew.

He watched as she remembered the sequence of events: A sailor delivering the captain's dinner and slipping out before either of them could see his face. Chou-Chou standing on the dinner tray, his furry face smeared with gravy from that dinner. Her pet lying on the hammock in a pool of his own vomit.

Her pale face blanched beneath the smears of soot. She'd spent a lifetime on pirate ships. She probably knew the crew's mood better than he did, even if she didn't know who'd orchestrated the poisoning.

He peered once again at the raw areas of burned skin around the lemur's short snout. He suspected they'd discover some missing poison in the stores...if the surgeon wasn't in on the poisoning.

First things first.

"Adriana," he said, "let me."

She didn't fight as he expected her to do when he slipped his arms under the lemur. She released her pet into his arms. He walked the limp creature to his bed and laid him down. He straightened the creature's legs and arms. Later, he would wrap the pet in a sail, let Adriana sew it up, and they'd all commit this little body to the deep, but only after he confirmed with the surgeon what he suspected.

When he turned back toward her, she buckled like a sail suddenly bereft of wind.

He seized her shoulders before she hit the floor. He pulled her into his arms. He felt against his body what he'd spent too much time imagining—a woman of subtle curves, warm and soft and lithe. He pressed his cheek against her short, cushiony hair as his hand found the hollow of her lower back. Molded against him she was tiny, weightless, too fragile to bear the burden of this grief. He waited for her to morph into a clinging, crying woman, but her grief was a cold, silent thing.

A vague, unfocused anger unfurled in his chest. Anger at the mutinous assassin, at the situation, at his own powerlessness in the face of her grief. Anger at the world she'd grown up in, the world that had taught her to bury her natural feelings deep. Her brow tasted salty. At the touch of his lips, she shifted in his embrace.

"Adriana?"

Her hands lay flat on his chest. Her lashes clumped in spikes around her eyes, but no tears fell.

Her expression was stone-still. He ran a hand over the curls on her head and found himself wondering what they would look like, long and tumbling down her back.

"The poison," she said, "was meant for you."

"Poison is a coward's weapon," he said, unnerved by how quickly she'd controlled herself and become alert, focused, and steady. "It's the work of one man, maybe two."

"But—"

"Had more men been involved, they'd be breaking down the door right now."

"Oh." The word was no more than a breath. "Of course."

Her brown eyes were fixed but he could see in the depths where she'd hidden her pain. His chest began to hurt in a strange way. He wanted to lower his head and touch those lips. He wanted to let her know that it was all right to cry. He wanted to thank her, because he was in her debt again. Tonight her pet had saved his life.

Instead, he thought about her hands, still flat on his chest, a subtle pressure.

He thought about what she'd once told him about women and choices.

And then he became alert, focused, and steady.

He quietly stepped away.

CHAPTER TEN

That night, the captain put out the news among the crew that Chou-Chou had died by choking. He brought in Drake. While Adriana sat in her alcove and sewed her lemur into his funeral cloth, she listened as the captain told the lieutenant the poisonous truth while her heart grew heavy as a stone.

The next day, after they stood on the deck and tipped Chou-Chou into the sea, the captain simply ordered everyone back to work.

Life went on as if nothing had happened at all.

She retreated to the crow's nest and went hot with anger and then cold with fear and then she started shaking for reasons she didn't know. She kept waiting for the captain to identify the sailor who'd delivered his dinner, then drag him on the deck to flay him bloody. She wanted whoever had done this to be keelhauled—hung from the yardarms in the blazing midday sun and then towed for hours from the stern, even if it meant his death.

She stumbled a lot, as if she'd forgotten how to walk without Chou-Chou's weight on her shoulder. From her place in the crow's nest, she watched everything. The stores of salted meat were dangerously low and the ale was gone. The sea grew violent and unpredictable at this latitude, and the sailors were constantly on guard for waterspouts and swells. Men grumbled in clusters. They looked thin and dirty. The captain kept them busy, but she could see he was careful not to work them to the point of exhaustion. Every night a different sailor was given the duty of delivering his supper. The captain casually asked them to taste it first as if he'd done that all along.

All this stealth, all this secrecy, all this careful maneuvering was futile—as was fury, mutiny, even vengeance. Nothing would change the fact that she was alone.

She didn't feel like herself anymore.

Maybe that's why, a few days after Chou-Chou's death, she found herself studying the charts on the captain's desk as midday light filled the room. She wasn't sure what she was looking for. Direction, maybe. A port that looked promising for a new berth, after she was off this wretched ship, away from everything and everyone. As she scanned the map, she noticed that the ship had made a sudden, northern change in direction days ago. That explained why the weather had turned, for they were north of the Tropic of Cancer.

In the back of her mind she knew she should wonder about this change, but she couldn't muster any interest.

Then the door swung open and the captain walked in. He stopped short at the sight of her, standing where she didn't belong.

His gaze was piercing as he approached. "When was the last time you slept?"

She shrugged. She'd spent years sleeping with Chou-Chou's warmth against her chest. Without him, she was cold, and restless, and hollow. In the middle of the night she would startle out of fitful bursts of sleep.

"I could get you laudanum from the surgeon," he said.

"Laudanum is like liquor, it makes people stupid."

He didn't respond to that, but his attention intensified. "You've washed the dirt off your face."

She frowned as she touched her cheek. She vaguely remembered doing that. She'd taken a wet cloth and ran it over her skin, over and over until the water in the bowl went muddy. It felt as if someone else had done that, not herself.

He came around the desk to her side. He radiated strength and something else, something that teased an old memory of better, kinder times.

He murmured, "You try so hard to be brave."

She didn't know who moved first. But all of a sudden her cheek lay against his shirt. The scent of him—salt and sea and wind and man—engulfed her. His arms curled around her back and she closed her eyes because he was warm and she was as cold as the deep blue sea. His heart beat hard beneath her ear.

"I'm sorry, Adriana."

Some sensible part of her knew she was reaching for his comfort to plug the lemur-sized hole in her heart, but she couldn't pull away.

I am just another problem on this mutinous ship, a needy woman forced into his life. Roarke is holding me because Chou-Chou lost his life in his place, and he feels some sort of obligation.

And yet even as these thoughts skittered through her mind, she felt a surge of other needs that came not from the hollow in her heart but from another hungry place, from some feminine part of her that until these last few days she'd been able to suppress.

She squeezed her eyes shut, denying it.

Still, she felt the movement of his fingers as he spread open his hands against her back. She felt the brush of his palm up her spine as he swept his hand up to touch the bare skin at the nape of her neck. He combed his fingers through her short hair while, beneath the linen binding, her breasts throbbed with sudden sensitivity.

This feeling was real.

This feeling was good.

He tugged her head back with great gentleness. Below thick and lowered brows, streaks of green radiated through his gray irises. It was strange to see such beauty in him. In battle and in storms, he looked fearsome, but now she only saw a riveting sort of intensity.

"So here she is," he murmured, "the woman you try so hard to hide."

She supposed a wiser woman would look away, but she didn't even know how to be a woman. She'd been raised to take the world as it came, to understand what she wanted, and to bargain hard for what she needed. So when the captain lowered his head to her throat, she tilted her jaw to make it easy for him.

The moment his lips touched her skin, she learned a new lesson of womanhood. All these years she had assumed that girls only surrendered their bodies for the sake of money. But here she was, feeling a weakening in her knees, a tightening knot in her lower abdomen, and a dampness between her legs. It was a primitive and undeniable ache, this thick, rising passion.

"If you want me to stop," he said against her throat, "tell me now and I'll—"

"Don't stop."

His arms tightened. "You don't know what you are asking for."

"I know how I feel."

He lifted his head from her throat. She caught a

glimpse of his tight, intense expression before he captured her lips.

His kiss was a spark shooting straight to her loins. She bowed back against the pressure of his mouth. She tried to mimic the movement of his lips against hers, but she was clumsy and he was quick, moving across her face as if he wanted to kiss all of her, all the time, all at once.

He pulled away, breathing hard.

She seized his head and kissed him again.

Every muscle in her body began to quiver. She became aware of odd things. Her clothing being tugged and yanked and jerked. A hot hand flat on the bare skin of her back. The scrape of his fingernails as he pulled her bindings down her ribs. A dizziness as she broke from his kiss to breathe.

The roughness of his palm as he cupped her bare breast.

"Your heart," he said against her face, "beats like a bird's."

"Don't stop."

Her feet left the floor. The room spun. The ceiling came into view just as the linen covers of the bed brushed against her back. He sat up to grasp the collar of his shirt and yank the linen over his head. She touched his flexing upper arm the way she'd wanted to, perhaps from the first time she'd seen him naked. She'd thought he'd feel cold and hard, like marble, but his skin was taut and pliable in the way it moved over the muscles beneath. He tossed his shirt away and then leaned over her. The world went dark for agonizing seconds as he tugged her shirt off her body and with it, the bindings that had covered her breasts.

"The sailors must be blind." He ran a rough hand from her breasts just beneath the gape of her breeches, to the valley by her hipbone. "I must have been blind."

He lowered his head and sucked one nipple into his mouth.

Gasping, she lost her fingers in his silky hair. Sensation rushed through her. He abandoned one breast to taste the other, rolling the abandoned nipple between expert fingers. She tried to understand the rush of feelings, not just from the tugging of his lips, but from how his touch made her feel in places he had *not* yet touched. A pressure and urgency tightened in the cleft between her legs.

He paused to span her waist with one hand. "You're too small."

"You won't hurt me."

She heard her words in a voice she didn't recognize as her own. A woman's voice, she supposed, dry and dusty from lack of use.

He hesitated, hovering above her. She tried to read his face, that beautiful face, the scar just above his eye, the sharp angle of his cheekbones, the thick, dark hair, and the way his lips parted so he could breathe better. He was thinking. She could see galloping indecision in the ripples of his brow. She didn't want him to think. She wanted him to kiss her again, press down upon her, touch her in ways that no man ever had.

She knew the moment he came to a decision because he plunged has hand lower beneath the waistband of her breeches. His fingers combed the tuft of hair that covered her mound before slipping between her legs to cup her sex.

She might have made a sound. She didn't know. It was becoming difficult to think. Her knees dropped apart and she felt her sex peel open against the heat of his palm. She tilted her hips up, she wasn't sure why. He accommodated her wordless demand and slid fingers into her sex.

She gasped.

He withdrew and slipped into her again.

Her inner muscles clenched.

He slipped his fingers deeper, and this time he used his thumb to roll around a place that ached.

Oh.

She stopped counting the strokes, stopped thinking of anything but his wet, quickening touch that made her ache even more but in a wonderful, intensifying way that had her writhing beneath him. When he lowered his head to suck her nipple into his hot mouth again, all her senses exploded.

Lights behind her eyelids. Music in her ears. Strange images flickered through her mind, of running in frilly dresses and the feel of long curls swishing against her back and the thrill of being swept up and twirled in the air. She struggled with a rising wave of emotion for the man coaxing out of her this woman's gift she hadn't even known she owned until this blinding, incandescent moment.

During the delirious throbbing that continued he still touched her. Her senses began to re-assemble and she realized that her back was arched off the bed, and her head was thrown into the pillow, and her mouth gaped open as if she couldn't breathe deeply enough.

She blinked once, twice, and looked at him through eyes whose lids had become almost too heavy to keep open. His face was full of astonishment, as if he were gazing upon something new in the world.

Beautiful, she thought. This is what it was like for a woman to feel beautiful.

He gently withdrew his fingers. She reached for him, running a hand over the craggy muscles of his shoulders and arms. She felt languid, heavy in the loins, but she knew what happened during a proper coupling.

She wanted more than just his fingers inside her.

He must have read the look on her face, for his gaze flared and he rolled onto his back to tug at the opening of his breeches. A fresh new tingling spread through her body, as if, now awakened, the woman in her understood perfectly what better pleasures could be had.

With shaking hands she pulled down her own breeches and tossed them off the bed.

Then she heard a sound. A creaking sound, a familiar sound.

The captain bolted up to a sitting position.

In alarm, she followed his gaze.

In the open doorway stood Gwynn Sayer.

CHAPTER ELEVEN

"Close the door," Roarke barked.

He seized his discarded shirt and tossed it over a naked Adriana, although, if he read Sayer's expression correctly, it was too late.

"Put the tray down, Sayer."

The sailor, stunned, clattered the food tray on the nearby table. He fumbled behind to find the door to shut it. He never once tore his gaze from the sight of Adriana's sweet breasts, the wet, little nipples straining upward as she struggled to pull the shirt over her head.

Damn it.

He should have paid attention. Since the poisoning, he'd insisted that each day a different sailor deliver his meal. Not every sailor had the wits to knock first.

"You," Roarke accused, buttoning his breeches,

"didn't knock."

Sayer stuttered, "You've got a woman."

"Lower your voice."

"You've been hiding her."

"A wise man," Roarke said, rising to his feet, "would shut his mouth fast."

"It's been a long time," the Welshman said, reaching down to rub his breeches, "since any of us have had a woman—"

"Hire one in Jamaica and get your eyes off mine."

The shock ebbed from the sailor's eyes as he shifted his gaze from her to him. The Welshman's expression of befuddled lust was replaced with something else, something wary and far more dangerous. A prickling alertness made Roarke keenly aware of the situation. Adrianna's safety depended on him handling this sailor very carefully. He prided himself on being a good swordsman, better with a pistol, but he'd rather not have to kill the man.

"Gwynn, you stupid fool," Adriana blurted into the silence. "Are you so blinded by a pair of tits?"

Roarke's shirt covered Adriana from neck to knees, but without the bindings, those gloriously responsive nipples poked against the weave.

"It's *me,*" she insisted, patting her chest. "It has always been me."

Confusion crossed Sayer's face. "What's this foolery?"

Adriana sighed, "*Look* at me."

His face fell. He shook his head. "You—you—you're not—"

"I am a girl, and I was, even on *The King's Arse* when I dragged your dirty self out of more than one alehouse fight."

Behind the thick black beard, Sayer's mouth sagged. "You sneaking whelp."

"Don't blame me. You couldn't see what was right before your eyes."

"All these years." Sayer's mouth opened and closed like a gasping fish. "You hid this from me all these *years.*"

"From you and every ship's crew I knew."

Roarke watched Sayer struggling to absorb the shock, waiting to see how the Welshman would take the news while he edged his way toward where his sword was sheathed.

"If the pirates of *The King's Arse,*" Sayer stuttered, his face contorting, "had ever found out that you were a woman—"

"But they never did."

"They would have sliced my throat!" He threw up his arms at her. "Those pirates would have killed me thinking I'd kept you to myself!"

"Mind you remember that," Roarke interjected, curling his hand around his sword belt, "before speaking a word about her to *this* ship's crew."

Sayer blustered, "But I didn't know until now!"

"Who's going to believe that?" Roarke looped the sword belt around him as if he were just calmly getting dressed. "If you say a word about her masquerade, she'll swear that you knew from the start."

Sayer's face tightened.

"They'll believe me," Adriana added quickly. "I've seen you more than once without your breeches."

Sayer snapped, "You won't dare."

"I dare *every day.*"

She glowered at the Welshman while sitting on the bed wearing nothing but a shirt. Roarke had that strange sense of double vision again, the kind he had all too often whenever he was around this woman. She had the undeniable shape of a woman, the passion of a woman, but in times like this she spoke, acted, dared, and even sat with her legs splayed carelessly just like a man.

Then Sayer turned his attention back to him. Roarke saw the dislike slither behind the Welshman's eyes.

"I might just keep my mouth shut," Sayer said, as he ran his fingers through his thick beard, "in exchange for a piece of her."

Roarke's ears filled with a buzzing. He heard his sword belt clank to the floor as he rushed the man. Suddenly the Welshman wasn't standing. A red haze came over his eyes as Roarke dropped to his knees and felt the jolt of the impact of his fist on Sayer's face again and again.

"Stop."

There was a weight on his arm, light but insistent.

"*Stop.*"

He stared down at the sailor trying to shield his face with his hands. Blood ran between his fingers. Roarke looked at his own clenched fist, the knuckles bloody. He glanced over his shoulder and met Adriana's dark gaze and saw in it the warning that rang in what reason still existed under his fury.

One dead sailor, and there would be a mutiny for sure.

Roarke yanked a dagger from his boot. He set the tip against the sailor's groin. "Welshman," he spat, "there are many ways to stop a man from talking."

Behind the screen of Sayer's broken fingers, one eye widened. "There'll be no need of that, Captain."

"Joubert," he said, never taking his eyes off the man, "you told me once that this sailor was trustworthy."

"He turned on me quick enough."

"'Twas the shock," Sayer sputtered, "I wouldn't have—"

"Aye, you would have," she said and Roarke heard the anger in her voice. "How many years have we known each other? Yet you would have treated me like a common whore and then thrown me to the crew."

Roarke shifted the knife from Sayer's groin to his chin. He pressed deep enough so that a bead of blood grew on its tip.

"A man without a tongue," Roarke warned, "can't tell tales."

"For the love of God, Captain."

Sayer's chest rose and fell. The man was terrified, but Roarke knew that terror would pass as soon as he lifted the knife.

He would have to kill this Welshman.

He changed the angle of the knife.

"Mercy, captain!"

Roarke thought of Captain Samuel Leighton laughing on his ship as he sailed it away from the strand where he'd marooned his brother and himself, Adam already half-dead from a whipping. Someday he would plunge a knife into the neck of his brother's murderer, just like this.

"Mercy," Sayer cried softly, his face crumpling. "Please—"

"Captain."

Her voice was calm and low but it filled his head. Her voice was the singing of reason and he heard the echo of it despite himself. He couldn't let passions overcome him. The death of a sailor by his bloody hand would be like a spark over a powder keg. Mutiny would mean a tortured death for him, for Drake— and for Adriana.

He glared at the sailor. "Do you want to live?"

"Aye!"

"Then swear." Roarke pressed the dagger's edge flat against the sailor's throat. "Swear you'll stay silent...or you'll die."

CHAPTER TWELVE

When four people knew the truth, was a secret still a secret?

Adriana contemplated this quandary as she stood in the cabin with the captain, Drake, and a bloody Welshman, discussing how to guarantee Gwynn's silence. Gwynn sprawled on the floor, curled in on his own ribs, still bleeding from what appeared to be a broken nose, watching her, Drake, and the captain with rolling, half-wild eyes.

"Tonight, Sayer walked in here and collapsed," the captain began, relating the story they would all stick to. "His nose broke as he hit the floor."

"So our little mouse," Drake continued, "raced over to see what happened to her friend. She—" Drake closed his eyes and composed himself "—*He* noticed that Sayer was feverish and his face spotted."

"Smallpox," Roarke said. "So Sayer must go

directly to isolation and stay there until the sickness passes."

"Smallpox won't work," Adriana said. "Make it the ague or something."

"Smallpox," Drake said, "strikes more terror."

"But Gwynn doesn't have any spots." She breathed out a frustrated sigh. "*I've* had smallpox. I know it doesn't look like this. The men will know, too."

"Not everyone has had the disease," the captain added. "I haven't."

"And even if they have," Drake interjected, "the disease is fierce enough that no man wants to test the idea that he can't get it again."

Roarke nodded. "It's a sure way to isolate him."

"Smallpox or not," she said, "they'll be suspicious. They'll try to see him from afar, to whisper to him."

Roarke sidled a glance to Drake. "Is the surgeon with the crew or with us?"

"With us. In an uprising, the surgeon will be the first to die just for the botched amputation he did on old Jean-Claude."

"Then tell him to set up an isolation area where the men can't get to this Welshman. And he has to guard Sayer personally, for the sake of the whole crew."

She insisted, "It will never work."

Roarke's face tightened. "It has to work, at least until we see land."

Drake headed toward the door. "I'll tell the surgeon to prepare the area."

"I'll announce it to the crew." Roarke pushed away from the desk and reached for his burgundy velvet coat. "Once they hear that he has smallpox, they'll clear a wide path for him. Nobody will be close enough to see the difference."

Drake said, "When I return, the mouse and I will carry him—"

"Me? He weighs a ton!"

"You and I have had smallpox. The captain hasn't. I'll bear the weight, you just have to pick up his feet."

"Adriana."

Roarke's voice was a calm rumble, and she felt the vibrations down to her toes. She braced herself to meet his all-too-knowing eyes.

"This is very dangerous," he said. "You need to be convincing."

"I'm very good at pulling the wool over sailors' eyes."

As Roarke predicted, the sailors kept their distance when she and Drake carried Gwynn out of Roarke's cabin. Sayer kept his silence, as well, probably due to the keen edge of Drake's dagger against his spine. While they brought Gwynn to the far end of the orlop deck, she heard the sailors' voices filtering down from the deck above. Oddly, many of their comments were directed at her. They kept telling her to buck up and be strong, as if the captain had made an unwilling peg boy out of her.

Not yet, she thought with a quiver. *Not yet.*

The bells had rung for the last dog watch by the time she got back to the cabin. Roarke was waiting for her behind the desk, a dark silhouette in the waning daylight.

He looked up at her with troubled eyes. "You're in terrible danger, *petite*."

Petite.

Like she was small, precious.

Like she was loved.

She shook the foolish, foolish thought out of her head. "I've always been in danger. Sayer's stupid but he's not a fool."

"I wasn't talking about him, Adriana."

He spoke her name and it was like music, somehow. Maybe it was the English accent, maybe it was the way his voice rumbled, but the sound of her true name on his lips was enough to make her knees go soft.

"You," she said, "haven't done anything that I haven't wanted."

He made a sound like he was sucking air between his teeth, and that's how she knew she'd surprised him. She'd been a boy too long to start pretending she was some ninny nursery-raised virgin or a fan-wielding flirt.

"Your honesty," he said, "is...unsettling."

"Would you have me lie?"

"To protect yourself? Yes."

"Why would I protect myself from something I want?"

She'd wanted him in an instinctive, deep-seated, purely feminine way that she could no longer deny. She knew he wanted her, too—he'd been at sea without relief for months, of course he reacted swiftly—but it was more than that. When they'd lain on that bed together, they'd been so absorbed that they hadn't even heard Gwynn open the door.

"Adriana." His voice was strangled, frustrated. "I thought you understood the drawbacks of being a woman."

"The drawbacks, yes." She raised her hands to her hips. "As for the benefits, I'm still learning."

"It's always women who pay for such pleasure, *petite*."

He straightened up and found interest in the darkness in the corners of the room. He ran a hand through his hair. She could practically hear his thoughts running amok. Then, suddenly he seized one of the charts curled to one side and, removing the weights from the chart beneath, smoothed the new chart across the desk.

He said, "I've made an adjustment in our latitude."

"I noticed." But the scratching on his map wasn't what she wanted to talk about. "We've veered northerly."

"We're not very far from the coast of the Americas."

Through her mind passed a flood of stories about impenetrable forests, roaming beasts, brutal winters, and red-skinned savages. From what she'd heard of that vast place, it was untamed and brutal, destroying any colonist who dared to settle.

"If the winds hold," he continued, "we should be at Charles Town any day."

"Charles Town," she repeated, as the word settled. "But Charles Town is an English settlement."

"As usual, you are remarkably well-informed."

Her heart skipped a beat. She glanced down at the chart, at his finger tracing the furrowed edge of land toward a spot at the edge of a river marked with an X.

"We're sailing on a French privateer," she said. "It'd be madness to approach Charles Town."

"My ship is fast. We'll veer wide around the city."

"Roarke."

His head shot up. She realized, in her distraction, that she'd called him by the name she'd found on his letter. With one look at his face, any doubts she'd nurtured that the letter she'd read was addressed to this man vanished.

He said, "How—"

"I was looking for a rag." She felt a rush of shame. "I found letters wrapped in a red ribbon."

"You read them."

A statement, not an accusation.

"Just one." She pulled on her own fingers in agitation. "A letter from your mother, concerning

Adam."

She knew his brother Adam was dead. She'd parsed together the stories she'd heard from the sailors with what she'd learned from the letter and what Roarke had told her outside Roscoff. She didn't know the details, but a girl didn't have to be lettered to assume that Captain Samuel Leighton was somehow behind his brother's death.

"Forget my name, Adriana."

She shook her head. She would never forget that name, any more than she could forget this beautiful man standing across the desk, trying his best to pretend they hadn't almost made love on the bed she could see out of the corner of her eye.

For that name was the name of the true man, the kind one, the honorable one who existed behind the mask of Captain Wolfe.

"Forget that name," he repeated, his eyes going flat.

"Why would—"

"I would have you curse Captain Wolfe for what I'm about to do—not the man whose name you discovered."

For what I'm about to do.

A terrible weakness stole over her.

"As soon as we get within rowing distance of the Americas," he said, "I'm sending you off alone."

Roarke turned his back to her. He could not bear

to see the shock, terror, and betrayal in those soft brown eyes.

We all wear disguises, he thought, as he fixed his gaze unseeing out the wide stern windows of his cabin as the day's light waned. The danger comes when you wear a disguise for too long, and you become the very demon whose sins you'd once hoped to shed.

"Jamaica," she said, sometime later, when the silence became too much to bear. "If you're going to maroon me, do it in Jamaica."

He flinched at the word *maroon*. He didn't want to do this. He didn't want to be responsible for her virtue. He didn't want to spend every waking moment thinking of her while the taste of her skin lingered on his tongue. But most of all, he didn't want to be a captain who maroons people, as Captain Samuel Leighton had marooned him and his beaten, broken brother on the coast of Madagascar.

"Jamaica," he said tightly, "is too far away."

"There are other islands."

"Any island in the Caribbean is infested with pirates."

"Heaven forbid."

He tightened his jaw at her flippancy. "If I leave you among pirates, you'll sign up for another ship and continue this farce until it's too late."

Her silence confirmed his suspicions. She knew no other way to survive, so of course she'd do the easiest thing possible. Images of her fate flashed through his mind—dirty, grunting men limned by torchlight groping her small white body sprawled naked on a deck.

Bile grew hot in his belly.

She said, "Tell me where I'm going, then."

A hot breath rushed out of him. This would be a hundred times easier if she were willing. He'd spent the last week charting the latitude of their voyage and estimating the longitude. He probed his memory for what he knew about the colonies that populated the American coast. Several cities from New York to Charles Town were bustling, thriving English seaports. They'd be difficult to approach in this French privateer without risking notice by any English warships that might be in the area. But there were other settlements, smaller towns with settlers desperate for men and women to join and help build their communities.

He turned around to lean over the desk again. "I intend to release you—"

"—abandon me, you mean—"

"—save you," he interrupted. "From yourself, if necessary."

He mustered the courage to look at her. She stood cock-hipped. She had her boy face on, immobile, steady of gaze, her little nostrils flaring. But it was too late, he saw the girl underneath the mask. He knew the softness of that cheek, the curve of her breast now crushed under linen bindings. The hollow of his palm felt warm, as if he still held the throbbing heat of her sex in his hand.

He dragged his attention back to the map. "The Santee River pours into the sea right here." He tapped a coastal area. "Upstream is a French Huguenot settlement called Jamestown."

"French?"

"Yes." He forced confidence in his voice though he wasn't sure if the settlement was still in existence. Settlements grew, struggled, and disappeared on a regular basis in this wilderness. "The English proprietors of this land are desperate to get it settled, and they're not particular about nationality. They've accepted several shiploads of French Protestants into their colony."

"But I'm Catholic."

"Hide it," he said. "You're very good at that."

He heard her footfall as she came around the desk. He fixed his attention on the map while the lines blurred in his sight. A perfumed creature in satin couldn't exude as strong of an attraction as this slip of a woman, now pressing her small, strong body against his side.

"Don't maroon me." She stretched her hand over his. "Don't leave me there to die."

Each word a dagger in his heart. Memories tormented him, of him and Adam scouring the shore, seeking fresh water, scrambling for food, wilting under the fierceness of the Madagascar sun.

"You'll have supplies," he said. "Food, water, a tarp for shelter—"

"In Jamaica, I could find work in the port. As a cordier or—"

"Don't lie."

His fears threatened to choke him. She still didn't understand that she couldn't masquerade as a boy any longer. Her secret was contained, but not for long. She needed to face her fate as a woman, and that's what troubled him the most. He now understood that the choices for women were few and well-defined. She would have to marry, or she would have to bargain her wares in one of the seaports that dotted the coast.

The thought of another man touching her made his ears buzz and his vision haze over, so much so that he didn't notice the pounding of footsteps on the deck above until Drake rapped on his door.

Roarke barked, "Enter."

Drake tumbled in, a smile splitting his face. "No worries now, Captain." Drake waved to the east. "Land-ho!"

Relief loosened his limbs. His longitude measure had been off, they'd reached the coast sooner than he expected.

He said to Drake, "How far?"

"If the wind keeps," Drake said, "then we'll be within rowing distance by sunset."

"Good." He tapped the desk, thinking. "Tell the men we need to restore our fresh water supplies. Set the sails to landward and make them prepare the barrels."

"Aye-aye, Captain."

"Drake," Adriana said, "one more thing."

Drake raised a brow as if amused that a pip of a girl would make a demand.

"When you return," she said, "make sure to knock first."

CHAPTER THIRTEEN

After Drake left, Adriana walked across the cabin and shot the bolt. Then she turned to the man determined to abandon her on a savage shore.

Roarke stood very still behind the desk, his gray-green gaze as bright as the sun hitting the water through the window behind him. Her heart did a strange looping drop. Something akin to fear made her limbs go numb, but she started toward him anyway.

He said, as she approached, "I will not change my mind, Adriana."

"I know."

He seized her jaw to stop her in place. "You'll hate me for this."

"I may hate you for marooning me," she said, raising her face despite his resistance, "but I won't hate you for *this*."

She met his lips with her own. She knew what she was doing this time, so she anticipated the parting of his lips, and the way his tongue brushed against hers. She ran her hands up his shoulders and stroked his chest, feeling his own nipples beneath the linen. He thrust his fingers through her hair and held her so tightly that she began to worry that he would do nothing more but kiss.

Then a sound came from his throat—low and long and rumbling—and she understood that he would not stop now.

He lifted her off the ground. She wished his hands were not dug into her sides, full of the linen of her shirt or the wool of her breeches, but rather full with her breasts or the curve of her backside. Her skin prickled in anticipation of his touch. Already her mind skipped ahead to nakedness though she was still fully dressed and the bed was just a shape on the edge of her sight growing larger as he hauled her toward it.

She jarred as her feet hit the floor. They separated for a dizzy breath. She stared up at him, that tight jaw, that muscle moving in his cheek, the sun-kissed skin with the flare of white crinkles on the edge of his eyes, that strange crescent-shaped scar, memorizing already the moment that she would dream about in the days, months, maybe even the years to come.

The tails of his shirt brushed her face as he yanked it off his chest.

She seized her own shirt.

Off.

She threw it aside and tugged at the bindings around her breasts. Roarke dipped to yank off his boots. She struggled with the bindings as he straightened to undo his breeches.

Off.

Everything—shirt, bindings, breeches, small clothes, modesty, hesitancy, fear—all tossed in abandon. With a racing heart she saw Roarke's body unveiled—the wide, muscled shoulders, the strange undulating ripples of his abdomen, the ridges on either side of his hips that her fingers itched to trace, ridges that tapered down to his sex—now hard and straining up.

A sensation like a shock shot through her body as he brushed a finger across the tip of her nipple. She'd always been grateful that her breasts were small, for it made it easier for her to pretend to be a boy, but when Roarke cupped one of her breasts in his hand she suddenly felt as if she had the bosom of a farmer's wife, spilling out full, swollen, and heavy.

Her curiosity overtook her. She wrapped her fingers around his sex and was rewarded with the feel of a jolt going through his body. He felt silky-smooth, like the well-polished railings of the quarterdeck, but warm and ridged and pulsing with life.

Her inner muscles throbbed with an unsatisfied ache.

He pressed his forehead against hers, and she

knew behind that hard skull doubts were growing.

"Don't," she whispered.

"Adriana—"

"You're the Sea Wolf, a brutal pirate without honor, remember?"

"But you spoke my name." His mouth pressed against her hair. "You know my name."

His sex slipped out of her grip as he hauled her onto the bed. She bounced on the mattress only to come up against his solid chest. He braced himself on one elbow as his other hand roamed over her—a swift pass across her breast, her waist, the curve of her hip, down over her thigh only to rise up inside it. His fingers scraped against the tender skin of her inner thighs as they traveled closer to where she wanted them to be. He found her cleft and stretched his fingers deep.

She grasped his muscled arm to brace herself for the sensations flooding through her. His tongue found the hollow of her throat and he mimicked there what his fingers were doing between her legs until both places were slick with moisture.

Though she loved this feeling, it wasn't enough.

She reached down and removed his hand. She nudged one knee against his legs as invitation. Groaning, he rolled atop her, then used his thighs to push her legs open even wider, so that her cleft was exposed to his perusal.

How wonderfully arousing it was, to look between them and see their naked bodies, so clearly made for this joining.

"Look at me."

He was breathing heavily above her, bracing himself on his elbows.

"It will hurt for a moment, *chérie.*"

No, she thought.

It will hurt forever.

It would hurt whenever she smelled the scent of pine wood or pitch, whenever she saw sails billowing in a harbor, whenever she smelled the sea wind on linen, or heard the rush of waves against a hull. If she lived through the next months, she would treasure this singular moment though she might resent him, for the rest of her life, for what he planned to do.

Then all thought flew out of her mind as the head of his sex probed where his fingers had once been. He moved with great tenderness, and her heart swelled with painful pressure at his kindness. She watched his jaw tighten as he eased himself a fraction deeper. The air in the room grew thin. An ache had grown to agonizing proportions in the core of her body. She felt full, but not full enough, so she surged her hips up, a silent assent for more.

With one smooth, insistent stroke, he slipped inside her, pausing briefly against a resistance that she felt as a stretching, increasingly sharp pain that ended almost as quickly as it started, leaving behind a twinging sensation overwhelmed by the fullness of his sex lodged deep inside her body.

He went still and watched her face. She trembled

though not from cold or fear or anything bad. The sensations rushing through her were just too many to parse. She had not expected such a perfect fit of their bodies. Not just his sex throbbing within her loins, but the way his hips fit between her thighs, his abdomen against her own, his chest just brushing her nipples which seemed to rise to meet his skin.

The way his hand cupped her face. The way his gaze held her own.

Skin to skin. Heart to heart.

A slow smile stretched across his face, and she felt a smile blossom on hers to mirror his own. How kind he looked when he smiled. She saw the boy still within him, the laughing, excited older brother setting off for adventures, coaxing his younger brother into the fun. She saw the commanding man he'd grown into, the confidence and the quiet assurance and the steady sense of right that had led him to command.

And she saw the hurt, too, rippling under all that. A pain that came from a sense of failure. He couldn't prevent that failure with his brother, just as he felt he couldn't stop what he was about to do to her. She traced the line of his jaw and wished she could wipe all that pain away—and sensed that maybe, in this wrapped embrace, she could.

Coupling was not always like this. She may be just new into womanhood, but she'd witnessed many a sailor having his way with many a woman in many a strange way. She'd never once conceived that giving herself bodily to a man would make her feel so completely whole. Yet she knew that there was still more to this coupling. That ache that she'd thought was only for the feel of his hardness inside her was growing.

She wanted all of him.

The sunlight had turned golden through the stern windows. They still had time. She wanted to live in this ringing joy for as long as fate allowed them.

Then he moved inside her.

She grasped his sides to brace herself.

He lowered his head to suck her upper lip into his mouth, and then he moved again.

Oh.

He took her lower lip this time, and moved again.

Beneath her gripped hands his muscles rippled. His stroking took on a slow but increasing rhythm. She tilted her hips to try to match his movements. Everything inside her grew taut and tense—too taut, too tense—she wasn't sure she could bear it. Her breathing started to match his thrusts as her senses went dizzy.

She gave herself over to an urge that was pure and fierce and undeniable and a hundred thousand times stronger than she'd ever imagined. It tangled up with all the other things she craved—warmth and compassion and love, yes, even love, she could admit that now—for it was one of the wonders she'd been denied when she dedicated herself to living a life that wasn't honest and wasn't true.

She knew he wanted her, too—even if it were only for her body. He spoke by the way he gripped her hair, by the tenderness of his movements, by the way his breath came harsh through his throat, and the way he dug his hand in the flesh of her hip to still her though she sensed he hadn't yet thrust as deep as he wanted.

His voice came, hoarse and full of desire.

"Come with me, Adriana."

She wasn't sure what he meant, but she knew she would follow this man to the very ends of the earth.

"Come with me," he whispered, "as you did before."

And then she understood.

So she threw her head back against the covers and followed the captain's orders.

CHAPTER FOURTEEN

He lay on his back with her head in the nook of his shoulder. She'd snuggled close to him, slipping almost immediately into a doze, but there would be no sleep for him.

She could not stay on the ship. That much he knew.

And yet...if he and Drake could maintain the smallpox farce for but a week, the ship could sail safely into the Caribbean among a dozen French ports. He could make arrangements in Haiti, Martinique, or Saint Martin for a place for her to live. She could eat beignets on her terrace in the morning, wear soft silks bought with his money, and spend her days raising her sweet face to the warm tropical sun.

He buried his face in her short, soft hair and breathed in the smell of the sea. Her body lay against his, small and lean with sleek muscles defining delicate curves. Her beauty was like a bud that would soon blossom into fullness.

He wanted to be the man to make her blossom.

He closed his eyes and tried to focus his thoughts. His privateering deal with the French did not specify where he took his prizes, but he knew they had expected him to hover around the mouth of the English Channel in order to deliver stolen ships straight to French ports. But there were plenty of English merchant ships plying Caribbean waters, and plenty of French ports for safe harbor. Technically, he would not be negating his contractual duties if he were to harry the English here.

After he found and destroyed Leighton, of course.

He could return to her between voyages. Drape fine jewels across her neck. Gift her with sapphire-blue or emerald-green satin that would set off her coloring. He wanted to see her hair grow below her shoulders, watch how it brushed against her little sharp chin. He'd buy her corsets to surge her plump breasts above the neckline, lacy garters that he could untie from her sleek thighs. He could lay her down on fine linen and sink his cock into her tight body and watch as she abandoned herself to sensation.

Then he became aware of her hand curled around his cock, already at half-mast.

She raised her head and showed him sleepy eyes. "I want you again."

Her directness sent his blood rushing southward.

She smiled as his cock tightened in her hand.

"You'll be sore," he warned.

"I don't care."

"Then you'd better captain this ship, Adriana."

He rolled on his back and pulled her on top of him, positioning her thighs so she straddled his body. Understanding lit her dark eyes. She shimmied down until he felt the heat of her cleft suck the tip of his cock.

He grasped her hips in warning. For all her enthusiasm, she was new to this and he didn't want to hurt her. But once again, she brushed aside his caution. She tipped forward and kissed him—a hungry, open-mouthed kiss. He tilted his mouth against hers to try to gain mastery over the moment, but she was eager. Their mouths merged, separated, merged again, and their tongues slipped past one another. The battle of wills exhilarated him. His cock strained up toward the heat she freely offered.

He let go of her hips.

He let her win.

With a little sound of joy, she slid down in one swift stroke so urgent that he nearly lost all control. He broke away from the kiss and dug his fingers into her hair. She lifted her hips again and slid down so far he felt her wet sex down to his root. She surged up again, this time so high that his cock slipped out of her. She paused an aching moment before she plunged anew.

His breath came fast. Was there ever a woman so

open to her own pleasure, so free of coyness or calculation?

He tried to focus so he wouldn't spill inside her before she was ready. He should have prepared her better before lifting her atop him. Right now he wanted to slip his hand between them to stroke her, but it was hard enough to hold himself back while she moved on him, her lids heavy, her lips plump and parted, so full of joy.

She chose, suddenly, to wriggle.

"Adriana."

She laughed at his gritted warning. Her laugh was a light, rippling sound that made him think of sunshine and cool water and long, unfurling days of leisure.

What are you doing to me, my little mouse?

He nudged her torso upright. The movement settled her weight on his cock and stopped the wriggling for now. It also exposed one tip-tilted nipple within reach of his mouth.

Then it was her turn to groan and clutch his head as he made that nub tighten against his hungry tongue. His cock throbbed for release, but at least for the moment she wasn't stoking him beyond all control. It was his job to coax that little hoarse gasp she made when she came, and he would do it before he found his own pleasure. He wasn't going to let this determined, tiny woman upend the natural order of things.

But she was strong. Even pressed down as she

was by his leaning grip, she managed to press her knees against the mattress to slide herself up his shaft a fraction. Then she changed the dynamics altogether by bracing herself on his shoulders to gain leverage. He sensed by the swift beating of her heart that she was perilously close to the brink of pleasure. So he did what he must—he slipped his fingers between them to find the other, hidden nub of a woman's sex so he could stroke it in rhythm with her movement.

At the first touch, her inner muscles tightened around his cock. She threw back her head and made that glorious sound.

He couldn't hold on a moment longer.

He rode this pleasure to its fullest, falling back on his hands so he could lift his hips off the bed and thrust every inch into her. She gasped with her head thrown back. Her skin—so pale where the sun had never touched—flushed pink from the plump mounds of her breasts to the top of her thighs. The sight of her made his cock pulse until he had nothing left to give her.

He sat up and seized her. He held her as close as skin and bone could be. Another kind of feeling swept over him, an unfamiliar, undeniable sensation that dragged his heart to places he'd never dared to go. He buried his face in the nook of her neck and smelled her—salt and sex and woman and tar and sun—a mélange of perfumes that he knew would from this moment on forever identify as the perfume of Adriana.

He could not send her off alone in the wilderness. The decision sank into him like an anchor hitting the seabed. He would risk another week on the ship. He would settle her on an island. He would arrange for shelter and food and safety and give her the life she deserved.

Then the world outside began to sift through his consciousness as they rocked gently on the bed. On the deck came the sound of throaty singing and the raucous sound of feet stamping, the joy of men knowing land was near. He started to speak to her, talking against the delicate ridge of her collarbone, words that he wanted to say but somehow came out only as *Adriana, Adriana, Adriana, Adriana.*

She answered him in kind.

Moments later, he heard the sound of footsteps just outside his door, followed by a banging, an infernal banging on the wood.

Her smile was the sun falling warm upon his face. "Your men," she whispered, "need lessons in timing."

"That they do."

"Can you pretend that you're sleeping?"

"Sir!" Drake interrupted from beyond the door. "Captain!"

Her little nose wrinkled with disappointment. With reluctance, he slipped her off him and tugged the sheet over her nakedness. He reached over the side of the bed for his breeches.

"Sir!"

"Damn it, Drake, give me a minute." He shoved his feet in his breeches and padded barefoot to the door to unbolt it. "What is so urgent that—"

"Captain."

Drake swung into the room. With one look at his face, Roarke knew something was terribly wrong. Then he realized that the deck above had gone quiet.

"It's Sayer," Drake said. He tugged on his belt as if his hand itched for a weapon. "He broke out of quarantine. He wasn't as hurt as we thought."

"Damn it."

"It's worse." Drake's jaw tightened. "They know about her."

Roarke reached for the hilt of his sword but found nothing but the waist of his unbelted breeches. In his mind he measured the path from his cabin to the boat, and thought of the hoard of mutinous sailors that would be in his path.

Think. *Think fast.*

He barked, "How far are we from land?"

"Within rowing distance." Drake threw up a hand. "But I haven't seen any settlements, no sign of life at all."

"Check the weapons chest and make sure it's secure."

"Done."

"Arm yourself well." He slapped a hand on Drake's shoulder. "Put down one of the *chaloupes,* and do it quickly. We'll meet you on the upper deck in five minutes."

Drake left. Roarke closed the door behind him and turned to face Adriana.

There she was, the ship's mouse again, fully dressed with a dagger tight in her hand.

She said, "I will fight beside you."

"This is a fight we can't win." His mind raced, counting the seconds. In his mind he heard the sound of an axe breaking down the door to the cabin. "I'm sending you off, Adriana."

"But you're coming with me."

He didn't answer. She was a sailor, she *knew*. This ship was his wealth, his livelihood, his identity, his blood and his bones. This ship was meant to sweep him across the sea in Leighton's wake, bring the bastard to justice for Adam, and then deliver the means to support a true life, a safe future. He couldn't leave this ship even if it was doomed to a grave on the watery sands of the deepest sea.

"Gather your things." He strode to his desk so he wouldn't have to see the betrayal in her eyes. "Here's a compass, some food, money." He searched through the drawer and gave her all of it—a clanking pile of pieces-of-eight. He shoved everything in a hemp sack and thrust it toward her. "Take it. We can't wait."

"Don't do this."

Her voice was plaintive.

His heart was a six-ton stone in his chest.

He told himself that he was different from Leighton. Leighton hadn't felt this bone-deep remorse as that wretch sent him and his brother to certain death.

But no amount of rationalization could negate the fact that he was committing the exact same sin.

"I told you," he stuttered, hating his own voice. "I told you that I wouldn't change my mind."

If he'd swung at her with a fist he couldn't have hit her harder. He watched as she stumbled back to her alcove to emerge out moments later with a sack across her shoulder. His arms ached to embrace her but he forced them to his side.

It was better this way.

She would be *safe*.

He grabbed his coat, his burgundy coat, and slipped it on for the edge of authority it might gain him. He yanked his sword out of its scabbard as he thrust the door open. The hall was quiet, unoccupied. Keeping her in the shadows behind him, he pushed the far door open and swung out onto the deck to see the men gathered, unnaturally silent, talking in clusters. With relief he noticed that they bore no weapons.

Drake stood up near a rope ladder swung between two wooden davits. He nodded and Roarke knew the boat was ready.

He pulled Adriana into the violet light of sunset. At the sight of her, the sailors began to murmur.

In a whisper she said, "You'll come for me later?"

His throat went dry. He didn't know what would

happen after she and Drake rowed away. The surgeon, now skittering up the stairs to join him, wouldn't be of any use in a fight. Roarke didn't want to leave her standing on the shore day after day, week after week, waiting for salvation in a sail glimpsed on the horizon. He wanted her to find help, shelter, and succor amid settlers. Unlike him and Adam, she would know from the start that she had no one and nothing to rely on but her own wits.

He shoved her toward Drake.

She would survive this.

Facing a ship full of mutinous sailors, he likely would not.

CHAPTER FIFTEEN

While Drake rowed them to the unbroken forest of the shore, Adriana held onto the gunwales of the *chaloupe* and stared over her shoulder at the ship, waiting to hear the blast of a pistol or the shouts of angry men.

"He'll hold them off," Drake muttered between pulls. "He'll keep them at bay until I return to help."

She could tell he was trying to convince himself. Her heart ached to believe him. She strained her ears, seeking any indication of what was going on upon the ship from which he'd cast her away.

She wanted to believe that he would survive. She wanted to believe a lot of things. She wanted to believe that he'd felt something special in their lovemaking, something more than just physical gratification. She wanted to believe that his soft, warm smile meant that he felt as she'd felt—joyous and safe and utterly loved. She wanted to believe that he would come back to fetch her, once he dumped this mutinous crew at some Caribbean port.

But he'd made no promise.

Adriana, Adriana, Adriana.

She felt the wetness on her cheeks and knew what it was. She couldn't blame these streaks on rain or sea-spray or anything but the fact that she'd become a woman, and would never again be able to pretend she was a boy.

Desperate for distraction, she pulled out the items Roarke had given her—a compass, a map, a sack of coins useless in a wilderness—palming each item as if it were a piece of his heart. She arranged them and rearranged them in her satchel while her mind raced, doubting everything, especially the idea that after just a few hours of lovemaking, she and Roarke were bonded in a way that would last forever.

He made no promise.

Too soon, the boat slid into the muddy shore.

"Out." Drake grabbed her satchel and tossed it over the bow where it fell with a thump on the dry shore. "The sooner I'm back, the better the captain's chances."

She swung a leg over the gunwale into the shallow water, gathering splinters in her palms as she clung.

She whispered, "Save him."

Drake's face, full of worry. "Push me off."

She splattered to the bow and put her weight

behind it to free the keel from the sand. She felt the moment it floated free.

She stood while waves washed her ankles, watching Drake pull hard on the oars. "Tell him," she shouted, "Tell him..."

Tell him that I love him.

"Follow the shore until you find the mouth of a river," Drake shouted without pausing in his rowing. "Colonists tend to settle upstream."

Adriana stumbled backwards out of the wash of the tide. She felt the hard sand beneath her feet. Still she backed up until she tripped over a piece of driftwood and fell hard to her backside. There she sprawled, breathless and unbelieving, watching the rowboat as best as she could in the gloaming. Dampness seeped through the seat of her breeches but still she sat as the first stars winked in the sky. Tiny golden lights lit on the ship, lanterns for the night watch, and she breathed in short, frightened gulps wondering if Roarke still captained it.

Those lights became dimmer, and then disappeared altogether.

Her breathing sounded so very loud. She sat on a shore of a savage country with the sea empty before her and the solid wall of untouched woods at her back. She threw her arms back and lay flat on the mud, waiting for fate to find her.

The tide washed soft and rhythmic against the sand, and in her mind it sounded like *Adriana, Adriana, Adriana.*

CHAPTER SIXTEEN

He will come back for me.

She woke up the next day shivering and hungry. She refused to move from that spot on the shore, despite the swirling storm clouds churning toward the land. From the water's edge she saw the wind kicking up whitecaps. She strained her sight seeking a sail on the horizon.

High tide came and she skittered back to the edge of the woods, where massive oaks with twisted branches gave some measure of shelter from the first, splattered drops. When she saw the foam of a surge race past the high tide line she fell back even further, deeper into the woods. The twisted branches bent back under the onslaught of the wind. She realized that this was no common storm, but very much like the tropical cyclones that plagued the Indian oceans, whipping the sea into a frenzy and on land tearing all but the massive Baobab trees from their roots.

Roarke couldn't approach land today and risk the ship being pushed into the shallows where the hull could be torn on some unseen rocks or reef. He would seek a safe, deep bay from what he could find on his map, or he'd ride out the storm's fury on the open seas.

So she found shelter deeper into the woods, on higher ground, in the burnt hollow of an oak that seemed as old as the world. To light a fire would be fruitless, so she huddled for warmth and pressed up against the grooves inside the tree, her nose filled up with the scent of moss and fungus and the sweet scent of lightning and ocean rain. To pass the time she fumbled in the sack he gave her, turning over in her hands each of the gold pieces he'd given her—more wealth than she'd ever owned. She discovered at the bottom of her own sack an apple she'd saved for Chou-Chou.

She ate the apple and ached for all she'd lost.

Roarke will come back for me.

She didn't sleep for a long time. She scarcely knew day from night because of the glowering clouds. When she finally did sleep, she woke to a world transformed. Sunlight slipped through the trees and glittered on the forest floor. Through the leaves she glimpsed patches of bright blue sky.

She came out of the woods and scoured the sea for any sign of a sail. She was so fixed on the horizon that she tripped over a plank of driftwood.

Only it was not the bleached gray branch she'd tripped over before. This was a sea-soaked wooden plank, cut and planed and polished to perfection.

A tremor rippled through her.

It's nothing, she told herself. A storm like that churns the seabed and throws up old, strange treasures.

She ventured a little farther north. There were lots of cockles and a conch of a remarkable size, but she saw no more driftwood. She kept glancing back to where she'd started, not wanting to get too far, in case Roarke sent a boat. She determined to venture as far as the little spit that jutted out into the sea. Then she would turn back, start a fire if she could find anything dry to burn, and wait for Roarke's return.

She reached the head of the spit and saw, on the other side, a deep inlet that narrowed as if it were the entrance to a river. The entrance was choked with debris and mud. With a start she noticed about a dozen people walking about on the shore, men and women, gathering things in their arms. They looked like they wouldn't have been out of place walking the streets of Saint-Malo.

Then she noticed two men trying to straighten a tattered white sail to dry in the sun. Only then did she realize the brown mud wasn't mud but a piling up of wooden boards.

With a cold calm, she told herself that surely there were many ships that sailed upon these seas. Many English ships must ply the route between

Charles Town and the other settlements to the north, passing across these waters to deliver goods from one part of the English colonies to another. One ship's planks, one ship's sails, they all looked the same.

The sand bit into her feet as she stumbled closer to the ocean's edge. Her throat contracted so that it took effort to force air into her lungs. A ringing began in her ears, so loud that she was only vaguely aware that someone had shouted in her direction. She stepped over what she knew now as a yardarm and tried not to tangle her feet in the stretched rigging.

She saw a leg jutting out from beneath the broken staves of a barrel. She saw a red, bruised, naked back, a hemp-rope belt, and the wide-legged breeches favored by sailors on merchant ships or private vessels or privateers.

"Garçon!"

The sound was a wasp in her ear. She ignored it as well as the people heading her way. She found another broken body. Crabs ran across his back as she pushed off some debris. She saw the glimmer of an ear-piercing and pulled her gaze away, unwilling to confirm if the dark gold loop belonged to the bosun. Such a piercing was common enough, she told herself. It could belong to any sailor. Yet her heart raced as she pushed away planks, though splinters dug into her hands and tore at her sagging, wet shirt. She found more broken bodies, and cutlasses and pistols and a belay pin and an enormous capstan and piece of the cathead and a metal davit and washboards and swollen salt tack and Gwynn.

Gwynn.

Black bearded and blue-lipped and swollen in the belly. A thousand memories passed through her mind. When she was young, he would let her ride his shoulders as he brought her to a seaside tavern in St. Mary's. He would rub her head for luck as he gambled, while she gorged herself on rice boiled in milk and drizzled with honey under the table by his feet.

Swift footsteps sounded on the sand.

"Garçon, ça va?"

She whirled around and stared unseeing at the man who spoke to her—a boy, really, tall and skinny with skin that turned a flaming pink as he got a good look at her—then she pushed past him to seek more bodies.

Behind her, the boy whispered in astonishment, *"Mademoiselle?"*

She couldn't suck in enough air. *Roarke is alive.* He would ride a plank through the storm. He would clamber upon a loose boat, drift on the sea until the waters calmed and he could row himself to the west. Right now he could be pulling up on the sand and seeking her amid the inlets. He wasn't here, she told herself, as sea-soaked wood slipped out of her bloody hands as she overturned another plank.

The boy's shadow fell over her. "Miss," he said in English. "Miss, can I help you?"

She realized she was making strange mewling

sounds, half-gasps and stuttered noises, as she recognized a ledger, a pillow peppered with glass, the little table where Chou-Chou had eaten the captain's poisoned dinner.

"Etienne." A woman's voice, calling out in French. "Stop staring at the poor girl and go help your father."

The sand sank under her feet as she hefted a broken section of the hull. This plank was heavier than all the rest, but she saw the toe of a shiny boot poking out from beneath. A sharp pain slashed through her shoulder as she heaved it up, a ripping of muscle that she ignored because she had to know.

This man's shoulders were broad.

His boots, made of leather and scaled with salt.

His black-haired head, crushed under planking.

His coat, fine burgundy velvet.

The world shrank to a pinpoint of light that vanished into nothing.

CHAPTER SEVENTEEN

Three years later

Adriana walked through the thick forest of swamp oaks and cypresses, bending to avoid the gray moss that hung from the branches. The winter air stung her cheeks, but she made no effort to cover her face. The Carolina winters were far milder than those of Brittany. In the three years of her stay, she had grown to appreciate the winter's chill after the sweltering heat of the southern summers.

She shifted the weight of the wild turkey that lay lifeless against her back. Using a musket as a walking stick, she waded through the underbrush near the bank of the flooded rice fields. Her leather moccasins brushed over the carpet of marsh grass and bulrushes, and the hem of her coarse woolen skirt collected thistles and dried twigs.

She surveyed the shallow lake that covered the fields for the winter. Flooded to attract migrating game, the fields bore no resemblance to the rolling green tracts of France. It was a constant wonder to her that so much life could come out of the reclaimed swamplands. In a month the cycle would begin again. The Gaillard family would have the field drained and dredge the canals. The rich, dark Carolina soil would thaw in the open air. The brook would swell as the melting snow coursed down from far-off mountains, and the sluice gates would direct the excess water into the tawny Santee River. Then summer would come, and with it, the humid, stifling heat, the endless, windless days, and the rapid growth of the green shoots of rice.

One year after another, three long years now, she had watched this place grow cold and wither only to come back to life again.

She was still waiting for the same to happen to her.

Now she veered away from the swamps and headed towards the old winnowing building. With each step, the head of the turkey bumped against the back of her legs. Adriana was satisfied that she had caught some fresh meat for the family she worked for. Monsieur Gaillard and his eldest son, Etienne, were due back from Charles Town any day. If she fed them a full dinner of freshly killed turkey, succotash and corn bread, she might coax them into telling a story or two about the English settlement, and take her mind off the predictable relentlessness of the days.

She smelled the odor of burning pitch pine long before she reached the plantation. Newly fitted with gleaming white weatherboarding, the Gaillard's residence seemed out of place against the untamed forests of the inland swamp. When she had first seen it, during those first hazy days when she was brought here, this house had been a simple log cabin made of cypress trees. The changes made since were visible reminders of how hard these French Huguenots had worked to build a new life for themselves—and a stark reminder of how little she'd done to rebuild her own.

She opened the back door and walked into the main room. A fire blazed in the fireplace. Madame Gaillard turned at her entrance.

"Where have you been? My husband and Etienne are coming. Claire glimpsed their canoe coming upstream."

"It's about time," Adriana said, as she heaved the wild turkey onto the large center table. "They're a week overdue."

Madame Gaillard poked the turkey. Her thin features struggled between pleasant surprise and matronly disapproval. "You borrowed Etienne's musket again."

"He gave me leave." She shrugged out of her woolen cape lined with beaver. "He told me I could use it before he left for Charles Town."

"Elisabeth!" Madame called her twelve-year-old daughter from her chores in the next room. "Take this turkey out back and have one of the women pluck it for tomorrow's supper." Then Madame's sharp, dark gaze returned to Adriana. "Adriana, is this the example you will set for my daughters?"

Adriana glanced down at her dress. A streak of reddish soil stained the front of the woolen skirt. She walked to a pail of water near the hearth and tried to scrub it out. Her corset bit into her side as she bent over. She suspected that she would never become accustomed to this awkward garment, no matter how many years passed. Many a day she'd been tempted not to wear one, but Madame Gaillard had strict ideas about feminine propriety.

And about me, she thought ruefully, as she dipped her hands in the water and scrubbed them clean. The Gaillard children—Etienne, Claire, Elisabeth and Martha—all treated her with sisterly affection, even when Madame shot commands at her like a bosun ordering his mate. Adriana knew that the eagle-eyed woman never really believed the story that Adriana had told them about how she ended up pawing through the wreckage of a pirate ship after a hurricane.

But the story she'd told the Gaillard family was no wilder than some of the stories the Huguenots told about their own emigration. Several noblewomen who now lived modestly along the Santee had escaped religious persecution by dressing up as shepherdesses and driving huge herds of sheep over the French border into the German states or Spain. Others had hidden in empty casks of wine and smuggled on ships heading to England. Her simple story of an emigration cut short by pirates, of dressing as a boy to escape the pirates' attentions, of how she'd clung to wreckage to survive the hurricane, certainly it paled in comparison.

But Madame had sharp eyes. The woman had watched her as Etienne had pulled her away from Roarke's lifeless body all those years ago. When her grief madness passed and cold practicality returned, Adriana had told everyone that the man whose head was crushed under the wreckage had been her brother.

Somehow, Madame had known that she'd lied.

Suddenly one of the Gaillard daughters tugged at her skirts, a snub-nosed little urchin with her mother's dark eyes.

Claire said, "I saw Papa."

"So your mother told me. Was he alone?"

"'Tienne was with him, and Joachim."

"Did he have bags and packages with him?"

"*Oui*. Bags and bags and bags." The little girl's eyes widened. "Full of dolls."

"Perhaps they're full of other things, Claire." Adriana gave up cleaning her skirt and went to the hearth to give the joint of meat a twist. "But there's always a chance."

"Claire," Madame said. "Put on your coat and go

outside to greet Papa, now, so Miss Joubert can get back to work."

Claire raced to where her cloak was hung by the door. Adriana gave the pot a stir, and then settled by the fire to take up a mortar and pestle to pound corn into a coarse powder.

"I've been meaning to talk with you for weeks," Madame said, as soon as Claire had left. "But now the men will be home so my time has run out."

Madame Gaillard focused on stirring stiff, lumpy dough with unnecessary forcefulness. Adriana had a creeping feeling that she wasn't going to like what her employer had to say.

"This concerns," Madame said, "my son."

Adriana focused her attention on pounding the corn into meal. She remembered how, three weeks ago, Madame had caught Adriana with her skirts hitched up into her waist while she waded into the marshes to retrieve an egret she and Etienne had shot for its feathers. She'd expected a good talking-to that time. When it hadn't come, she figured Madame had decided to let the incident pass.

"Adriana," Madame said on a sigh, "when a woman lifts up her skirts in the presence of a young man, she incites sentiments in him that are not altogether holy."

Adriana fixed her face so she wouldn't grimace at Madame's efforts at delicacy. "If you're talking about when I fetched that egret in the marshes," she said, "I was simply trying not to soil this good English tweed."

"My dear." Madame's bosom rose and fell on a sigh. "I'm not privy to what you and Etienne do when you wander off into the woods—"

"We hunt," she said. "Our kills prove that."

"You are not killing something every moment of every hour you're gone."

Adriana stopped grinding corn in irritation. "How can you accuse your own son of anything dishonorable? He's a fine boy."

"I know." She knocked the spoon on the edge of the wooden bowl. "Perhaps that's why he's itching to marry you."

Marry.

The word rang in her head.

Her mind balked.

"You are well aware," the lady continued, "that there are few women here in the up-country. Few enough to be considered proper wives, that is."

"I know that well enough." Men stared at her whenever she gathered with the Gaillard family at the Huguenot church in Jamestown, though she wore the same plain clothing as everyone else. "But I don't see—"

"Etienne is a young man, and young men think about these things." Madame kneaded the dough with more force than necessary. "I have to assume, because you two spend so much time together, that it's natural that his interest has focused on you."

"It's not interest, he's just kind." Etienne was just

a boy—a few years younger than herself—skinny and long-legged and always getting dirty, at ease in the wilderness as if he were part native. She'd never thought of him in any other way but as a boon companion, as she had for many a sailor upon the sea. "He is like a brother to me."

"A brother? Is that truly how you think of him?"

"Of course." After she'd lived only a few weeks at the homestead, she'd picked up a musket and followed him into the hunt. Etienne hadn't blinked—he'd welcomed the company, and she was grateful for the friendship. "Etienne has said nothing to me of this sort. I'm sure you're mistaking his intent."

"You're as bad as any man ignoring a flirting young woman." Madame shook her head. "You're blind to his feelings."

Her first instinct was to deny the words but Adriana hesitated. In the first few months Adriana had tried to settle in the Gaillard's household as a young woman, she'd tripped over her borrowed skirts, sat with her knees splayed, walked like a lumbering boy, and referred to herself as *Français,* not *Française.* No one but Madame Gaillard had truly noticed how different she really was.

So now a memory floated back to her, of when she'd last said good-bye to Etienne before he left for Charles Town. He had hesitated before climbing onto the canoe. His gaze had fallen to her lips.

"You're not right for him, my dear. He is meant to have a quiet wife who will serve him well. Not a wife who—"

"Who can shoot better than he," she interrupted. *Who can swear like the sailors of Charles Town.*

"He would not make you happy."

Her mind balked at this, too. Happiness was not something she had strived for since she'd lost Roarke, but Etienne's friendship did bring her a quiet contentment. Etienne was sweet, kind, gentle. Hardworking, uncomplaining, and strong. In those early days, she'd cried on his shoulder, back when she still had tears left to shed.

"You would be bored with him within a month," Madame persisted, "and then what would you do? Would you stay complacently by his side for the years to come, bear him his children, and cook his meals? Or would you escape and leave him heartbroken?"

Adriana sat with the pestle tight in one hand and the mortar cupped in the other while her thoughts swirled. Yes, Etienne was young, but it was strange, really, that she hadn't considered this before. She couldn't stay in this house forever, she had known that from the start. Yet as a single woman, the opportunities this bountiful new country offered were difficult to access without the help of a husband.

She shook her head to leave off the strange thoughts.

She could not marry Etienne because she did not love Etienne.

Adriana knew what it meant to love.

"So," Madame persisted, "you have no intentions

of being his wife?"

No.

Her heart blurted the word.

But her tongue remained silent.

Then the front door opened with a bang and put an end to the discussion. Pierre Gaillard stepped into the room and his wife straightened to attention. Pierre's blue eyes twinkled as he approached and threw his arms out for an embrace. Madame Gaillard, blushing like a girl rather than a matron well into her forties, crossed the room to suffer the enfolding. She scolded him as he lifted her clear off the ground.

"Why, I've been away for nigh four weeks!" Pierre exclaimed. "Don't I deserve a sweeter greeting than this?"

"Depends on how well you've done in Charles Town," Madame said as she extricated herself from her husband's arms.

"I made enough to buy you wheat flour, sugar, some strong English tweeds and enough molasses from Jamaica to make sticky cakes for years." He winked at her. "I've bought some rum, too, to keep us warm during these long, cold winters."

"You've been trading with pirates again, Pierre Gaillard—"

"Of course I bartered with pirates. I bargained with the Sewee and the Kiawah and Santee Indians, as well. If I hadn't, we wouldn't be able to afford such luxuries with the English-controlled prices."

Etienne squeezed by his father into the kitchen.

Though as tall as his father, Etienne was thin and leanly-muscled where his father was broad and thickly-made.

She felt a flush of heat and anger at Madame for suddenly making her conscious of such things.

Etienne came to her side, his grin wide. "You would have liked Charles Town this season, Adriana. It was full of trading ships with their sails unfurled."

Her mind suddenly flooded with images of Saint-Malo bay and the vessels that crowded around the walled city. She felt a strange longing, but suppressed it because Etienne was looking at her with an expression she didn't want to read.

"Don't tempt her with talk of Charles Town, Etienne," Madame said, a bit too sharply. "You know I cannot do without Miss Joubert here, and once the outer kitchens are built we'll need more help, not less."

Etienne rolled his eyes. "So, Adriana," he said, "what did you kill for dinner to welcome us home?"

"A wild turkey it was." Madame answered for her, trying to capture her son's attention. "It's unseemly for a lady to be hunting in the brush."

"I suspect Adriana would hunt with or without my permission, *Maman.*"

Adriana knew better than to respond. Etienne's cheeks were flushed red from the cold, his hair stuck up in odd directions, and he looked as irresistibly happy as a half-grown pup as he gazed upon her.

"So where is this turkey?" Pierre lifted his

daughter Claire and tossed her up high above his head. "Etienne and I have traveled long and far today."

"The turkey is still being plucked, so tonight we're having venison." Madame glanced at Adriana, a wordless command. "I'll serve it as soon as the table is set."

Adriana set the mortar and pestle aside and bustled around the rough wooden table, setting down the pewter dishware that Pierre Gaillard had bought for his wife during the last trip to Charles Town. After the family had seated themselves, she served them corn bread and bean stew from huge wooden platters, then filled a plate for herself and sat nearby, by the hearth. Pierre Gaillard carved the haunch of venison with relish.

The family joined hands and prayed, as was their custom, then began to eat.

"What news do you have of Charles Town?" Madame asked as everyone dug into their food. "Is Governor Joseph Blake as bad as his uncle, Archdale?"

Pierre's blue eyes twinkled as he looked at his children. "At least she waited until the prayers were said."

Madame ignored the amusement rippling around the table. "Come, Pierre. You've been gone nigh three weeks and I've heard nothing about the new governor. The old governor was nearly the death of all Huguenots."

"Wife! Such sour sentiments."

"He didn't let you vote, husband."

"Well, things may be changing." Pierre speared a piece of meat. "There's a petition in the Assembly to grant full privileges to Huguenots who swear allegiance to England. Including voting."

Madame made a little gasp. "Including letting us build our own ships?"

"*Oui.*"

Madame Gaillard slapped her pewter spoon by her plate. "Then you *didn't* secure a ship this trip! That's what you're telling me, yes?"

"It was impossible," Etienne said before his father could reply. "Each time we broached the subject, they heard my accent and they turned away. No foreign-born can hold deed to a ship out of Charles Town."

"They don't trust us," Adriana said from her place by the hearth. "Because the English are still fighting the French."

"Yes, yes, but it's a faraway war." Pierre waved his hand. "It's King William's war, not ours. How does it affect us here? There have been no French raids on Carolina. Of course, it doesn't help," Pierre added, "that they've heard rumors that the French intend to settle at the mouth of the Mississippi. According to some backwoodsmen, that land belongs to the Carolinas."

Madame Gaillard, ever practical, said, "So who, exactly, is shipping our rice?"

"An English middleman, of course."

"Those thieves take nearly half the profits!"

"Wife, what choice did I have?"

Madame sighed through her teeth. "Did you ask the Guerrards if they had room on their ship?"

"Their ship was full when it left weeks ago, Lise. *Must* we discuss this now, in front of the children?"

"It affects our children, too, and they may as well know the full of it. How can the Guerrards hold a title to a ship and not you—"

"They have more power in the Assembly."

"Indeed," Adriana interjected. "Monsieur Guerrard was wearing French silks at church last Sunday." She remembered the detail because of how the color stood out in the very plain, very simple Huguenot church in Jamestown. "I'd wager he knows some men in the Assembly on a first-name basis."

Madame Gaillard said sharply, "And what do you know of such things?"

"Sharp eyes," Etienne answered. "They help her in hunting and in seeing things others would overlook."

Was his smile particularly tender, Adriana thought, or had Madame's scolding colored her perceptions?

She shook off the thought. "It was hard to overlook the coins he gave the churchman after services. You don't get clean, shiny doubloons from the English merchants. He's been bartering with pirates, for much more than the necessities like

Monsieur."

"Our young lady is right," Pierre said. "You don't like when I trade with pirates, wife, but it is the only way to get coin in this colony, and coin is the only way to gain influence in the Assembly."

Madame pursed her lips. "There must be another way."

"Perhaps there now is, as I tried to say in the beginning." Pierre rolled his eyes at his wife's impatience in perfect imitation of his son. "That petition in the Assembly—it *passed*. All French who swear allegiance to England within the next three months will become naturalized citizens. We'll have the same benefits as Englishmen."

"So you registered us?" Madame Gaillard tapped the table in impatience.

"Yes, Papa registered us all." Etienne turned briefly to Adriana. "All the family, that is."

Adriana blinked. "I'm not registered?"

"I tried, child," Pierre said. "They said because you had reached your majority, you would have to go and register yourself."

"Well," she said, as calmly as she could. "I suppose I'll have to go to Charles Town now."

"Come, come," Pierre said, as he exchanged a glance with his son across the table. "There are easier ways for you to become naturalized, though it's not as important for a woman—"

"It *is* important," she retorted, "if I ever want to own a ship."

Pierre laughed and the girls giggled in suit, and Adriana realized that she'd said something preposterous again.

But she'd spoken truth, and she felt it ring through her body with all the solemnity of funeral chimes.

"Perhaps," Madame Gaillard said, "it's a good idea for Miss Joubert to go to Charles Town."

Adriana glanced at her employer in unabashed surprise, and saw Etienne do the same.

"I think there's even some silk left upstairs," Madame continued, "from the early days when we experimented with those silkworms." Seeing Adriana's gape, Madame shrugged her thin shoulders but there was calculation in her eyes. "You can't go and show yourself off to all those English people in your work clothes, Miss Joubert. I think our young helpmeet has earned one good dress from us, wouldn't you say, Pierre?"

CHAPTER EIGHTEEN

When Adriana approached the town overland with Etienne and his father Pierre, she lifted her face to the cool breezes to catch the familiar, briny scent of the ocean. As they swept deeper into the town, she realized how much she'd missed the rush and tumble of a vibrant city. When she glimpsed the straight wooden masts surging high over the eastern fortifications, her heart began to pound.

She couldn't help herself. She swept onto the beach and scanned every one of those ships in search of the familiar rigging of *L'Aventure*.

Foolishness.

How strange the mind worked. Roarke was three years gone and still she struggled to believe what she'd seen with her own eyes at the mouth of the Santee River. Her lover was dead and she had to accept that, and the sooner she did, the better. Frustrated at her inability to let the past go, she vowed to stay away from the port in the week that followed. The Gaillard men went about their business which allowed her to spend leisurely days riding a mare through the sandy streets. But her own urges tested her resolve, for her gaze was always drawn to those things that made her heart beat faster and her memories churn.

She saw sailors lounging in the taverns. She heard a bawdy pirate song and brazenly hummed a few bars as she passed the punch house whence it came. She glanced at a trader's horse and saw muskets, axes, daggers, and bottles of smuggled rum strapped on the beast's back. Nearly everyone on the spacious street—backwoodsmen, natives, pirates—stowed a pistol or a knife in their belts. Throughout the town, the scent of pitch and powder drifted on the wind. The screech of terns filled the wide sky.

She found herself strangely exhilarated as she slipped into the bumping traffic, following a line of Indian women, their backs bent under a mountain of deerskins. Then suddenly—unwittingly—she discovered she was at the port again. Every urge seemed to lead her to this place, so this time she lingered as the breeze tangled her hair. She watched a pirate ship lying low in the bay while *chaloupes* passed between ship and shore, transporting anyone willing to unload the pirate's stolen wares.

Perhaps it *had* been a deep, hidden spark of hope

that had drawn her thoughts to Charles Town, but the more time she spent by the ramparts watching the sea, the more she realized that it was something far deeper that caused the swelling emotion in her heart. Charles Town was young, rough, and vibrant. Improbable dreams, unlikely ventures, and crazy ideas might just burst into full bloom in this rough-and-tumble place.

So on the day they were all due to return to the plantation on the Santee River, she rode her mare to the harbor once again. This time she tied her mare at a hitching post and, pulling her beaver-pelt cape around her silk dress, she headed toward a particular dugout canoe among the dozens on shore.

Etienne, standing in the half-laden canoe, straightened carefully and lifted a hand in greeting. "Still dressed like a grand lady?" Etienne ran an admiring gaze over her fur and silk. "It would have been better to wear your wool for the journey, Adriana."

She turned accusing eyes on Etienne's father. Monsieur Gaillard flushed crimson where he sat in the canoe, but he continued to take cargo from his slave Joachim and stow it on board as if he hadn't heard a thing.

"It would be silly to change clothes," she said as evenly as she could, "when I'm only here to see you off."

Etienne's brow furrowed. His gaze fell to her hands, which were empty. "Where's your satchel?"

"It's back at the house that I'm renting from the St. Julien family." She had hoped to be spared a confrontation with Etienne, but his father had clearly said nothing. "I've decided to stay in Charles Town for a while."

"What?"

"Come, Etienne. You must have guessed this would happen."

He twisted to face his father. "Did you know about this?"

His father's shoulders rose and fell in a shrug.

"Etienne," she said, bracing herself, "Over the last week, I have mentioned many times how much I love this city—"

"But you can't stay," he said incredulously. "Not alone."

"Joachim will be staying with me for the summer."

She glanced to Joachim, who stood by the canoe helping Etienne's father load the last of the bales. Joachim was too old to be working the rice fields, so having him work as her helpmeet in Charles Town would be far easier for the elderly slave. That's the only reason she agreed when Etienne's father had insisted. She attributed her ambivalence about Joachim's presence to an uneasy, thrumming sense of kinship she always felt for the dark-skinned men, women, and children forced into servitude.

Everyone wore shackles of a sort, but the shackles worn by the Charles Town slaves were heavier and far more visible.

"You're not serious." Etienne's dark brows lowered. "Joachim is mute."

"And he's faithful," she said. "And strong."

"You can't do this. You'll be alone."

"I know the Ravenels now," she said. "And I know the St. Juliens."

"Acquaintances, no more." Etienne jumped out of the cypress canoe, making it rock wildly. "You work for us. You're needed at home."

Etienne strode toward her and then stepped closer than he should. She became very aware of exactly how tall he'd become since she'd first met him. And how dark his jaw became when he hadn't shaved for a few days.

"This is not a town for innocent women." His voice was a rumble of disbelief and worry. "What will you do? What will you live on?"

"I have three years' wages put away."

"Wages?" His laugh was rough and very unlike him. "Is that what you call a few coins gifted to you at Christmas and Easter?"

"I have other resources."

He lifted one brow, waiting for an explanation. She dropped her gaze to her satin slippers, soaking up the moisture from the damp marsh grass. She'd never told Etienne, or any of the Gaillard family, about the sack of coins Roarke had secreted in her satchel on that terrible day. In those early months, her mind had been a bruised, soft thing, and her heart held its secrets close.

"I have a fortune in pieces-of-eight taken from the pirate captain's cabin."

Etienne's eyes went wide, and she knew then that it was right to have kept this secret for so long. The coins hadn't been stolen, but there was no way to explain how she'd obtained them without making him think less of her. They were friends—good friends—and she could not bear the thought of his disapproval.

He lifted his hands to his hips and squinted off to the battlements of the city. She sensed the uneasiness within him. She suddenly remembered a day when Etienne had caught her in the woods weeping over the compass that Roarke had put into her hands. Etienne had held her while she cried—without demanding to know the reason—and when she finally calmed down, she had noticed that Etienne was also trembling.

"Etienne," she said, taking a deep breath. "Listen. I can help your family in Charles Town more than I can help at the plantation. My English is better than yours." She placed a hand on his arm and tried not to act surprised at how hard his muscles felt under her palm. "You have probably figured out that I know how to deal with pirates, as well."

"My mother," he said, as he turned back to her with a curious intensity, "doesn't know about these other resources of yours."

It was a statement, not a question, and she could only nod in acknowledgement.

"Yet she knew you'd stay here in Charles Town."

"Etienne, I don't know what your mother was thinking—"

"I do." He stepped dangerously close. "She knew you'd stay. She's pushing you away from me."

Her heart did a strange skip-beat. When he stood this close, no longer was he the awkward young man racing her through the deep woods, dappled sunlight pouring across their faces, their laughter rising to join the songs of the birds. She noticed that his shoulders strained the seams of the shirt she'd just mended, not three weeks ago. He didn't flush as he used to when he looked down at her.

His deep, brown gaze was unwavering.

She could have stepped back, out of the reach of his grasp, but she knew that rejection would hurt him deeply. So she flattened her hands on his chest to keep his body at a distance. Then she tilted her chin to accept the kiss he lowered his head to give her.

He had kissed before. The knowledge was a gentle shock. She had assumed that Etienne didn't think about such things, didn't imagine them. After all, she'd never caught him with his hands in his breeches as she'd caught shipboard sailors many a time. Suddenly the wide, shamefaced grin he wore whenever he returned from Charles Town took on a new meaning. His kiss lingered, hungry but controlled.

Her eyelids fluttered closed.

When he released her, she blinked, dazed, into

his soft brown eyes.

A slight smile tilted the edge of his lips. "I should have kissed you years ago."

"If you'd tried I'd have slapped you silly."

And then the vague, pleasant sensations that Etienne had ruffled in her body settled as quickly as they'd begun. In their wake came an awkward discomfort, as well as wistfulness for a different man, a fiercer kiss.

With the flat of her hands, she pressed him away. "This is not a good way to begin my stay here in Charles Town. People will talk."

"It doesn't matter—"

"It does to me."

His kind smile dimmed. "So I can't convince you to come back with me."

"I'll see you soon." She lifted her skirts and stepped back. "After the August harvest."

"You'll see me sooner than that." He took a swaggering step back toward the canoe. "I'll be back during the stretch-flow, then again during the harvest-flow."

"Your mother will not approve."

"No," he said, his brown eyes twinkling. "My mother will not approve."

"Send the gentleman in, Joachim."

Joachim left her alone in the large sitting room, furnished with hand-wrought wooden chairs and a mahogany table. Adriana smoothed her green silk skirts over her thighs and took a deep breath, despite the bite of her corset. Her breasts surged above the low décolletage that spread from shoulder to shoulder.

A man entered the room. She stood and approached him with her hand extended in the fashion of the other ladies of Charles Town. He wore a wide-skirted cassock coat made of dull wool. His sleeves were frayed below the cuffs. "Mr. Elsworth. Thank you for coming. I am Mademoiselle Joubert."

He stared at the extended hand with cold blue eyes. She lifted a brow, waiting. He took her hand and barely brushed the back of it against his dry mouth.

"Please come and sit," she said. "There is little tea in Charles Town these days, but I have chocolate for the two of us."

"I am in no need of refreshment," he said. "My time is short."

"Oh?" She led him deeper into the room and settled in one of the hard-backed chairs. "Shall I congratulate you, then? Your business improves?"

Mr. Elsworth visibly stiffened.

"I mean no offence, monsieur," she said, spreading her skirts and giving him what she hoped was a simpering smile. "But you must know that Charles Town is full of talk about your..." She hesitated, searching for the correct English word. *Failure* would send the man stiff-backed out the door. "Your hardships."

"You have me at a disadvantage, mademoiselle." He spoke the French word like he was trying to tongue a bone out from between his teeth. "Your slave was insolent and said nothing to me about the purpose of this meeting."

"Joachim is mute. And what I have to discuss with you is careful."

His face went blank in that way she'd become familiar with, a way that suggested she'd botched the words. Over the past month her English had improved considerably with the help of the local Anglican priest, but she still found it a challenge to grasp the subtleties.

"Delicate," she corrected. "What I have to discuss is of a...delicate nature. I have invited you here to offer business."

His fair brows rose on his ruddy forehead. "What business could possibly interest you?"

"Business interests me. Very much. Strange, *n'est-ce pas?*" She tilted her head and startled at the feel of a curl brushing against her shoulder, like a spider dropping from the yardarms. "I understand that you work as a factor."

"Yes, I have been a facilitator for Charles Town shipping concerns for many years now."

"Successful?"

"Your point?"

She resisted frowning at his insolence. She had been warned that he was a bitter man. That's exactly why she'd chosen him. And if he didn't want to play silly drawing-room games, she was happy to comply.

"I understand," she continued, "that you were once a middleman between some of the wealthiest planters in the Carolinas and the merchants of London. I also understand that your current difficulties arose when it was discovered that you had a relationship with a certain lady. I believe she was the wife of one of your clients, *n'est-ce pas?*"

"The sordid details of that incident have been widely gossiped. It is no surprise to me that a woman of your like has heard them."

Her eyes narrowed. "You speak quickly for a man who was once considered a good businessman."

"This is not business. This is digging for gossip."

"Look around you, Mr. Elsworth."

His frigid gaze slid across the room, noting the lace-edged curtains, the whitewashed ceiling and walls and the fine mahogany of the table. Though the house was rented from the St. Juliens, and therefore none of the furniture was hers, she saw no need to inform Elsworth of that detail.

"Your lover," he said, "must be a very wealthy man."

It was an insult of the gravest kind, but Elsworth's arrow missed its mark. She'd grown up not caring a wit about something as airy and useless as a reputation, and she wasn't about to let it bother her now.

"Perhaps I have a lover," she said, shrugging, "perhaps I do not. But the wealth you see around you is no illusion."

Neither were the pieces-of-eight she'd hidden in a drawer upstairs.

Adriana settled back in the chair to give him a better view of the cream silk lining the slashing of her sleeves. The French milliner she'd hired to fill her wardrobe also came to fix her hair and advise her on what wrap should be worn with what shoes. She'd soon discovered that acting the boy had been a lot simpler—and less expensive—than putting on the mask of a well-bred young woman. It was a lot of frippery and foolishness in her opinion, but the wealthy people of Charles Town put great stock in it.

Now she watched Mr. Elsworth's appraisal and waited. Finally, he shoved away the skirt of his cassock coat and took a seat on a hard-backed chair.

"Ah, so now we can talk business." A frisson of excitement charged through her. "What you see in this room is but a reflection, sir. There is more money in the Santee district with the people who have become my family. But, you see, we have a small problem. We are French, and even after the recent petition passed in the Assembly, we are restricted in what kind of business we can take up."

"I know plenty of Frenchmen doing quite well despite the laws."

"Please, Mr. Elsworth, let's be frank. Just last week a French-owned ship was seized outside of Charles Town. Owned by the Guerrards, people I know. The Carolina courts condemned it as an enemy vessel."

"The Navigation Acts *do* forbid foreign ownership of ships out of the Carolinas."

"The man was naturalized according to the law."

"Mademoiselle." He sighed and closed his eyes for a moment. "I cannot help you with the policies of the government."

"Men make those policies and profit by them as well. Men like Governor Joseph Blake."

She saw him flinch at the name and took a measure of pride that she'd found a weakness.

"I am told," she continued, "that Blake will receive one-third of the profits from the sale of that ship and its cargo. It is a pity you won't be sharing in his newfound wealth, Mr. Elsworth, for I know that the governor was once a faithful customer of yours—"

"Once again," he interrupted, "I am a businessman, not a politician."

"I only mention that event as an example of what happens to the loyal French of the Santee. Despite all the promises of the law, we are still treated like enemies."

"We are at war. Englishmen must protect our colony."

"Protect yourselves from warships, then, not honest merchantmen." This argument was getting her nowhere, so she waved it away. "I did not bring you here to discuss King William's war. I understand that many of your clients have moved their interests to other factors."

His face turned an alarming shade of red.

"I also understand," she said, "that you have a long-standing agreement with one of the caciques of the Catawba nation."

"Yes." The word came with force.

"I've also heard that this agreement is in danger of lapsing."

His gaze cut cold through her.

"You have not been able to supply the materials that the Catawba demand."

"A need I am in the process of fulfilling."

"And it must be done quick, no?" Adriana toyed with the curl that had fallen against her nape. "The governor has shown interest in supplying that tribe, as well as the Cherokees and the Choctaws to the west. Will your agreement with the Catawba survive, in the face of the far greater wealth of Mr. Blake?"

His gaze narrowed. "You are irritatingly well-informed."

"The governor's dinner parties can be very productive for those who have the patience to listen."

"I am well aware of the governor's ambitions, and I have already planned to counter his offers."

She smiled without showing her teeth. "Where, Mr. Elsworth, shall you get the money for that?"

"The Indians want rum and guns and trinkets and brightly colored cloth—"

"Which cost money."

"Not much," he countered, "when you buy it from pirates."

"Oh, I suspect you'll have to bargain long and hard to get the amount of goods you need for the amount of money you have."

"And what would a woman know of bargaining with pirates?"

She kept her smile though all she wanted to do in that moment was speak to him in her own tongue—her Saint-Malouin French—and barter for his coat right off his shoulders like a true urchin of the sea. But she was no longer the tough little ship's mouse. She'd peeled that mask off and put on an entirely different one that required a whole new set of weapons.

"I know something else, Mr. Elsworth." She leaned forward. "You've approached an acquaintance of mine—a prominent French Huguenot—for a loan."

He couldn't mask the shudder of distaste. "A moment of weakness."

"Or desperation."

This time he had the dignity not to deny her words.

"My dear sir." She rose from her seat and took her time walking to the window. "I am in a position to lend you a modest amount of money on certain conditions."

"The legal interest rate in Charles Town is ten percent."

"I'm not offering you a loan."

"Then what in God's name are you offering me,

woman?"

"I want a percentage of the profits on your trade with the Catawba."

He laughed. A strange burst of a laugh. She recognized it for the scorn, the dismissal, the amused disbelief of an arrogant man.

"If your agreement is as strong as you say," she continued, ignoring the moment, "then the money you spend on trinkets and rum should bring you a wealth of deerskins and beaver furs. When you sell those skins to the English, I'll take a percentage of the profits. *Plus* my original investment back in full."

"A loan," he said, clearing his throat, "would be sufficient."

"I also want a written contract between us for further investments. The contract will last no less than five years, unless I decide to break our partnership."

"Partnership?" That strange laugh again, but less certain now. "Mademoiselle, I don't think you even know what that means."

"Don't I?"

She heard the clock in the hall sound tick, tick, tick, as she waited for this desperate man to overcome his pride and to come to his senses.

"Quel dommage." She sighed into the lengthening silence. "It seems our discussion is over, then." She swiveled on one foot and gestured toward the door. "I am ever so sorry to have wasted your time, Mr. Elsworth."

The factor hesitated. He gripped the arms of the chair as if to lift himself out, then caught sight of his own frayed cuffs. He sat back down. Stiffening his narrow shoulders beneath his cassock-coat, he swept off his tricorn hat and placed it on the table.

She gave him what she hoped was a sweet smile. "I had just about despaired of you, sir."

"I am not fond of the French."

"You share common sentiments with most of the English in Charles Town, then."

"Why me?"

"That's very simple." She came around and prevented herself, at the last moment, from flopping into the chair like a boy. "I need your name."

He startled.

"I have two disadvantages." She ticked them off on her fingers. "I'm French and I'm a woman. Yet I have all this money, aching to be invested." She glanced out the front window, where she could just see the tips of the masts peeking over the battlements. "But if your English company owned the deeds to those ships, and that company name was on any agreements with London merchants, then all would be legal—and the two of us could profit greatly by it."

"You are asking me to break the law."

"What laws? The English Navigation Acts?" She shook her head. "You know that those laws are twisted daily by the English themselves. How many times have you bartered with pirates for French goods?"

"Bartering with pirates may be against the law, but no one has ever gone to jail for it."

"No one has ever gone to jail for what I have suggested, either. It may not even be illegal. After all, you're an English citizen and all our investments will be in your name. I'm just an anonymous investor, taking my cut of the booty."

She pulled her lips. Booty was not a word a well-raised woman would have used. She hazarded a glance toward the factor, but he seemed too involved staring at the back of his knuckles to have caught her slip.

He ventured, "If you're interested in an investment, there is a certain pirate ship in the harbor now, looking for—"

"No." Her heart squeezed. "No pirates."

"But there is nothing more profitable—"

"Pirates are dangerous clients and make for volatile investments." She swept out of her chair again and turned toward the window so he wouldn't see the strain on her face. She couldn't risk tripping over the past she was determined to bury, along with her grief.

"I've heard," he said, "that you've had dealings with pirates. Dressed as a boy. So the story goes."

"Monsieur," she said, feeling the wave of smugness coming off him, "you are irritatingly well-informed."

"The streets are full of talk, *mademoiselle*."

She let the insult pass. His nascent sense of

superiority would work to her advantage, as would the gossip. She didn't care what he thought about her, as long as he would bend to her will.

"Do we have an agreement, monsieur?"

"Indeed." Mr. Elsworth reached for his feathered tricorn and smiled a yellowed, stiff, humorless smile. "We do."

CHAPTER NINETEEN

"But who the devil *is* this mysterious investor?"

The governor of the Carolinas, Mr. Joseph Blake, scowled over his dozen guests from where he sat at the head of his dining table. Adriana glanced around as if seeking an answer herself, blinking her eyes in feigned ignorance.

"No one knows," said one of the landowners at the other end of the table. "And Elsworth, despicable character that he is, won't say a word."

"Elsworth is still your factor, isn't he, Edmund?" The governor lifted a glass of pirated Bordeaux to his lips. "You've asked him about this devilish silent partner, then?"

"I have, and he has kept his lips as puckered as a—" the landowner caught himself before he scandalized the ladies. "Whoever this new investor is, he's becoming as rich as Midas with Elsworth's help. He's as sharp as you, my dear governor, in his investments."

"Too sharp for his own good," Mr. Blake added. "He'd best watch himself or I might use that new court of Vice Admiralty for its intended purpose."

"Come, governor." Nicholas Trott, seated at Adriana's left, leaned back in his seat. "Would you jail a man for cutting into your business with the Catawba? It was his business first. And there is plenty of opportunity for this sly ghost, and for all of us, here in the Carolinas."

"There's plenty of opportunity, indeed!" Blake protested. "Why, then, must he trade with the same tribe I've been wooing for a year?"

"You are not the only wooer, Governor. You have simply been, until now, the richest and most powerful one."

Adriana frowned, wondering why the governor always seated her next to this tactless attorney general.

"Well," the governor sputtered, "I suspect Elsworth has been funding pirates, undoubtedly with this nameless investor's money."

"Pirates or privateers?" Nicholas asked.

"What difference is there?" Blake retorted. "Name me a privateer who hasn't at one time or another been a pirate. I can call into question at least one of Elsworth's investments, and then I'll have him and the pirate hanging off White Point—"

"Governor Blake," she heard herself saying,

knowing the governor was powerful enough to accuse Elsworth of anything whether it was true or not. "Are you truly talking about hanging good businessmen?" She leaned forward so her breasts surged above the décolletage of her new emerald-green silk. "Then wherever would the women of Charles Town get such necessities as these?" She patted her mouth with a napkin made of Dutch linen and then raised her Spanish goblet filled with French wine.

The governor grinned, his wine-dazzled gaze slipping over the expanse of her shoulders. "I would not want to inconvenience the ladies, that is true, dear mademoiselle. I'll have to find another way to thwart this man."

"Ah, look," said the governor's wife suddenly, shooting Adriana a dark look. "The next course is served."

The house slaves brought in the next course. She tasted the venison, drowned in molasses, and then quietly put down her fork. Reaching for her wine, she strained to hear the conversations around her. From the provincial nobility in the Carolinas, she learned what ships were in port, what ships were expected, and how the sporadic Indian wars affected trade in the backcountry beyond the settlement. She had no fear that these men would guess that *she* was the investor Blake hated so much.

She sat among them like a French spy among English generals.

"Something amuses you, mademoiselle?"

She found Nicholas Trott's close-set gaze focused on her in that greedy way. It was so predictable it made her sigh.

"I was just thinking," she said, pondering what information she could tease out of him, "about how angry the governor becomes in the face of competition."

"Name me a governor who hasn't used his power to line his own pockets," he mused. "Still, I'd like to meet this investor who challenges him so well. None of the rest of us dared for fear of the repercussions."

"Then it would be wise to guard your tongue around him. The man you just challenged is the most powerful man in the Carolinas."

"Governors come and go in this settlement." He shrugged. "Blake will leave soon enough and another will take his place. But certainly we can think of a more interesting subject than politics." His gaze slipped to the lace of her chemise peeping from the edge of her bodice.

She said, pointedly, "Politics intrigues me."

"A strange interest, for a woman."

"In politics lies power, does it not?"

"Not always." His brows raised. "Often it lies in money, or influence. And such things shouldn't muddle your mind."

"Like this wine?"

She took a small sip of wine and wondered if men ever tired of these silly verbal games. Then she caught a snatch of conversation from the governor's end of the table and tilted her head to hear better.

"...I wanted to meet him this afternoon but he had other business to attend to. He claims that the war with the French is over."

"Governor, every year comes word that the war is over."

"Yes, but he said he heard it announced, and that, sooner rather than later, we'll get an official notice..."

Adriana started as she felt warm breath by her ear.

"You're a cruel, heartless woman, Adriana," Trott whispered, leaning close. "I'd been told that blood runs hotter south of the English Channel, but with all your strange chatter, now I'm not so sure."

"Mr. Trott." She spoke in irritation, having lost the thread of the governor's conversation. "I didn't think you liked the French."

"Who could resist a Frenchwoman with eyes like a mulatto and skin the color of burnished gold?"

"As attorney general," she said, "I was sure you'd resist quite well. After all, many French natives like myself have such a difficult time winning in your courts."

It was an unwise comment, but sometimes even in the disguise of a fine young lady the street urchin came out.

"Trott," came a voice from across the table, "are you bothering the charming Mademoiselle Joubert?"

The voice belonged to a prominent rice planter whose name Adriana had forgotten. His open, blue-eyed gaze rested with unabashed admiration on her face.

"She has no need for your defense, William," Trott said. "At times her lips have the venom of a water moccasin."

"Well, if Trott says anything amiss, Miss," the planter offered, "just let me know."

She smiled sweetly at her protector in a way she'd practiced in a mirror, and watched the color rise on his face. She wondered if the attention she received at these dinner parties was due exclusively to the dearth of women in Charles Town or whether all men were susceptible to a pair of white shoulders.

Truly, it was a wonder that women didn't rule the world.

Finally, the governor's wife stood up and announced that they would all retire to the nearby sitting room. Adriana breathed a sigh of relief, and not just because she'd be free of Nicholas Trott's brooding attentions. The day's heat had become oppressive despite the efforts of the slaves waving cane fans in an attempt to whirl a breeze in the closed room. At least in the sitting room the windows were thrown open to the Cooper River.

Adriana and the three other women sat in the carved mahogany chairs near the unlit fireplace. She refused a glass of strong brandy in favor of keeping a clear head. One of the plantation wives, a nervous woman with wispy brown hair, pulled her small silver flute out of its case and began to play a melody.

Adriana remembered her Breton horn, which lay wrapped in cloth with Chou-Chou's harness buried in a drawer in her bedroom. She had not touched the horn since Chou-Chou had died. She wondered what these genteel guests would say if she brought it in and played a pirate jig. It certainly would be more entertaining than this reedy flute.

She waited patiently for the music to end so the men could go back to discussing business and she could continue to gather information.

She heard a rustling outside the sitting room. The front door opened and closed and she heard the murmuring of male voices as a new guest arrived. She could just see him through the open doors, an unfamiliar figure standing with his back to her. He wore a blue satin waistcoat embroidered in gold. His hair was his own, pulled back and knotted at the nape of his neck. She knew instantly that he was a seaman, a merchant captain most likely, considering his dress. He stood with his feet braced apart as if to balance the rocking of the deck. There was an angle to his neck that suggested he was used to staring long distances and measuring his position by the stars.

A pang shot through her—a pang of forgotten memory, a sudden longing for the prickly feel of ropes against the arches of her feet, the tingle of sea spray on her skin, the lift of a salt-breeze in her hair.

Then the man turned around.

Adriana's heart stopped.

CHAPTER TWENTY

R*oarke.*

Adriana saw his figure as if through a haze of smoke and heat and waited for it to disappear as quickly as it had appeared. Since she had arrived in Charles Town, she imagined she had seen Roarke a half dozen times, a tall figure out of the corner of her eye. Occasionally she thought that she glimpsed him on the forecastle of a ship in the bay, or saw him roaming the beach among the privateers on shore. She heard his voice in the laughter of the sailors in the taverns along the waterfront, or in a sharp, barked command from commander to sailor.

But Roarke was dead, dead, dead, his head crushed, lying amid the wreckage of *L'Aventure,* and what she imagined in Charles Town were only ghosts.

Now she blinked once, twice, and then a third time. Still there he was, standing in the doorway of the sitting room, exuding vitality like a burning torch exudes light.

Their gazes met and locked.

The music of the flute stopped. What muffled conversation there'd been had dissolved into a hushed silence. A stormy breeze blew in and shifted her heavy skirts against her legs, and that's how she knew she'd shot out of her chair. She stood by the hearth staring at his face, the face she had treasured in her memory, summoning it out only in the darkest, loneliest nights, pushing it away quickly lest it fade from handling.

Her corset tightened around her torso, cutting off her breathing, blurring her vision even more. She suddenly understood why the well-dressed ladies of Charles Town fainted so very often.

Abruptly, Roarke approached, his eyes like the green sea hit by sunlight—bright and sharp and intense. He reached for her hand and took it in his own. The feel of it, hot and strong and *real*, shocked her heart into a racing gallop.

"I am overwhelmed," he said in English, "by your beauty, madam. I beg you, tell me your name."

You know my name.

How cool he was, despite the recognition in his eyes. He was unruffled enough to speak in English, instead of the French in which they had always conversed. She'd completely lost her tongue for both languages.

In the stretching silence, she drank in the sight of

him, looking for reasons for his existence. His skin, sun-bitten, still bore a flare of lines by his eyes. No amount of finery could hide that he'd grown tauter, more muscular, in the years that had separated them. He had grown, if possible, more savagely handsome.

She remembered his head crushed, the bloody pulp in the sand, the clothes that belonged only to him.

"Sir." The governor stepped up, his face alight with curiosity. "My man tells me that you are Captain Roarke Cameron?"

"Governor Blake, forgive me for this unorthodox entrance." Roarke didn't drag his gaze away from her. "This lady has enchanted me."

"Yes, she has enchanted most of Charles Town." The governor raised his brows and rocked on his heels in amusement. "May I introduce you to Mademoiselle Adriana Joubert, a French settler from the Santee district. Mademoiselle, this is Captain Roarke Cameron, a ship owner new to Charles Town."

"Enchanté." Roarke lowered his head to lay a kiss, like a spark, on the back of her hand.

"A pleasure to meet you, sir." Her voice was throaty, breathless, betraying. "You have missed dinner."

"I came to speak with the governor about some private business." He seemed indifferent to the attention they were getting from every single person in the room. "Had I known there was such lovely company, I would have intruded much earlier."

"Yes, well, Captain," the governor said, placing his hand on Roarke's arm. "If I can tear you away from the lovely Miss Joubert, I'd like you to join me in some Madeira. I'd like to discuss that business immediately, and I wouldn't want to bore the ladies with it." He turned and gave his wife a decisive nod. "I believe Mrs. Axtel was about to sing?"

"Indeed," his wife said drily. "Mrs. Axtel?"

Roarke whispered, "Another time, *mademoiselle.*"

When he released her hand, her knees went wobbly. She seized the arm of her chair so she wouldn't lose her dignity by bouncing to her seat. Roarke turned to follow the governor out of the room as she sank down with as much grace as she could muster. Mrs. Axtel rose belatedly to clear her throat. Ignoring the looks cast her way, Adriana sat mute while Mrs. Axtel's thin, reedy voice rose and fell in the room.

Roarke, Roarke. *Roarke.*

Alive.

Memory rushed through her like a freshet running down from the mountains of the backcountry. She could no more stop it than she could stop the rice fields from flooding. Standing on the deck of *L'Aventure,* playing with Chou-Chou and talking to him, soaking in his kind affection as they stared at the milky sweep of stars. The astonished look on his face as he first laid eyes upon her as a woman. His warning kiss, and the undeniable surge of passion she'd felt at the touch of his lips. His hands roaming across her naked body.

The joyous rush of sensation when he'd made her a woman.

A full glass of ruby Madeira appeared in front of her. She glanced up at the man who held it, too bereft of composure not to show her disappointment that it was Nicholas Trott who offered the glass.

"I know you usually avoid drinking at these dinner parties, mademoiselle." His lips twitched in his all-too-perceptive face. "But you look as if you need it."

She didn't bother to deny the truth. It was not every day a woman sees her lover risen from the dead.

She took the glass. Mrs. Axtel's reedy singing continued. Trott took a position just behind her chair, close enough that he could lean down and whisper in her ear.

He said, "You know him."

"I've never seen him before." She'd answered too quickly, she could feel the wave of Nicholas's skepticism.

"Come, mademoiselle. You aren't going to tell me that you were simply struck by Mr. Cameron's rather barbaric looks?"

She sipped the Madeira and felt the burn down her throat. "I would be lying if I didn't admit that he's an exceedingly attractive man."

"I thought your tastes would be more refined."

"You act as if I'm the only one in this room

struck by our new visitor." A quick glace showed many woman talking behind their hands, and not just about her.

"I've always granted you more sense than they," he said.

"Have you?" She wished he'd leave her be. "Wasn't it you who told me that intelligence is unattractive in a woman?"

"I've been known to be wrong."

"A confession of weakness. How wonderfully refreshing."

"I'm coming to realize that, among certain of the female species, intelligence can even be an aphrodisiac."

Flirting, again. How dully predictable. She lifted the glass to take another sip, but found she'd already drained it.

"So," Nicholas continued, "what, exactly, triggered such a passionate display? Was it love at first sight?"

"Shock." That was honest enough, for the surprise still rippled through her. "Mr. Cameron bears an uncanny resemblance to a man I once knew. A man long dead."

"A man you loved."

She didn't bother to deny it. It was a simple explanation and a true one. She could even pass it off to the women of Charles Town and they'd swallow the story whole. They adored swooning over tales of thwarted love. She could dodge the true details by burying her face in a handkerchief and insisting the story was too painful to share.

"I hope," Nicholas said, "that Mr. Cameron doesn't become as fortunate in your affections as the man he resembles."

The thought of Roarke becoming fortunate in her affections sent an unwitting jolt through her body. The tingling shot all the way down to her feet and made her toes curl in her slippers.

"My dear woman, be very careful." Nicholas's voice was a shivery breath on her hair. "You'll have every eligible bachelor in Charles Town challenging the man for your affections."

Mrs. Axtel finished her song and a few guests clapped politely. Governor Blake stepped back into the room, and Roarke stepped in right behind him.

She didn't breathe for a good long time.

The governor raised a hand to quiet the gathering. "Mr. Cameron has brought some news that you will all want to hear." The governor paused a moment, relishing the tense expectation. "The war against the French is over."

"Nonsense," Nicholas blurted through the gasps and cries of the guests. "Captain Roarke, how do you know this?"

"I spent the last few weeks in Jamaica." His gaze flittered to Nicholas's hand where it rested on the chair, inches from her bare shoulder. "Before I left to sail for Charles Town, a messenger arrived from the court of William III. The announcement was public.

The war between England and France is over."

"It's a hiatus, no more," Nicholas retorted. "There'll be no permanent peace until King Louis XIV stops attacking foreign territories and claiming them as his own."

"They are in the process of signing a treaty at Ryswick." Roarke shrugged. "Soon enough, your proprietors will send word of the peace."

"Not any time soon, I hope," the governor said gruffly. "When they do we'll have to call off our privateers, and then how will I possibly get good French wine for my table?"

Everyone laughed light-heartedly, and then Mrs. Blake rose from her seat and directed the guests into the coolness of the garden in the hopes of catching a breeze before the coming rain. Adriana stood up though she could barely feel her own body. Her stomach dropped as she approached the door, where Roarke waited, but the governor spoke into his ear, took his arm, and then led Roarke out ahead of the ladies.

It was a small garden, fresh and full of the heady scent of magnolia. The snowy white petals of a dogwood tree shimmered in the uncertain light of the cloudy sky. Other flowers—jessamine, Joe-bells— filled the inner plots but she did not know their names. She walked boldly into the garden, in the opposite direction of Roarke and the governor, hoping for a moment alone, but she sensed Nicholas hanging back, watching her. She drank that Madeira much too fast. The act of standing and walking forced the dizzy fumes straight to her head.

She came to the edge of the Cooper River and fixed her gaze on the slow-moving water. Lost in her thoughts, she did not know how much time passed before she heard footsteps on the grass behind her.

"Ah, Mademoiselle Joubert," Governor Blake said as he drew near. "I came to apologize to you."

She braced herself as she turned. Roarke stood at the governor's side as she knew he would. In the shadows beyond, she saw Nicholas Trott lurking amid a small circle of men.

"My dear." The governor's face was full of sympathy as he bowed. "I know how grating it must be for you to have to listen to all these Englishmen roundly abuse the French. You've become so much an accepted part of our society that we are probably not as sensitive as we should be to your origins."

"You need not apologize, Governor." She was pleased to hear that her voice sounded normal, despite the trip-beating of her heart. "There are plenty of French families who were hounded out of the country, who reject France nearly as much as you do."

Roarke said, "You don't miss your native land, mademoiselle?"

Her grasp of English suddenly faltered. "It is difficult...to forget the country in which I was born. But France has treated my family badly."

"Your family?"

"I speak of the people who took me in after they found me at the mouth of the Santee River. They were forced out of France because of their religious beliefs."

"Huguenots?"

"Of course," she said, "though all of us have become naturalized. We've taken an oath of loyalty to King William III."

Nicholas swung into the conversation, a half-empty glass in his hand. "Naturalized, or not, that accent alone is enough to drive a man into a frenzy, wouldn't you say, Captain?"

Roarke stiffened.

"Mr. Trott." The governor's voice held a warning. "You've had too much to drink." He grasped the attorney-general's arm and turned him away from the river. "And I think you've monopolized this lady's attention for long enough today."

"Monopolies." Nicholas finished the glass. "Well, Governor, you know all about those."

The governor didn't answer. His grip tightened on Nicholas's arm as he drag-trotted him through the garden in the direction of the back door.

She watched their retreat for as long as she could.

Then Roarke stepped so close that she could feel the heat of his body in the small space that separated them.

"Finalement, petite," he began, lapsing into French. "We are alone."

CHAPTER TWENTY-ONE

"We are *not* alone."

Adriana forced herself to step back. She moved up the bank until she could feel the pebbles of the path beneath her slippers. Out of the corner of her eye, she noticed several groups of people casting curious glances their way. She needed the protection of their gazes as a brake to her tangled impulses.

If he touched her now, she would be lost.

"Adriana." His voice was soft. "You've grown into a wild, beautiful blossom, *petite*."

His words flummoxed her. She was thrilled at the compliment yet at the same time it annoyed her. She'd worn the mask of a woman long enough to know that sweet words came easily to a man's tongue if a woman's bodice was cut low enough.

"After all these years," she said, her voice husky,

"and that's the first thing you say to me?"

"I hardly know what I'm saying—"

"You seem to be poetic, nonetheless."

"I'd rather speak the truth than insult your intelligence." A strong emotion rippled across his face. "In all the ways I thought we might meet again, never did I expect it to be in the house of the governor of the Carolinas."

Her mind did a stutter-jump. "Then you knew I was alive all along."

"I *didn't* know." He shook his head hard. "I only hoped."

"Well I knew *you* were dead." She spoke the word through a throat gone tight. "I *saw* you dead."

She would never forget the sight of all those bodies washed up on shore. She would never forget Gwynn's swollen, half-eaten face. She would never forget the man in Roarke's clothing, the man whose head had been crushed to a pulp.

"That explains why, when I walked into the room," he said, breathing hard, "you looked at me as if I were a ghost."

"Yes."

"I took your hand so you wouldn't faint." He raised his hand as if he were going to touch her, but dropped it so it lay by his side in a fist. "You thought me dead because you heard the gunshots?"

"Gunshots?"

"That night I sent you to shore, the men attacked. I tried to shoot, but they wrestled the gun from me."

"Mutiny."

"Yes." His palm drifted to his shoulder. "They shot me and I toppled over the gunwale. I don't remember anything else until I woke up in the *chaloupe* with Drake."

She didn't remember hearing gunshots during that terrible first night, not over the crash of the waves upon the shore. Now her breath came hard and fast as she tried to make sense of his story.

"You were in a boat," she said, "during that terrible storm."

"Was there a storm?"

"A hurricane." It hurt to trace the familiar lines of his face. The last time she had observed him so closely, they had been naked in bed. "As bad as any cyclone in the Indian Ocean."

"I don't remember it. Drake spent a lot of time rowing before he found landfall."

"Your ship was destroyed. Days later I found pieces of it washed up by the Santee. I found Gwynn. I found *you*." Her voice broke. "Your burgundy velvet coat. Your boots—"

"I'd taken the coat off," he said, understanding lighting his eyes, "preparing to fight unencumbered."

She whispered, "Somebody else—"

"Yes, some unlucky soul sported my coat. Such fools, those men," he said, in a voice that almost seemed as if he mourned the deaths of mutineers. "Not a one of them knew how to handle a ship properly in a storm."

"They got their just deserts."

"It's done then." He nodded. "Captain Wolfe is well and truly dead."

Captain Wolfe did not look dead as he stood before her. Her mind ran with questions but she had enough of her wits to hold her tongue, for some of the governor's guests drifted their way and now stood dangerously within earshot.

"We can't talk here." He dropped his voice so only she could hear him. "Let me come to you tonight."

Her heart raced in her chest. She had so many questions. She could barely think straight, but under the murk of her confusion one single, disturbing thought rose like a bubble floating up out of molasses.

Roarke had been alive all these years.

Yet he'd never tried to find her.

"Adriana," he said, with urgency.

She met his eye.

"Come to me an hour after this gathering disperses," she said. "I shall leave the back door unbolted."

As promised, the back door to her house was open.

Roarke slipped in and closed the door behind him. He stood in the gloom waiting for his vision to adjust. A golden glow spilled from a hallway. He followed that light until he found a room with a large wooden table strewn with papers and lit by two single candles.

Adriana stood behind it, still laced tight in her jewel-green dress. She gripped in her hand a crystal glass filled with the same liquor that gleamed in a nearby decanter. Even if she finished the bottle, he didn't think it would make this reunion any easier. If he had to wager, he'd say that Adriana could handle her drink better than any woman in Charles Town.

It made his chest ache that she looked so guarded and so breathtakingly beautiful.

He nodded to the room. "You've done well for yourself, Adriana."

"I've heard the same said about you."

He'd seen her approach the governor later in the evening, talking in low tones. "It's true that I've prospered."

"Astoundingly, for a man risen from the dead."

"Only Captain Wolf is dead," he corrected, hearing an edge in her voice that he'd dreaded but expected, now that the shock had worn off. "The respectable Captain Roarke Lee Cameron has taken his place."

He tried very hard not to stare at her. He knew his presence unnerved her. He'd noticed that in the garden when he called her *petite* and her little nostrils had flared and her chin had gone tight. But he still couldn't quite reconcile the tiny beauty he saw before him with the dirty-faced girl he'd known upon the ship. He couldn't yet discern whether the fine satins, ribbons, and lace were just another disguise, or whether she had finally come out from behind all her masks.

"What I would like to know," she said, "is what you've been doing since you marooned me on the shores of the Santee."

He flinched as if she'd hit him with a splintered spar.

It was no more than he deserved. "It's a long story, *petite*."

"I'm in no particular hurry tonight."

She kicked back her foot, juddering the chair behind her a few inches, before dropping into it like a sailor onto a coil of rope.

He filled his lungs with air. He would tell her the truth. He would tell her all of it, from beginning to end, even if it meant that, when he was done, she would hate him for the rest of his life.

He gestured to a chair across the table from her. "May I?"

A lift of her glass was her only assent.

"As I mentioned at the governor's house," he said, settling uneasily into the hard-backed chair, "I was wounded during the mutiny. Drake fished me out of the water. I only came to when our *chaloupe* was very far from the ship. Drake was in a panic, trying to find landfall in the dark."

Sharp needles of rain had awoken him, he

remembered, the rain and Drake shouting curses toward the sky. The boat rode the growing swells in a way that lifted him off the boards and slammed him back so that his shoulder exploded with pain. He must have lost consciousness several times, because he remembered little else until he woke again somewhere on shore.

"We put in to shore just north of Charles Town." He hadn't known it at the time, because he'd been beset with fever-dreams of Adriana lost in the woods. "Drake was concerned about being caught by the English authorities. Once I was strong enough to take to sea again, we made our way down the coast."

"*Down* the coast?"

Her eyes glittered in the candlelight. Sharp little darts piercing his conscience. He supposed he could tell her that he'd argued with Drake to sail north to retrieve her from the wilderness. He could tell her that he was too weak with blood loss and fever to convince his own lieutenant. It was all true.

But that was nothing but a litany of failures— failure to convince Drake, to muster the strength to physically overwhelm him, and a failure of heart, as well, for reasons it took him a long time to grasp.

That was the heart of his shame.

"We had no food, no water, no coin." The words were like rocks in his mouth. "We'd heard that in the inlets south of Charles Town we might find friendly faces."

She swirled the liquid in her glass. "You went

looking for pirates."

"As long as a man knows a foresail from a jib, pirates don't ask uncomfortable questions about nationality or loyalties."

He held out his hand toward the decanter and raised his brow. She waved for him to pour.

She said, "You gave me the impression at the governor's house tonight that you put Captain Wolfe firmly in his grave. Yet now you tell me you went looking for pirates."

"Not as a captain, but as a common sailor." He pulled the stopper out of the bottle. "Drake and I found transport on the first ship we could. We jumped ship weeks later, in Jamaica."

"And then?"

"Drake and I had nothing but the clothes on our backs. For a while, we worked on merchant vessels, doing some shipping among the islands. St. Kitts, Barbados." A man had a lot of time to think about his life's bad choices when swabbing decks on someone else's ship. "Eventually, I made the acquaintance of a man who owned a ship and a sugar plantation, whose captain had died during a smallpox epidemic. He put me in charge of his cargo."

"Fortuitous."

"I've discovered," he said, "that a man doesn't have to be a pirate to succeed in this new world."

"Thus you put Captain Wolfe in his grave."

"It had been my intention from the very start," he said. "It's the reason I took a false name." He searched for some explanation she would embrace. "I was Captain Wolfe in the Indian Ocean, and, for a very short time, in the waters outside Saint-Malo. There are few people in the Caribbean waters who know my face or my name. It seemed the opportune time to let him drown in the Atlantic."

"Fortunately, most of the men who would recognize you," she murmured, "went down in *L'Aventure*."

"Which explains why I never came face-to-face with any of the mutineers, as I expected to, eventually." He took a sip of the brandy and felt it burn down his throat. "This new world," he said, "allows fortune among common men."

"And women."

He thought he saw a flicker of a smile on her face, but it was there and gone too quickly.

"Is fortune what you were striving for," she said, "while you sailed on those merchant ships? While I spent my days grinding corn and sewing skirts in the swamps of the Santee?"

"They weren't my ships," he said, trying not to wince at her words. "I sailed under other men's orders until I finally had saved enough to purchase my own vessel."

"How very respectable of you."

"The minute I bought my ship, Adriana, I came here to look for you."

It was a bald confession that had little effect on her. She made a moue with her mouth, a lovely shape that he wanted very badly to kiss.

"It seems," she said, "we've both had adventures in the three years since we've seen each other."

"You haven't told me yours."

"Another time."

In the golden light of the candles, he watched the perfect mounds of her breasts swell against the constriction of her bodice. His cock noticed, too, stirring in his newly-bought breeches, in a way that made him wonder for the thousandth time since she'd promised to unlock the door to her house whether she would welcome him into her bedroom as well.

He didn't deserve forgiveness. He didn't know how to ask for it. But he couldn't stop hoping.

This woman had every reason to despise him for what he'd failed to do. He couldn't erase the past. He couldn't make her believe that he'd spent every hour of the past three years thinking about her. All he could do was tell her the truth and see if some of it slipped by her defenses and stirred old feelings.

"I knew that you would survive this new world, my strong, resilient Adriana." He tried to catch her suddenly elusive gaze. "I knew it in my heart three years ago. And here I am, finally returned, and I discover you dressed like the finest of Charles Town ladies, with no need of the fortune I spent three years raising so that I might finally—"

"Stop." She clattered the glass upon the table. "Don't talk of what you might *finally do* if you *finally* found me."

His chest tightened. He saw the color on her cheeks, her swift breathing, the way she tried so hard not to show how much his return had affected her. He sensed that she balanced on a knife's-edge of indecision, the kind of decision that an honorable man would allow her to make without influence.

She stood up suddenly. "I'm very glad to find you alive, Roarke." Her throat flexed as she swallowed hard. "I wish you the best of prospects in your business here in Charles Town."

It was a cold, undeniable dismissal. She met his gaze with all the street-urchin courage he remembered. He pushed himself up from the hard-backed chair, taking his time about it, debating whether he should press the subject or let it lie, whether he should try to step around the table and take her face in his hands, debating whether truly he'd become an honorable man in all the years he'd been away, whether he'd become the kind of man that a woman like Adriana deserved.

"As for your pirating past," she continued, with a nervous wave of her hand, "you need not have any fear in that regard. I will never refer to you as Captain Wolfe. Your secret is safe with me."

He didn't give a damn about his secret. He didn't give a damn about anything except kissing the soft lips he'd dreamed of. He didn't give a damn about anything but making her love him again.

"Adriana," he said. "That's not why I came here tonight."

CHAPTER TWENTY-TWO

Adriana stood frozen in place as she watched him take long, lithe strides around the table that formed the only barrier between them.

Since she'd first come to Charles Town, she'd battered off the impertinent attentions of dozens of interested men. She'd closed doors in the face of late-night, drunken visitors. She'd removed hands from her thighs, slipped away from fingers skimming her spine, and pushed against the chests of men who examined too closely the jewelry lying upon her bosom. She knew she could skitter away from Roarke's determined approach. She could hold up a hand to stop him in his tracks. Perhaps a single, sharply-spoken word would be enough, for if she'd learned one thing from this dangerous gambit of inviting him into her home, this man had changed in ways she did not yet fully understand.

But as that single, sharply-spoken word rose in her throat, it came up against the barrier of her swiftly beating heart. She did not want to stop him. The truth made her blood race through her. Strange, faintly-remembered sensations pooled in the secret places of her body. Maybe she *needed* him to kiss her, to see whether his touch would still bring the thrilling madness that she half-remembered but had begun to suspect she'd dreamed after so many years of embroidered fantasies. Perhaps the reality of his kiss would clear away this dense, swirling fog of emotions that had tangled within her at seeing him resurrected, so vital, so alive.

He stepped around the edge of the table, tall and lean and broad of shoulder, and suddenly she couldn't breathe. She closed her eyes as if against the brightness of the sun, and then braced herself for the slam of his body and the bruising grip of his hands.

But his hands were cool and smooth as they slid up her cheeks. His fingers were gentle as they curled against her scalp. He didn't force his body against her as he nudged her head up. She blinked her eyes open as his warm breath fell upon her face. Her heart squeezed as her gaze drank in the sight of him—the slight bend in his nose, the fall of black hair across his brow, the crescent-shaped scar at the corner of his eye—a feast her senses couldn't devour quickly or thoroughly enough.

Then the world blurred as he captured her lower lip with his mouth.

If he'd been forceful or demanding, perhaps she could have pulled away from him. She might have bucked under his attempt to control her, or found some trailing resistance to the thwarting of her will. Perhaps she could have finally mustered the anger she had every right to feel for the way he'd left her to her fate.

That's what she told herself, as she laid her hands on his chest and clawed at the fabric of his shirt.

She felt floaty, weightless, as he took his time exploring the contours of her mouth. The memories of another time, a hungrier kiss, galloped through her mind. Upon his warm, bristling cheek she smelled the perfume of Roarke—sea air and pitch and hemp and ink. Beneath her hands, his heart thudded as fast and furious as her own, as it did three years ago when he had taken her in his arms and taught her what it meant to be a woman.

She was a woman now. She'd never felt more so, through and through. She wanted Roarke to keep kissing her until she could think no more.

She parted her lips for his touch. She felt a sudden vibration through his body. His fingers curled deeper into her hair as he merged their mouths and touched her with his tongue. She stepped closer until she felt the buttons of his waistcoat press against the swell of her breasts. How she ached for their clothes to melt away so that they would be flesh against flesh, heart against heart. Her breath quickened as she envisioned them lying on the rug beneath her feet, their limbs entwined as he sank himself deep inside her. She slid a finger through a buttonhole and flicked it open.

He pulled away from her. She glanced at his buttons, eager to undo every one of them, but he nudged her face so she would look up at him. His eyes had gone dark gray, stormy like the sea during a gale.

"Adriana."

He spoke her name in question. She knew what he wanted, but she could not gather her breath. She swallowed, but still no words came. Why, why, why would he make her speak words of acquiescence when nothing about this was simple? Kissing him didn't mean she loved him.

Making love to him didn't mean she could forgive.

She turned her attention back to his buttons, her fingers fumbling, inept.

"Adriana," he repeated, more softly this time. He released his grip on her hair and instead wrapped his arms around her shoulders. "Adriana, Adriana, Adriana..."

Her heart squeezed so tight that black spots appeared before her eyes. She pressed her forehead against his chest as, in a flash of painful memory, she relived the thousand nights she'd gone to bed alone with this voice in her head lulling her into sleep, lulling her into the safe and harmless fantasy that Roarke had truly loved her during their hours upon the ship, and if he'd lived...if he'd lived...if he'd lived...

Suddenly she was staring at the back of her hands splayed flat on his chest, and her elbows were locked tight. She struggled to control her breathing. Her body throbbed with frustrated desire as her mind grappled with a simple truth.

I cannot do this.

She dared to look at his face. His brows were drawn in confusion and curiosity and something that looked oddly like concern. She let her hands drop to her sides and took a step back, willing her body to stop throbbing with desire.

If there were nothing but passion between them, she might consider bucking the conventions of good Charles Town society. She'd unlace her corset, let it drop to the floor, and willingly give herself over to a night's pleasure. Men did it often enough. She saw no reason why a woman shouldn't, as long as she was discreet and the man took precautions.

But nothing between her and Roarke was simple.

Someday, she might agree that he was justified to send her off the ship to save her from a worse fate. Eventually, she might be able to forgive him for taking three years to find his way to her in Charles Town. Those hurts were deep, but she'd already forgiven him the first when she thought he was dead.

She supposed, with time, she'd forgive him for the second.

But what she kept thinking as she stood there breathing hard under his perusal was that she was not the hapless, desperate little ship's mouse that he'd once known. Three years had changed her from a woman in disguise to a woman on her own. She'd learned how not to depend on a man—or *being* a man—to make her way in a man's world. She stood on her own heels now. She would never have to worry about survival again.

She wasn't yet ready to hand any man—least of all Roarke—her vulnerable, confused and still-aching heart.

"It's late." Her voice was rough, husky. "You need to leave."

He did not try to convince her otherwise. He left on silent feet. A long time after she heard the back door close, she stood there wondering when and how the pirate she'd once known had become a gentleman.

Roarke sat in his cabin with a map of Charles Town spread in front of him. One of the boxes on the grid was marked in black ink with a strong "X." He had been considering buying this lot and another—one for his warehouse, and one for his private home. After the events of the past week he was more determined than ever.

Charles Town was perfect for his ambitions. It lay on a finger of land riddled by streams and swamps, in the confluence of two major rivers. The only English city of any note was nearly 500 miles north in Virginia. St. Augustine, a Spanish settlement, was 250 miles south. The huge Carolina backcountry stretched as far west as the Mississippi River. Unlike the northern English colonies, the westward trails beyond the town were not hindered by mountains. Carolinians roamed deep into the heart of the New World. All the commerce of hundreds of native nations focused here, in this small port town less than one square mile in area.

And then there was Adriana.

He stood up and walked over the gently rocking floor to stare out the stern windows. Small boats wove between the ships anchored in the bay. The sweaty, muscled backs of their slave crews gleamed in the June sunshine, but the only thing he could see was fixed in his mind, a petite spark of a woman whose kiss he'd never forgotten.

She was alive.

He slapped a hand on the rim of the window as relief swept over him, the same drowning wave that had baptized him when he'd first seen her standing in the governor's parlor. This time, alone in his cabin, he let the feeling weaken his knees. He hadn't realized how heavy the guilt and self-recriminations had pressed upon him until, with one glance, he felt a terrible measure of undeserved respite.

He should have sailed to Charles Town sooner. He should have found a way, no matter how difficult. He should have found *her*.

Now he suspected she might already be taken.

For her kiss had been passionate—and her dismissal final.

With his thoughts darkening, he remembered the governor's party. Every time Adriana spoke, the governor's wife had shot darts at her with her eyes, and the other women in the room set their shoulders against her. Only men surrounded Adriana, and he couldn't help but notice that the attorney general—Nicholas Trott—had been particularly possessive. Roarke's inquiries to various citizens about Adriana's precise status in Charles Town society were met either with vague details about her Huguenot 'family' on the Santee, or, more often, with the cold, territorial looks that people gave to outsiders who asked too many questions.

An unmarried woman with the appearance of wealth suggested a very particular occupation. At the governor's house, she looked like a ripe, dusky rose among wilting daisies. He couldn't forget that she herself had once flippantly commented that a woman only had three choices in life—laundress, wife, or whore. But the idea of Adriana being forced to entertain a series of lovers made his belly churn.

A knock interrupted his roiling thoughts.

"Come in," he said, turning to see his first lieutenant smirking in the doorway. "What is it, Drake?"

"Some fop who calls himself Elsworth is here to see you. Something about investing in our ship."

Roarke recognized the name. Elsworth was a

factor who'd had a falling-out with a number of Charles Town businessmen, most prominently Governor Blake. At the governor's house, Blake had cursed the man's name up and down because Elsworth had some kind of monopoly with the Catawba tribe. Roarke recognized the jealousy of a thwarted investor when he saw it, which made Elsworth suddenly interesting.

He said, "Send him in."

Elsworth burst into the room, or at least, he gave the illusion of it, because suddenly color entered the dimness of his cabin. Elsworth's wrists, shoulders, and garters fluttered with scarlet ribbons. Lace cascaded from his throat. The gold embroidery on his coat approached garishness, and his full-bottom wig wilted in the humidity of the day.

Still, in the powdered, painted folds of his face, Elsworth's eyes were calculating. "Captain Cameron, I presume?"

Roarke nodded and gestured to a chair near his desk. He hadn't had much chance to furnish this room. A hammock on the port side served as his sleeping quarters. A desk and a few chairs finished the furnishings. Elsworth perched on the edge of the rough wooden chair.

"I apologize," Elsworth began, "for not approaching you in a more public space before seeking you out in your ship. But given the situation with the war, my investor thought you might leave the harbor before I had a chance to set my proposal before you."

"Peace or not, I'll only leave the harbor when my hold is full."

"Then do you intend to sail out of Charles Town soon, Captain?"

Roarke shrugged, and then steepled his fingers and waited for Elsworth to continue.

"Well," Elsworth said, reaching into his pocket to pull out a small snuff case, "it matters little. I meant only to ease the mind of my investor, who was quite eager to engage your services."

"Do I know the man?"

"Perhaps only by sight." Elsworth pinched out some powder and spoke while fragments dusted his knees. "This particular client has heard about your prowess as a merchant captain among the islands, as has all of Charles Town, of course. We've been told that you made a number of Jamaican and Barbadian planters quite wealthy. Their relatives in the Goose Creek section of the Carolinas have spread the word."

Roarke knew a few Goose Creek men from when he and Drake had searched for help with pirates after the mutiny. None struck him as being sensitive about anonymity in their business dealings.

Elsworth snorted the snuff and then flicked off powder remnants from the tip of his nose. "This particular client," he said, "has left it to me to choose exactly how to financially support your next venture. His primary objective is to get this ship—the *Neptune,* is it?—on the high seas in pursuit of profits as soon as possible."

An admirable enough objective, Roarke thought, since he made no profit while his ship sat in the bay. "I'm listening."

"My investor has a considerable amount of rice to be sold," Elsworth said, waving a hand, "and searches for a trustworthy merchant to ship it to farther ports."

Charles Town was full of merchant ships captained by men better known than he. He wondered if Elsworth's anonymous investor was a native, or a Huguenot, who he'd heard had trouble in the shipping business.

He didn't care—rice was cargo, and that meant money. "I'm heading north," Roarke said, "toward Boston, though I can stop in any port—"

"Yes, yes, certainly you can sell it in some coastal settlement," he said, waving a hand. "But personally, I think you should consider a privateering expedition."

Roarke's shoulders tightened. "King William's war is over. I announced that in the governor's house only a few nights ago."

"Of course, we've heard the rumors, but Charles Town has not yet received official notice of the peace. Until then, Governor Blake is free to issue privateering letters."

"You're asking me to attack ships after hostilities have ceased." Roarke lifted a brow. "That's piracy."

"Now, now." Elsworth's stained nostrils narrowed slightly. "All I am saying is that there's one last chance for tremendous profits."

"Profits," Roarke said darkly, "that are best made from trade. This investor of yours, has he asked to fund a privateering expedition?"

"My investors only concern themselves with profits. They surrender the making of them in my hands." Elsworth gave him a sidelong look, a conspirator's look, as if he knew they were playing at words. "I'm sure of your abilities in such a venture, Captain, you have the look of a privateer, and your ship, I noticed is well-cannoned."

"Against pirates, ironically."

"My investor is in possession of a considerable amount of gold. I'd be able to obtain several hundred pounds, if you were to consider my proposal."

"Your hearing must be failing, sir."

"A thousand pounds, then. In specie." Elsworth snapped shut his snuff case. "That should be enough to buy powder and shot, refit your ships, pay your sailors, and, perhaps, buy even more cannon. I can connect you with men willing to sell such things, of course."

One thousand pounds was a considerable sum under any circumstance. His investors weren't natives, or Huguenots, or even Goose Creek men. That narrowed the list of possible investors to a small caste of society: the landed gentry, the politicians from London, a handful of risk-taking businessmen.

"I see," Elsworth said, "that you are reconsidering?"

"You are mistaken." Roarke stood up, shoving the chair back behind him. "Good day, sir."

"Understand that I'm only trying to maximize profits." The man rose and smoothed the lace of his cravat. "Opportunities like this don't come along often, Captain. If you are still interested in the rice—"

"Drake!" Roarke called to his first mate, who was waiting outside the door. "Show Mr. Elsworth out."

"I suppose twelve hundred pounds wouldn't change your mind?"

It was this last offer, so above and beyond what any man would risk, that convinced Roarke of his suspicions. Somebody very rich wanted him out of Charles Town.

Roarke knew that people push away that which they fear. He knew this, because it was his own shame that had kept him away from Charles Town for too long.

"Mr. Elsworth," he said, "tell your investor that even if she offers me five thousand pounds, I will not leave Charles Town." Roarke saw his suspicions confirmed on the factor's face. "Better yet, I will tell her myself."

CHAPTER TWENTY-THREE

Adriana paused just outside the fortifications of Charles Town, watching the bustle of activity in the harbor. The sea breeze tugged at her pinned-back hair, freeing strands to fly wildly around her face. She lifted her chin to the sun, not caring that it might multiply the freckles on her skin. If she closed her eyes long enough, listened to the swearing sailors and the sound of the tide knocking up against the bows of boats, and filled her lungs with the briny scent of the air, she could imagine that she was still a girl sitting in a crow's nest, drowsing and dreaming as the ship rocked on an open sea.

Then a cool shadow fell upon her.

"With your hair pulled back like that," he murmured, "I can still see the urchin you once pretended to be."

Her whole body tingled with awareness. That

voice had haunted her dreams last night. Lusty, carnal dreams that had left her restless and unsettled.

"Your ship, the *Neptune*," she said, not meeting his eye, "is that sleek three-masted barque by the brigantine now passing by, yes?"

"You must know every ship in the harbor."

"It's the rigging," she said. "The fore and mainmasts are rigged square and the mizzen is rigged fore-and-aft."

"Your eyesight hasn't weakened since your days on the crow's nest."

"I make a point to see things clearly."

"Then it's no wonder you've fooled the men of Charles Town. You're twice as educated in sea travel and have a street-urchin's ruthlessness in business."

Uneasiness rippled through her. What could he possibly know about her business? Or was this just a strange compliment, a reminder of how well he knew her?

"If you'll excuse me." She turned on one foot and headed toward the river. "I'm already late to meet some friends."

"Your rice planter family, perhaps?"

"Yes, by coincidence." Clearly, he'd been asking about her. "They have affairs to attend to in town."

"I have some affairs to attend to as well." He fell into step beside her as shamelessly as if she'd invited him. "In fact, just a few hours ago, a man named Elsworth offered me more than the usual price to ship some rice up the coast."

She made a point not to stumble. Roarke was sharp, but certainly he couldn't guess that she was the person who'd sent him.

"I confess," she said, determined to change the subject, "that I'm astonished to realize that you've become such a respectable man of commerce."

"Respectable wasn't what that man had been looking for, apparently, for he also offered me a tremendously large amount of money to return to privateering."

Sand sprayed as she stubbed a foot deep into the sand. She made the mistake of turning to face him.

There he was, with the sun haloing his dark hair, his gray-green eyes intense, reading her face as if she were a freshly-drawn chart of just-discovered seas.

Her heart made one painful, hard thump.

"They're all fools," he whispered. "Every one of those beribboned men in the governor's house, staring at you and imagining how grateful you'd be with an offer of a little house on the edge of the settlement, and a few hundred coins a month, when all the while you're scheming—"

"Yes, they are fools." She wished he'd stop whispering like they were conspirators. Or lovers. "Why didn't you accept Elsworth's offer?"

"I'm not a pirate anymore. Did you put him up to it?"

"Of course not." For the love of heaven, what did Elsworth *do*? Though she had given the man great latitude when it came to encouraging Roarke to hurry his business along, she'd drawn the lines clearly. "I would never make such an offer. Privateering is too risky a stake."

"Ah. The ever-practical Adriana."

"It's also illegal," she added. "The official news of the war's end might very well have arrived on that brigantine now dropping anchor in the bay."

"You always were clear-thinking."

"So this meeting with Elsworth," she said, her mind turning to business. "Despite his ridiculous privateering proposal, you'll ship the rice, yes?"

"For your Huguenot friends, I assume."

"Huguenots or not, you'll charge the customary percentage or the deal is off. Otherwise, they may as well sell it to the English captains who take advantage—"

"The customary percentage it is." His lips twitched as he squinted down the beach toward the mouth of the river. "I should meet your planter friends, if we're going to be partners."

Partners.

The word rang in her head. She didn't like the idea of *partner.* How on earth had she gotten into a situation where she would be working in any capacity with Roarke? She'd sent Elsworth to urge Roarke to sail away, not to stay and form a relationship with her—whether it was purely business or not.

"We could be partners," he murmured, as if he could read her mind. "I trust you."

"It's a strange kind of trust," she said, "when we

both hold damaging secrets about one another."

"You have the better hand. Who is going to believe that the lovely Adriana Joubert spent her whole life as a ship's mouse? That would be as preposterous to the men of Charles Town as the fact that you now sit on your own pile of gold, gauging investments like a savvy London broker."

She couldn't help the pride that swirled up in her. She'd worked hard to parlay those pieces-of-eight into a quantity that would support her well.

"I hope you'll indulge me," he said. "There's one thing that piques my curiosity."

"Oh?" She lifted her skirts from the sand and headed toward the river, knowing he would keep doggedly by her side. "Just one?"

"Why did you do it?"

"Do what?"

"Send Elsworth to send me away?"

Her throat went dry as she fixed her gaze on the tips of her shoes kicking off sand with every swift footstep. She scrambled to find an excuse that wasn't the truth.

I want you gone because when I see you I yearn for you to kiss me, tear off my clothes, and touch me until I can't think anymore.

I want you to love me, as I imagined you once did.

"Smallpox," she blurted.

"Smallpox?"

"The Gaillards told me that there had been several cases upriver on the Santee."

She wondered if he remembered the day when he told her he'd never had the disease. They were trying to figure out how to keep Gwynn silent until Roarke could get her safely off the ship.

He might not remember it.

But she remembered everything.

"There was an epidemic in the area a few years ago," she continued. "Worse than anything I've seen. Etienne's grandfather and his youngest brother died from it. It swept through Charles Town, too."

"It pleases me to know that you don't wish me dead."

"Of course not," she said, increasing her pace as her heart raced. "Vengeance is a terrible waste of time."

"Then you are of a far better character, Adriana, than I could ever hope to be."

She suddenly remembered his determination to destroy Captain Leighton. He'd hurled himself across the Atlantic Ocean in pursuit of that man, a heedless odyssey that led his own sailors into bloody mutiny.

She wondered if he'd ever consummated that vengeance.

But this was none of her concern. What did concern her was the future between them, especially if he had no intention of leaving Charles Town. The past was done, and the sooner she could put it behind her, the sooner she could focus on her own future.

"Roarke." She hefted her skirts another inch above the sand, more to give her hands something to hold onto than any concern for soiling her hem. "I've been thinking about what you told me the other night about your years away."

She expected him to say something, but his silence was a gentle thing, patient and calm and unnerving.

"I now understand that you saved more than my virtue when you put me on that shore near the Santee that evening. In truth, you saved me from drowning along with the rest of the crew."

She saw his jaw tighten and shift.

"If you'd tried to keep me on the ship, both you and Drake would have been murdered trying to protect me—"

"I would have died a better man."

Regret thrummed in his voice, a rumbling, disturbing sound. She hadn't expected such a response. She didn't know quite how to absorb the implications.

So she moved on instead. "I also understand," she continued, "that it was impossible for you to come searching for me."

"Don't forgive me so easily, Adriana."

His hand was gentle on her arm, but it wielded a power that didn't come from brute strength. She'd been walking fast, breathing hard, and propelling herself across the shore as fast as her legs could take her to reach the shade of the trees that lined the banks of the river. Now with his touch she stopped, just as the river boats came into view.

She met his turbulent gaze. Whatever he would say would change things. That frightened her.

"Roarke." She was hardly able to breathe. "You owe me no explanations."

"I owe you much more than explanations."

He touched her chin. Her gaze fell upon his lips, that firm and hungry mouth, and she knew that she wouldn't be able to stop herself.

"Adriana!"

She startled at the sound of her name. The sound came from the river's edge. She glanced in that direction and saw the familiar silhouette of a tall, young man, stretching up to wave at her with enthusiasm.

Perhaps it was fate that Etienne would appear just at this moment, when she couldn't control herself one breath longer.

Roarke's hand fell away. She intended to walk with some dignity toward Etienne, but she must have shot toward him at a run, because Etienne met her halfway and caught her up and swirled her around while his laughter filled her ears.

Etienne's kiss was unexpected and thorough.

"That," Etienne said, as he placed her sputtering back down on her feet, "is the kind of welcome a man dreams of."

Roarke's shadow fell over them both.

"Adriana," he said, his green gaze as brittle as glass, "you'd best introduce me to your young friend."

CHAPTER TWENTY-FOUR

"I don't like him."

Adriana sighed as she took Etienne's arm and drew him away from the riverbank. "Etienne, at least wait until we're out of earshot before you insult the man."

"He can't hear us." Etienne hazarded a glance over his shoulder to where Roarke remained standing at the banks of the river. "My father hasn't stopped chattering with that captain since you introduced them. They'll be drunk in the tavern by dinner."

"And I thought your father didn't drink."

"Not in mother's presence." His dark gaze returned to her, unsettled and full of questions. "Who is he?"

"He's an English merchant captain who speaks flawless French and is willing to ship Huguenot rice at ten percent profit and without further questions."

"Why?"

She raised her brows. "For profit?"

"He could ask for better terms and we'd give them without argument."

"He's new to Charles Town. I suspect he doesn't know any better."

"But he knows *you*."

She prayed that Etienne would blame the brightness of the sun for the sudden flush that rose to her cheeks.

"Etienne," she said, in her sternest voice, "I've managed to find someone willing to take the Gaillard's rice to other ports. It's why I came to Charles Town in the first place—"

"That's a lie."

His words lingered on the air. She let go of his arm and put some space between them, walking in a tense silence as they neared the fortifications.

"What I mean," he said, his voice controlled in a way she'd never heard it, "is that you've always wanted to come here. You love the sea, and the rush of people. I don't blame you. I understand the attraction, the...excitement."

She thought about the kiss he'd laid upon her, a kiss that suggested a sexual education she was sure he hadn't received in the wilds of the Santee.

"And what else am I to think," he added, "when I return and find you walking about in a new dress, trailing some rough-looking sea captain behind you?"

"You are to think that I'm doing exactly what I

came here for."

"I don't like the way he looks at you."

Roarke hadn't like the way Etienne looked at her, either. There had been a terrible, brittle silence after she'd made the introductions. If the two men had had antlers, she suspected they would have locked them, then and there.

"Etienne," she sighed, "I don't even know what to say to a comment like that."

"Tell me he's not your lover."

She startled. She'd become inured to the gossip that she knew was tossed about that she was connected to one man or another—Nicholas Trott, or even Governor Blake—but she'd never expected such gossip to come from Etienne's mouth.

"I think," she stuttered, "that I should be insulted."

"Then he's not your lover?"

Not now.

Not yet.

"He's not my lover." She pushed the last thought away. "What exactly do you think I'm doing here in Charles Town?"

"Avoiding me." He pulled her aside, out of the way of a horse and rider racing dangerously fast through the street. "Foolishly searching for someone more exciting. Someone who feels less like a brother to you."

Ah.

Madame Gaillard had been right all along. She

felt a stab of guilt. Etienne had expectations, and now that Adriana was established here in Charles Town with many male acquaintances, her good friend felt his chances growing slim.

"Come to the governor's dinner with me tomorrow night." She took his arm and pressed her head against his shoulder. "You'll see that all the men of Charles Town are free with their looks. The good captain I just introduced you to is no different than any other."

"You are not easing my mind."

"You're not thinking like the good friend that I know you are."

"It's difficult to think like a friend when you're wearing a dress like that."

"My pretty dress has a purpose, Etienne." She resisted the urge to sigh again, because that made her breasts swell up from the hem of her bodice. A useful tool, but not in this particular situation. "It's like a mask I wear, to put myself in a position to smooth this misguided animosity the powerful men of Charles Town have against the French."

"I don't want you to be around powerful men." He reached for her hand and grasped it tight. "I want you to be around me. Tonight."

She knew what he was asking as he glanced hopefully at the door to her house, and it wasn't for a bed in a separate room. "Etienne, you stay at the tavern, not here."

"We are not children anymore. My mother's eye

isn't upon us."

"Your father—"

"Won't say a word. He knows how I feel."

His gaze fell to her bosom again. A shadow of disappointment darkened her heart. She didn't want to believe that Etienne couldn't see past her cleavage any better than the men of Charles Town. This man had seen her in breeches. They'd hunted in the woods around the Santee together, stepping as quietly as natives through the underbrush, the silence between them the easy companionship of friends.

"So you come here and accuse me of taking a lover," she said, releasing him and stepping away, "and then would take me as a lover yourself?"

He sensed her displeasure, for his shoulders drooped and a rueful look crossed his face. "I shouldn't have said all that, Adriana." He shrugged. "I just miss you."

He smiled a bashful smile.

And she looked at him and looked at him and looked at him until she once again saw in his face the shy and sweet boy she knew.

That evening, Adriana stepped out of the house and gasped as the wind whipped her skirts against her legs. Her hair strained against its pins. "The storm's so close!" She glanced beyond Etienne at the turbulent sky. "I didn't realize—"

"Shall we send word that we won't be coming?"

A speculative gleam came into his eye as he approached. "We could share a private dinner."

"We're going," she said, frowning at him. "The Blake's house isn't far from here. It won't make a difference whether we're in the governor's house or this one during the storm."

"Well, it's not hurricane season yet." Etienne held out his elbow for her grip. "The storm will wear itself out in a few hours."

She approached the horses. Joachim held the mounts firmly, for the whistling of the wind and the scattering of leaves frightened the beasts. Etienne held out his laced hands for her foot. She hefted herself up and settled in the worn leather saddle. The mare pranced beneath her as she pulled the reins from Joachim's grip.

Then Etienne struggled with his own mount. He was a rice farmer, more at ease with a dugout canoe and an oar than with a lively gelding. He also looked decidedly uncomfortable in his borrowed clothes, but his lips were set in what she had come to know as determination. He would take advantage of his situation tonight, because Adriana knew how much he wanted to be the man escorting her to dinner.

She needed Etienne, too. With her friend's strong arm under her hand, she was less likely to make a fool of herself with Roarke, who was sure to be one of the invited guests.

A little while later, she and Etienne dismounted outside the governor's house. Through the windows of the lower rooms, the golden glow of candlelight spilled over the lush, front gardens. A servant in broadcloth livery took the reins of the horses while another led them into the foyer, beyond which the guests of the dinner party mingled.

The governor greeted them in the foyer. "Madame Joubert! I am so pleased you braved the storm to come." He scrutinized Etienne's tanned face and his ill-fitting suit. "And who is this strapping young man?"

"Etienne Gaillard," Etienne said, thrusting out his hand and speaking passable English. "A pleasure to meet you, Governor Blake."

"Gaillard," the governor mused, tilting his head toward Adriana. "Of the family from the Santee?"

"Why, governor," Adriana said. "I'm flattered that you remember so much about my family."

"I make it a point to know everything I can about the good people under my jurisdiction. Especially the pretty ones." He winked at her before turning his attention to Etienne. "Welcome, young sir. I look forward to quizzing you about how you came to know this lovely young Frenchwoman that all of Charles Town adores."

They followed the governor into the parlor. She saw the usual crowd of proprietor's deputies and judges, Carolina landed gentry and their wives. There was one man she had never seen before, dressed in a brilliant scarlet coat with medals glittering on his breast. He sipped a glass of brandy with one arm bent behind him, as if standing at military attention.

Roarke, she noticed, was not among the guests.

"You were right," Etienne said, as the governor made his excuses and then stepped out to greet another arrival.

"Right about what?"

"The governor looks at you in the same way that captain did."

She raised a brow. "I did warn you."

"I still don't like it."

"You're not going to make a fuss now, are you? You are the man I chose to escort me, after all."

"Yes, and that gives me some ideas." Etienne took a glass from a tray a servant was circulating through the room. "The governor wants to hear stories. Should I tell him that you're a fine huntress?"

"Don't you dare."

"I could tell him," Etienne continued, speaking in low French, "that I've seen you wade into a rice field to retrieve a turkey you'd shot straight through the eye."

"You should remember how good my aim is before you anger me."

"You were happy then, Adriana."

She raised her brows, wondering what he was babbling on about, because never once in these past years had she felt anything as fierce as happiness.

"But since you've moved to Charles Town," he added, "I haven't heard you laugh once."

"Oh, Etienne." Her heart gave a little squeeze.

She ran a hand over Etienne's sleeve, feeling blessed with friendship and guilty about it at the same time. "I'm sure you'll have me laughing before the night's end."

Then she fanned herself with her free hand as she nodded to the many guests. Compared to the fresh, rain-washed air outside the house, the parlor seemed close and stifling. She took a cushioned seat by a window in the hope of a breeze. The patter of rain on the wooden sides of the house increased. The wind shook the locked shutters until they banged against the thick, greenish glass of the windows. The light from the myrtle-berry candles flickered in the drafts. The women gasped in unison as a particularly vigorous wind battered the side of the house.

"Well, Madame Joubert, you're looking more flushed and beautiful than ever. Storms suit you."

She glanced up to find Nicholas Trott's rheumy gaze on her. The strong scent of rum floated on his breath.

Etienne stiffened, but she placed her hand on his arm. "Nicholas, may I introduce to you a friend from the Santee, Etienne Gaillard. Etienne, this is Nicholas Trott, the attorney general of the colony."

The men bowed like they were testing the weight of their antlers. They exchanged stiff pleasantries, but she hardly heard them, for just at that moment she glimpsed Roarke as he stepped into the foyer.

Her heart did a little skitter-step. She suspected she may have gasped, too, because suddenly Nicholas turned to follow her gaze.

She slapped a hand on his arm to forestall him—and the gossip that would follow. "Nicholas," she said, letting his name roll over her tongue, "Etienne and I were just wondering about the new guest."

She gestured with a tilt of her head to the military man in the middle of a small crowd, all while watching Roarke chat with the governor in the foyer.

"That buck?" Nicholas frowned. "He's the naval captain of the brigantine that came into the harbor late this afternoon."

"Ah, a naval captain." Out of the corner of her eye, she watched as Roarke handed his hat to a servant.

"He's the guest of honor tonight," Nicholas continued, "for he brings us the news of the end of the war."

Etienne's eyes lit up. "Is it true?"

Nicholas shrugged. "He brought all the necessary papers."

"Perhaps now," Etienne said, "Englishmen will not hate us French so much. Will you introduce me to this man?"

Adriana knew that she should rescue Etienne from his own foolish candor, but Roarke had turned toward the parlor doors and saw her.

Their gazes locked.

"Oh, young man," Nicholas laughed, "I would not be so foolish as to introduce a Frenchman to Captain Samuel Leighton."

CHAPTER TWENTY-FIVE

Adriana remembered very well how quickly the world went mad during a storm. The undulation of the sea was not a steady, predictable thing, but a thrashing creature that toyed with the vessel as if it were a small wooden boat in a young boy's bath. A sailor had to be flat-footed, with a sure grip, and have lightning-fast impulses, if a sailor wished to live.

So now, she shot off the cushioned seat. She seized Etienne's arm and dug her fingernails into his sleeve as if struggling to stay upright. She stared at Roarke—her mind a wordless scream—and then she slid her gaze to Leighton. She saw confusion ripple across Roarke's face at the same time she saw Leighton turn toward the parlor doors.

"Oh!" She cried out, and then "oh!" again until every eye was fixed upon her. She swayed toward

Nicholas Trott as she loosened her grasp on Etienne. "I don't feel well," she stuttered, knocking her wineglass against her bosom. "I don't feel..."

The damn idiot didn't even catch her as she fell. She went boneless in the assumption that he would. Instead she cracked her back against the edge of the window seat—cushioned, but the edge was hard underneath—and then she nearly knocked herself silly as she hit the floor.

Her glass clattered out of her hand, spilling wine everywhere. She shook her head to dispel the black spots in front of her eyes. She'd been knocked unconscious by a swinging rope more than once, so she knew that she'd be sporting a lump when all was said and done.

Her ruse seemed to be working, because she heard ladies squeal and footsteps shuffle. A crowd surged around her. As she blinked her eyes open, she felt a jolt of triumph to see Captain Leighton frowning down at her amid the crowd as if she'd breached some rule of protocol.

"Adriana!" Etienne threw himself on his knees.

"Move aside, boy." Nicholas rustled a linen out of his pocket and then set to pat her bodice dry. "The woman needs space to breathe."

She feigned ignorance of Nicholas's attention to her bosom—and Etienne's fierce attempt to knock the man's hands away. She blinked up at the crowd as if dazed. Through the stocking legs of the men and the skirts of the women she strained to see if Roarke had heard her mental warning. The wall of skirts parted for a moment as Governor Blake pushed his way to the center of the crowd, but not long enough for her to see anything.

"What are you all gawping at?" the governor exclaimed. "Why, Mademoiselle Joubert."

"Forgive me," she said, in her huskiest voice, clutching her brow as Nicholas continued his ministrations. "I don't know what came over me."

"The heat," Etienne said in his imperfect English, his dark eyes swirling with questions. "She is overcome."

Still, she saw no Roarke amid the onlookers. The British commander with the pockmarked face hadn't moved.

"Fetch some wine," the governor ordered.

"Oh, I have wine enough," she said, raising her hands to stop the tug-of-war going on between Etienne and Nicholas and the wet linen. "I'm quite soaked with it."

"Trott," the governor said sharply. "Let our young lady dry herself."

Nervous laughter rippled through the crowd. Nicholas's nostrils flared, but he released the damp linen. Etienne seized it and handed it to her.

"If only," she said, clutching the wet cloth, "I could retrieve my dignity with as much alacrity."

"I'm sure you fell with the grace of a gazelle," the governor said.

She touched her head where she'd hit the floor

and winced more than warranted, for she hadn't even broken the skin. "I felt so dreadfully light-headed."

Etienne said, "Shall I fetch a doctor?"

"No, no. I may have a bruise or two, but otherwise the only thing that appears to be hurt is my pride."

"None of that, now, none of that," the governor said. "If it weren't for this blasted storm, I'd open every window in this parlor."

"But then I'd worry about my hair."

"My dear, every man in the room has wondered what your hair would look like free of its pins," the governor said. "We'd welcome a monsoon for that delight alone."

"There you go, flattering me," she said, as masculine laughter rose, "when I'm sprawled on the floor like a clumsy child."

"Then rise up and join us, mademoiselle." The governor held out a hand. "A glass of brandy and a moment's rest will do wonders."

She took his hand and gingerly stood up. "Perhaps I should retreat to my lodgings to regain my health, and dignity."

"No, no," the governor protested, "I won't hear of it. There's a storm out there, and we have plenty of room upstairs—"

"Your kindness touches my heart, governor," she said, "and I'm sure my weakness was nothing but a touch of the heat." Beyond the crowd, she noticed the foyer was empty. "But considering the reports we have heard of smallpox in the vicinity, perhaps it is best I depart.”

The mention of smallpox caused a sudden tension in the room, like a communal indrawn breath.

The governor released her hand. Suddenly there was plenty of space around her. Even Nicholas Trott toddled back.

“Mademoiselle speaks the truth.” Etienne slipped his arm around her waist to brace her. “I shall see her home.”

She played the part of the light-headed maiden as Etienne guided her through the parlor, then the foyer blessedly bereft of Roarke, and finally out the front door. While he bundled her onto her horse, she scanned the path for signs of a retreating mount, but the wind made tracking impossible.

Once they made it to her lodgings, Joachim ran out and took the reins of her horse. Etienne threw Joachim the reins of his own and then followed her up the steps as if he were master of the place.

“Etienne—”

“Not a word.” He swung open the door and gestured for her to enter.

Inside, she tossed off her cloak and tilted her head in the mirror to better gauge the extent of the bruise. Feeling Etienne’s gaze upon her, she wandered into her dining room and took out two glasses, filling them with brandy. Etienne took his glass and tossed it back. Then he set his glass down and dropped into a chair.

"You," he said, "have some explaining to do."

"It was just a temporary weakness," she said. "The heat, as you said."

"I've never seen you faint."

"I've never worn a corset as often as I do now."

"Any man can see that you don't lace it tight."

She turned away, disturbed that he'd noticed such a thing. She didn't want to think about Etienne in her home right now. She wanted to know where Roarke had gone. If Captain Leighton somehow found out there was a Captain Roarke Cameron in Charles Town—and it could happen so easily, just through a casual remark by the governor over a glass of wine—then Roarke's lodgings would be the first place the captain would look for the pirate who'd hounded him across the Atlantic.

"I've seen you pull intestines out of a buck's belly," Etienne persisted. "You're not the fainting kind."

"It's not the first charade I've played."

"Yes, but I couldn't help notice that you fell like a stone the moment Captain Cameron appeared."

His perception surprised her.

"Who is this man?" he said. "What is he to you?"

She wandered to the windows, sucked by the shifting breezes so they rattled in rhythm with the storm. How she wanted to fling them open and let the breeze pull the pins from her hair and the rain soak her, as if she stood on the crow's nest in a rolling sea.

"I knew him before," she said, offering a nugget of truth. "He was on the same ship as me."

"The ship that went down in the storm, three years ago?"

"Yes."

"But he wasn't among the bodies on shore."

"I thought he was."

"But now, years later, he reappears in Charles Town as a merchant captain." Etienne spoke in an even voice, as if he were making sense of hoof prints and signs in order to find his quarry. "He was a pirate," he finally said, "just as you were a pirate."

"A woman pirate?" she said, with not nearly enough dismissiveness. "Who has ever heard of such a thing?"

"You once compared a buck's intestines to a tangle of hemp rope," he said. "I remember the way you used to climb trees, swift and confident, one hand over the other like you were climbing rigging. You loved when the wind made the treetops sway, you with your feet braced on a branch while holding on to the trunk with one hand, smiling down at me."

"We were playing. We were children."

"*I* was a child." He found interest in the buttons of his suit. "But you were never a child, Adriana."

She looked at her friend, sprawled on the chair, his gaze as intense as ever she'd seen it. He was just guessing, certainly.

Had she given herself away so thoroughly?

"It's all becoming clear," he said. "You risked a

knock on the head tonight to get that pirate away from a British naval officer."

A pressure grew in her throat, an urge to tell Etienne everything, from her youth dressed as a boy, to her time as a ship's mouse, to these past months in Charles Town when she finally felt like she had some control of her life.

But Etienne was changing before her very eyes. He was no longer the gawky young man too awkward to make his own desires known. To reveal Roarke's past was to put a weapon in the hands of a jealous, full-grown man who knew Roarke only as a rival.

"Etienne," she whispered, "the situation is complicated."

"It's not complicated at all," he barked. "You're hopelessly in love with Captain Cameron."

Roarke stilled in the shadows of the next room. He had just slipped through the back door and followed the faint glow of candlelight, arriving here in time to hear the last of the conversation. Now the French boy's words rang in his ears. He willed Adriana to turn around so he could see her face.

She did not oblige. She went unnaturally still, and then, after a moment, she swayed as if the boards beneath her feet were not nailed to a foundation, but were rather the deck of a ship that had dipped into the trough of a swell.

The Frenchman shot up from his chair. A knot

tightened at the back of Roarke's neck. If that boy approached Adriana, touched her, kissed her...

Bloody thoughts filled his mind.

"All this time," the boy said, "you treated me like a brother. I welcomed your affection because I didn't know how else to be close to you. I thought, if I just showed you that I'd become a man—"

"Etienne, please stop."

"Your heart has always been taken, hasn't it?"

"You don't know what you're talking about."

"I know that the days are numbered for pirates, now that the war is over. The more English proprietors and naval officers who find their way here, the more civilized this place will become, and the less hospitable it will be to high-seas thieves. Soon your pirate captain will have no place to hide."

"He's not a pirate," she said. "Not any longer."

"He can never give you what you need. If you stay with him, you'll always live under the shadow of danger. He cannot offer you a home, children, a safe and comfortable life. But *I* can."

With those words, Roarke felt as if he'd ran into a wall he didn't see. The drive that had propelled him here—racing through the wind and the storm, ducking under eaves, sidling his way through alleys, his mind filled with the thought of Adriana—that forward motion stopped short at the truth in the Frenchman's words.

"Please leave, Etienne." Adriana flexed her narrow shoulders. "You shouldn't be here. If anyone saw you enter my home—"

"—they'll think I took shelter from the storm—"

"They'll think worse than that, and you know it."

The boy tugged on the hem of his waistcoat. Roarke saw the struggle on his face, and understood exactly what the boy was thinking better than the boy would ever know.

"I'm not giving up on us." The boy's shoulders rose and fell. "But for your sake, I will leave."

The boy headed toward the front door with a swagger in his step. Roarke heard the flap of a cloak being thrown over shoulders, then the sound of a door opening. The wind whistled throughout the house and made candles on the table where Adriana stood flicker. From outside came the sound of harness and horse's hooves, and then he knew the Frenchman was gone.

He curled his hands into fists to stop himself from stepping into the candlelight and making his presence known. He stared at Adriana until his eyes hurt. Maybe the young man was right. Maybe Adriana was better off with some inland planter, rather than with a man who would be forever hunted.

"You can come out of hiding now, Roarke."

The soft voice broke into his thoughts. She didn't look in his direction. She was transfixed by the dregs at the bottom of her glass.

"Please tell me Joachim didn't let you in," she added. "I won't have him think it's acceptable to allow men in this house."

"The back door was unbolted." He stepped into the room and saw how her knuckles tightened around her glass. "Joachim was busy dealing with your skittish horse."

"So." She took a breath that made her breasts surge. "You saw Leighton in the governor's parlor."

"I'd recognize the slouch of that man's stance from five hundred yards."

"Would he recognize you?"

"Instantly." At the battle outside Roscoff, he'd looked through the spyglass at Leighton standing on that British warship. Leighton nearly dropped his own spyglass as the naval captain recognized *him*. "Leighton is one of only a handful of people who know my real name," he said. "And he saw me attack his ships."

With him, you will always live under the shadow of danger.

"You must leave Charles Town now." She planted the glass on the table. "Take the *Neptune* and find some safe harbor—"

"Still trying to get rid of me, *petite?*"

"Please. There's no time for foolishness."

"It gives me ease that you never gave your heart to that young Frenchman."

"Do you understand," she said, her little nostrils flaring, "that the governor might have noticed your absence by now? That he might have mentioned your name out loud within Captain Leighton's hearing? That Captain Leighton might even now be sending men to your lodgings to arrest you for piracy?"

"Fortunately, I am not there."

"Then he'll send men to confiscate your ship, the cargo, and all the sailors aboard. He'll brand you a pirate, ruin your name, your prospects, everything you've spent three years building."

"Always thinking practical, my little Adriana."

"And if he catches you, if he arrests you—"

"He'll have me swinging by the neck tomorrow."

She was breathing hard now. Her bosom pressed against the restriction of her corset's edge. He didn't move, not consciously, but suddenly he was standing in front of her, looking down at her hair, n disarray from the tugging of the wind so that locks fell in tangles over her shoulders. He smelled the perfume she was wearing, a drifting, shifting sandalwood scent that reminded him of the breezes and the beaches of the Indian Ocean.

She looked up at him while splaying her hand against her stomach. "You are planning to kill him, aren't you?"

"No, *petite*."

"That had been your plan from the beginning." A note of accusation rippled in her voice. "You'll do anything, hurt anyone, and even disregard common sense and self-preservation all for your damn bloody vengeance."

"Adriana." He took her hand and lifted it to his lips. "I gave up on vengeance the very hour I marooned you on shore.

CHAPTER TWENTY-SIX

Undone, she whispered, "Why?"

He dropped his fierce gaze. Ripples tightened on his brow. A lock of hair slipped out of its binding and fell across his temple. She ached to reach up and push it out of the way, to urge him to look at her again so she could see what deep thoughts had put those lines on his brow.

But he remained mute, focusing such intense attention on the back of her hand that she became increasingly conscious that she'd spent her early life scrubbing decks with lye soap. No amount of leisure could ever make them feel as soft as a lady's hand.

She tugged gently. He released her hand and she instantly regretted it. He turned away from her and pressed his forearm against the mantel to stare into the cold ashes of the empty fireplace, and it was as if he'd stepped back a hundred thousand miles.

"I'm a damned fool, Adriana." He'd spoken the words so softly that she had to strain to hear him. "I was always so sure I was doing the right thing."

Her instinct was to remind him that she'd forgiven him for marooning her, but she sensed that he was talking about something else, something very distant, and so she hugged her own midriff to still the urge to say anything.

He began, "My brother and I grew up in Devon. My father wanted both of us to become blacksmiths like him, pounding iron staves for flour barrels and horseshoes for merchants' geldings. But we preferred running around the wharves of Bideford, gathering pay by hauling barrels and crates and sacks from the waterfront to the warehouses." He ran his hand over his jaw. "Adam and I would spend hours just watching the ships set sail. So when I was fourteen I signed onto a British naval ship. My brother signed on with me. He was only twelve."

She couldn't imagine Roarke that young, maybe as young-looking, gawky, and skinny as Etienne had been when she'd first met him. She tried, but any attempt was extinguished by the very real presence of the tall, broad-shouldered, deep-thinking man peering with increasing intensity into the mouth of the hearth.

"Leighton wasn't my first captain. I'd had another captain before him, Captain Pierce, a good man who taught me more than a common crewman had a right to know about rigging and sails and wind and navigation and discipline and seafaring. I was lulled into thinking this was the way every British naval ship was run.”

She stepped closer to the hearth. She had the strange, unnerving sense that she was hearing the voice of the young man he’d been, long before he’d put on the hat of Captain Wolfe.

“When Pierce retired, I signed onto a new ship. Leighton’s ship.” His voice rumbled with anger. “I soon found out that Leighton chose a whipping boy for every voyage. He picked a sailor he didn’t like. Adam had a sharp tongue and he didn’t have the sense to muzzle it. He was the unlucky one.” A muscle moved in his cheek. “I couldn’t abide the way the captain treated him.”

“Of course you couldn’t.”

“I put myself between them,” he said as if she hadn’t spoken, “so that Leighton would whip me instead. But I would rather bite through my own cheek than cry out when I was tied to the mast, and that’s what the bastard really wanted. He wanted to hear someone screaming under the lash.”

She’d heard such tales before from her own fellow pirates. Many of them had abandoned naval ships and chose the danger and uncertainty of a life as a thief rather than be a piece of meat for a naval whipping post and a cruel, all-powerful captain.

“So one day, after whipping Adam, he marooned both of us on a remote section of coastal Madagascar.” He rat-tat-tatted his fingers against the marble mantel. “Adam died within the week.”

His shoulder was within her reach. She wanted to place her hand on it, to wordlessly tell him that she understood. No man had the right to brutalize another with impunity. One of the reasons she took up the pirate life was because there, to a greater extent than anywhere else, all men were considered equal, even if women were not.

"I'm a damned fool, Adriana," he repeated, as he dropped his head between his shoulders. "I was so sure I was doing the right thing."

She spoke his name, her voice nothing but a breath, but he drew in a breath as if he couldn't finish the story fast enough.

"After I buried my brother, I joined a crew of pirates. I worked my way up to captaincy. I treated my men well." He curled his hand into a fist. "But the minute I caught scent of Leighton outside Roscoff I disregarded my crew. I dismissed all expectations that we'd be hunting prizes at the mouth of the English Channel. I set off across the open ocean like a mindless dog with the scent of a fox in his nose."

"To avenge a dead brother," she said. "To stop Leighton from his pleasure at hearing men screaming at the mast—"

"That drowned crew of mine had a right to mutiny. On the day I marooned you alone on that shore, I finally realized that I'd twisted myself into exactly what I most hated: I had become no better than Leighton."

The windows rattled as the wind blew debris

upon the glass. The roof began to thrum with a hard rain. His story held an element of truth that her instinct tried to reject, but reason forced her to examine. Long before she'd signed on the trip, she'd heard such terrible stories about the Sea Wolf. But her experience of him was of a hard leader, but often an unexpectedly kind one, for he'd shown her leniency even when she was just a ship's mouse.

How much he must have struggled during those long months to come to terms with the disparate angels of his nature.

"That's why I didn't come back to find you, Adriana."

She glanced up to find him staring at her with a wild expression in his eyes.

"I was ashamed." A muscle flexed in his cheek. "I was afraid what I would see, if I looked into your eyes."

He looked at her now like he'd never looked at her before, with such open and unabashed vulnerability, this man who'd captained a privateer, battled naval warships, and drove a crew to mutiny. He looked as bereft and undone as she'd felt in those terrible months after she'd assumed he was dead.

"What do you see now, Roarke?" she asked around the lump growing in her throat. "When you look in my eyes?"

"I see the beautiful, self-assured, confident woman who always existed underneath all the soot you used to smear on your sweet, young face."

She caught her breath.

"I see a woman," he said, as his voice broke, "who deserves safety, security, a home—all the things this ex-pirate may never be able to give you, now that Leighton knows who I am. All those things your good and ardent Frenchman offers."

"Etienne was wrong," she said, gripping the mantel so that her knees wouldn't give out. "In some things."

"Adriana—"

"Etienne believes that what my heart desires above all things are security, a home, and a normal life." She managed a shrug. "That's what most women want."

"Most women."

"But what Etienne doesn't understand," she said, daring to step toward him, "is that this house, these clothes, all the money I've managed to gather, it's not for security, for safety, or for a place I can call my own."

He breathed heavily through his nose, like the soft huff of a bull.

"All of my wealth," she said, "I earned for one thing alone: *Freedom.*"

His hand cupped her cheek. "You have the heart of a pirate still."

"I never felt more alive than when I was a ship's mouse without a shilling in my pocket." Her voice was swiftly failing her. "And when I was in your bed, I never felt more loved."

He touched her face with growing wonder as emotions rippled across his brow, more than she could name. Later, she wouldn't remember who moved first, whether Roarke bent his head toward hers or she raised herself on her toes to kiss him. Her mind was a blur of sensation as their lips came together and her nose pressed against his cheek. He hadn't shaved that morning, for she felt the stubble raze her face as he turned his head to deepen the kiss. She smelled him—sweet rain and pitch pine and warm linen. His clothing was damp. Her hands slid over the ridges of his muscles as she tried in desperation to draw closer.

Then came a flurry of undressing, buttons slipping between her fingers and her bodice ties flying, his coat tossed into the darkness. He yanked her bodice off her and seized her by the waist to lift her out of her skirts. Later, later, they would find a bed, but now the rug was soft enough as it pressed against her shoulder blades. A humid draft swept over them, shunted through the chimney flue, a breeze that smelled of ash and sea. It chilled the rainwater that dripped off his hair and slipped in rivulets over her naked breasts. He caught the droplets with the rough surface of his warm, warm tongue and spread them until her nipples tingled with tightness.

She wanted more than just kisses. She pushed his linen shirt off his shoulders, shoving it down so that she could feel his back under the aching hollows of her palms. She pressed up against him to feel every new inch of his skin exposed, but he frustrated her ambitions by sliding down, dragging the shift he caught in his hands, dragging it down and tossing it aside until she wore nothing but stockings caught by ribbons above her knees.

He looked at her body, tracing the swells and hollows of her torso with the same intensity and reverence with which she'd seen him concentrating on a new sea chart, taking in unexplored territory.

She couldn't bear it any longer. She grasped his head, curling her fingers into his hair, lifting from the ground to urge him up to kiss her mouth. Memories of their first joining made her heart race. She wanted him to plunge deep inside her. She wanted to feel him filling her up. She wanted his body to love hers.

But he cupped her breast and pressed her down against the rug, all while he trailed a line of moisture over her bellybutton and lower with his tongue.

She cried out at the first touch of his mouth between her legs, and then quivered as he explored the folds of her sex. Circling, circling, slipping in so that her inner muscles clenched, then slipping out to focus on the one swollen, sensitive area that in the years without him she'd discovered herself, usually in the midst of a fevered dream about their time together.

He held her tighter and tighter so she could not wiggle away from the intensity of this kiss, until all thought slipped away and stars started to burst behind her eyelids. She cried out and arched up with excitement.

She was still breathing hard when his shadow crept over her. She blinked her eyes open to find him haloed by the flickering light cast by the candles on the table. He smiled down upon her, and suddenly she saw him as he must have been before Captain Leighton darkened his heart. His hair was tousled, his eyes danced, he looked bold and reckless and light-hearted.

Her heart turned over in her chest.

Etienne was right.

She was hopelessly in love with this man.

Then he nudged her knees wide and positioned himself. With his gaze locked on hers, he slid his shaft against the cleft of her sex and then eased himself in.

She tilted her hips to welcome him. She thought she would burst from the joy of feeling him throbbing so deep inside her. The scrape of his thighs against the tender skin of her legs was almost enough to tip her into a sort of madness. He braced his hands on either side to stabilize his position. He pulled back a fraction and then plunged gently, waited a moment and then did it again, as if he were afraid of hurting her.

No, no, none of this.

She half sat-up, reached below her hips, and seized what she could reach of his backside. Digging her fingers into him, she shifted herself against him so that he sank his shaft into her all the way to the root. She urged him to match her own heart's frantic pace.

His gaze flared. He flattened one knee against the rug and then stroked her hard and fast, sucking her lower lip into his mouth until her head dropped back and, for all she knew for a few blissful moments, the storm could have brought the sea over Charles Town and swept her away in it.

He waited still, waiting until she could breathe again, and only then did he make one final plunge.

He swelled inside her and filled her with warmth.

"Adriana, Adriana, Adriana." He dropped his head upon hers and whispered against her hair. "I have always loved you."

CHAPTER TWENTY-SEVEN

A sharp series of raps woke Adriana from sleep.

She shot up in bed, feeling disoriented. She recognized the familiar walls, the draperies and furniture of her bedroom, but everything seemed different. The crimson drapes were brighter, the linens more tangled, the room suffused with a subtle, earthy scent that teased her but she could not quite identify it.

Man, she thought. *Sex.*

She looked beside her and saw Roarke stretched out on the bed in all his naked glory, his beautifully proportioned body gleaming in the light seeping through the windows.

She breathed in a long, slow breath. Memories of the evening flooded her mind, from the hungry mating on the parlor rug, the passionate interlude that followed halfway up the stairs, and finally the drowsy, teasingly slow way he entered her from behind when they finally made it to her bed.

Her whole body flushed. She dared to lay her hand on the rounded temptation of his warm buttock.

Rat-tat-tat-tat-tat-tat-tat.

"I'm coming, Joachim." She slid her hand away before Roarke stirred. When he finally woke up, she thought, she would tease him about how she'd worn him out.

She rifled in the chest at the end of the bed and decided to forgo stockings, shoes, and a corset. She slipped on a shift, ran her fingers through her hair, and shrugged. Back at the Santee, Joachim had seen her stumble in to the house wearing a dirty shirt and Etienne's old breeches. The elderly man could certainly put up with seeing her in well-loved morning disarray.

She swung the door wide. Joachim made motions that indicated that someone was downstairs.

The door to the house suddenly shook with pounding.

"Open up!" The masculine shout filtered up the stairs. "Open up in the name of King William!"

A chill shot through her.

It *couldn't* be.

It had to be.

Leighton.

Adriana clutched the doorjamb as her mind raced. Leighton must have found out that Roarke was in Charles Town. Leighton must have already searched Roarke's lodgings—maybe he'd already confiscated Roarke's ship. And now Leighton had come here, probably concluding that last night's parlor drama had somehow contributed to Roarke's sudden departure.

"Roarke." She sped to the bedside and shook his shoulder. "You have to dress and leave through the back door *now*."

He made a strange noise, but didn't move. She frowned at him. His skin looked flushed. Spots of color glowed on his cheeks. She pressed her hand against his forehead and realized that he was burning up with fever.

Bang Bang Bang.

She threaded her fingers through her wild hair, her thoughts racing. "Joachim, fetch the captain's clothes from the parlor." She had to get Roarke away from here now. "When you return, wake him, even if you have to roll him off the bed to do so. Get him dressed, take him out through the back stairs, and hide him in the woods somewhere. Do you understand?"

Joachim, wide-eyed, nodded.

"Hurry."

She seized her rouge pot from her vanity and used it as she knew she must. Then she flung open the chest at the end of her bed and pulled out a wrap. She walked to the top of the stairs just as Joachim returned, bounding up two stairs at a time, with

Roarke's clothes crumpled in his arms.

Bangbangbangbangbangbangbang.

"I'm coming," she sang-shouted, glimpsing a flash of a red coat through the window. "Just a minute, if you please."

She hoped it was the sound of her high-pitched voice that stopped the banging on her door. She took her time descending the stairs, fussing with the wrap to hide the lack of a corset and the fact that she'd dressed in haste. She figured by the slant of the light through the parlor windows that it was mid-morning, long past time for the respectable women of Charles Town to be done with their toilettes. She just hoped that Leighton's nose wasn't too sensitive, for she was keenly aware that she carried the smell of her lusty evening like a perfume.

As she reached the foyer, she startled as she heard her name whispered from the shadows. She turned to see Etienne standing loose-limbed in the parlor.

"Etienne," she gasped. "What are you *doing* here?"

"I came here to warn you," he said under his breath. "I came by the back and sent Joachim up to fetch you."

"You knew?"

"I heard a rumor in the tavern this morning." His gaze devoured up her rosy dishevelment and then returned, guarded, to her face. "You're hiding him."

She didn't state the obvious. She gripped her

temples with her hands, trying to stop her thoughts from swirling. She was an unmarried woman in a house with two unmarried men, one of whom was about to be arrested for piracy.

"Hide," she ordered. As a Frenchman, Etienne would be accused of piracy just like Roarke, if he were found here. "Don't let anyone see you. You can't be a part of this."

With reluctance, he slipped back into the shadows. On the other side of the door came the order to knock again. She swung the door open to a navy officer's upraised fist.

"My goodness," she said, pulling her wrap close. "It's quite early in the morning for so many handsome gentleman callers."

Six of them, she counted, as she forced a smile. Her sudden appearance had the intended effect, for several of the soldiers were suddenly unsure where to settle their feet or their gazes. She tilted her head and did the wide-eyed blinking that men found so oddly beguiling, hoping her face was full of curiosity instead of terror.

She recognized in the rear of the phalanx the unbending form of Leighton.

The man who knocked asked, "Am I speaking with Miss Joubert?"

"Yes?"

"We have reason to believe there may be a fugitive from justice in this house."

"A fugitive?" She allowed the door to gape wide

as if she didn't have a care for who saw what. Her bedroom couldn't be seen from here, anyway, so the soldiers wouldn't be able to observe Joachim carrying Roarke down the back servant stairs. "Has someone escaped the jail?"

"No, Miss," the soldier said. "We are searching for a man accused of crimes on the high seas."

"My goodness, I wouldn't know anything about that. Are you quite sure you have the right house, sir? I can't imagine—"

"Are you acquainted with Captain Roarke Lee Cameron?"

"Why, yes." Blink blink. "He's a merchant captain, isn't he? I've met him several times in the governor's house. I believe he has business with the governor. He's a tall, savage-looking type. Though not quite as tall as you, sir."

The soldier had the delicacy to blush. "We have a writ of arrest for him, signed by the governor, on the charges of piracy."

"Piracy?!"

"Yes, Miss."

"But he's a *gentleman*." She heard a sound in the house behind her, in the general direction of the kitchen. Her heart gave a little tumble but she pressed on. "I was told he came from Jamaica with letters of introduction from some of the very best families."

"Miss, who is in this house with you now?"

"Why, just myself and my servant, Joachim. He has been with the Gaillard family for decades. He joined me here because he is becoming a little achy in the knees, and can't do the work in the rice fields that he used to—"

"Enough of this."

Leighton stepped through the phalanx and pushed the young soldier aside. He cast a drooping, lazy eye over the length of her.

Never did she feel so thoroughly undressed.

"Step aside, woman," Leighton said. "My men will search your house."

"Captain." She straightened her spine. "There's no need for such a tone. I'd be more than happy to allow your men to search the premises, though I have to say that a gentleman would accept my word—"

"If you were a lady, I might accept your word," Leighton interrupted, "but by all accounts, you are a French whore, to whom a gentleman owes nothing but a few coppers."

Shock immobilized her. She found herself utterly bereft of breath.

"Step aside, woman," he continued, "or I will give my men leave to search much more than your house."

She opened her mouth to speak with the true voice of a well-seasoned sailor, but a familiar voice cut her off.

"Threatening a woman, Leighton? You never did have the bollocks to pick a fight with someone who could beat you."

Her heart skipped three beats. She turned.

Roarke stood shirtless, wearing only his half-buttoned breeches. He bore no weapon, no knife, no musket, no loaded pistol, and no defense whatsoever. He stood in the foyer, his gaze fixed on the British naval officer. She glanced beyond Roarke to where Joachim stood on the stairs, lifting his hands helplessly.

"At least I pick a fight," Leighton said, a ripple of triumph in his voice, "instead of hiding like a coward."

Roarke spread his arms. "I'm not hiding."

"Because I've trapped you. Tell me, do the stripes I left on your back still sting?"

"No more than when you first lay them upon me. I nearly forgot that you ever wielded a whip."

Leighton's pockmarked face colored. "Bold talk for a condemned man. I did not forget you, pirate."

"I made very sure that you wouldn't."

"You'll hang before the sun sets."

"That leaves hours and hours," Roarke said, "to count who has more friends in Charles Town."

"What friends? The governor himself gave you up." Leighton's nostrils flared. "I should kill you where you stand and save the colony the rope."

"If you shoot him now," she said, stepping out onto her stoop so that the neighbors peeking through their drapes could see her plainly, "you'll have to shoot an innocent woman as well."

Leighton's eyes were as cold and dead as the eyes of a fish. "What a naive little strumpet you have here."

"Careful," Roarke warned, "or you'll feel the sharp edge of her knife."

She stared at the pockmarked captain as boldly as if she did have a dagger hidden among her clothing.

"To the jail it is, then." Leighton stepped back to give way to his soldiers. "I'll take pleasure in the few hours you'll spend in a cell, Cameron. As much as I'll take pleasure in your death in a hangman's noose."

She slapped her hands on the doorjamb to block the approach. "Reconsider, sir. For the health of your soldiers."

Leighton waved her words away. "Push her aside."

"Your men, have they all had smallpox?"

Her words bore more force than the crack of a gun. The first soldier stopped short just at the threshold, and the men behind him stuttered back.

"She's lying, you idiots," Leighton snapped. "Seize him."

The first soldier gave her a terrified, pleading look. She spread a welcoming hand toward Roarke. Roarke tried to stand firm, but he swayed where he stood and his chest gleamed with sweat. His hair was damp where it clung to his temples and brow. His shoulders rose and fell as if he labored to breathe, though he held his jaw tight. His gaze blazed with defiance far greater than his fever.

"Arrest him!" Leighton shoved one of the soldiers. "That's a *direct order.*"

"The warden of the jail will not take him in," the

lead soldier said. "He will not put his guards at risk."

Leighton pulled his sword from the scabbard and knocked the soldier aside. The man fell back and lay motionless on the ground, blood pumping from a head wound.

The rest of the soldiers still hesitated. In the ensuing silence, Leighton's face turned an angry, mottled red. He glared at the men, and he glared at her, and she felt the smoldering heat of his fury.

"Surround this house." Leighton raised the point of the sword in Roarke's direction. "You are hereby quarantined until God determines whether you will die by His hand or mine."

Her whole body shuddered with relief. She and Etienne and Joachim and Roarke would be confined to the house, but this would give Roarke time to recover from whatever fever had seized him during the night. It would give her time to get in touch with Drake or one of Roarke's other men. It would give her an opportunity to contact Governor Blake and the influential men of Charles Town with her adamant denial of Leighton's charges. She could put her ample coin to good use to buy men's loyalties, Etienne's freedom, and to plan her and Roarke's ultimate escape.

She heard Roarke shout *No!* just as a knobby hand seized her arm.

"This woman is hiding a fugitive pirate." Leighton thrust her toward his soldiers. "If I can't arrest you, Cameron, I'll take your whore instead."

CHAPTER TWENTY-EIGHT

Adriana leaned against the wall of the jail and pulled her sweat-soaked shift away from her chest. Leighton had imprisoned her in a cell on the land-side of the fort, thus no sea breezes sifted through the barred window or winnowed through the ill-fitting logs of the Colleton Bastion. Instead, the foul, noxious swamp fumes filled the small room.

She pulled her shift higher, exposing her limbs to whoever cared to glance through the slit in the door. The dirty cotton hung loosely from her shoulders after two weeks of poor rations.

She'd slept in worse places before. She'd gone hungry before. She'd eaten worse food, too. What she couldn't bear were two weeks starved of information from the outside world. Her only human contact was the jail keeper who arrived once a day to deliver her rations. He took her old tray and slipped the new one through the opening at the bottom of the door, then rushed out of the bastion each time she addressed him. The only thing she knew for sure, from the fragments of whispers she caught as people passed below the window of her cell, was that smallpox was sweeping through Charles Town again.

She buried the heels of her hands into her eyes to stop her thoughts from spinning. Always, always, her heart whispered, *Roarke.*

When she heard the scrape of the bastion's outer door opening, she shot to her feet. She saw the scarlet cloak of Captain Leighton as the door swung open.

He looked her up and down from over the lace edge of the linen pressed to his nose. "Wallowing like a pig in your own refuse, I see."

She couldn't help herself. "You, of course, would be familiar with the stench."

"I see your condition hasn't humbled you."

"Was that your intent, Leighton? To humble a woman?"

"I don't treat traitors with any preference, even if they happen to be of the gentler sex."

"To an innocent woman imprisoned for a crime she did not commit, shame falls upon her captors."

"As a pirate's wench, you clearly don't understand the way our justice works."

"The way *your* justice works."

"I am an English naval captain on English land," he snapped. "I *am* justice."

She curled her hands into fists until her long,

jagged fingernails bit into the skin of her palms. She couldn't refute that he spoke the truth. Half the pirates she'd known in her life had once been members of the British Navy. They bore the scars of the justice meted out by men like the one standing before her. They'd escaped and become outlaws rather than live under that tyranny.

Now she was trapped within it.

"English law," she said, "doesn't prevent me from having visitors, or obtaining counsel for my defense." She jerked a chin toward the door, behind which the jail keeper lurked. "Yet when I request what any prisoner deserves, my jailor acts as if I have smallpox, and that I can transmit it with a single word."

"Perhaps you can spread the disease. Everyone knows that you have enjoyed carnal delights with a smallpox victim."

Victim.

She caught her own gasp. She had been waiting for word—any word at all. Roarke had been feverish when she'd left him, a certain sign of the start of the disease. If Roarke had recovered, Leighton would have arrested him and then gleefully informed her. Since she'd heard no word, she'd assumed that Roarke was still suffering in her home with Joachim, who'd already had smallpox, and Etienne, who had not.

Victim.

"Ah," Leighton said, drawing out the word. "I

was beginning to think you were incapable of shame."

She could not speak though words gathered pressure in her throat. She batted away mosquitos and told herself that Roarke was not dead. Leighton's silence on the matter was his twisted way of making her think so.

"Maybe now you understand," he said, "that my importance in Charles Town is not imaginary. You'll know it in truth when you sit in the court of Vice Admiralty for your trial."

The word *trial* needled through her thickening cloud of worry. Intellectually, she knew what he had just said should make her knees quake, but right now it had no more effect than the pinch of a bug bite.

"What charges," she asked, "did you create to convince the governor to put me to trial?"

"I didn't have to create any, my dear." He wandered further away from her slop bucket and more toward the window. "A factor by the name of Elsworth supplied enough information to charge you with a great deal of criminal behavior."

Of course. Elsworth had hated his dependence upon her from the very first day. With a little encouragement, he probably happily supplied false documents to implicate her in some forbidden-on-paper business with pirates. Her imprisonment meant he would be free of his debt to her.

Leighton said, "I see you do not deny my charges."

"I do deny them." They meant nothing to her

while her mind loped and twisted and flexed, trying to justify the word *victim* in any way but the most obvious. "I did all my business through Elsworth, forbidden as I am to do it myself, as a woman and French. If he incriminates me, he incriminates himself."

"His name is not on those papers."

"There's the proof of falsification. He is a man of known questionable character."

"As are you, my dear."

He gave her an oily, condescending smile. She hated that smile. She hated this man. She hated that he held back the news she most wanted to hear. She could see in his eyes that he was waiting for her to ask. To beg was to cede to him the power that he wanted most to hold over her. To ask was to invite the answer she feared.

She had a single advantage over him and so she used it. "You are unfamiliar with this colony, aren't you, Captain Leighton?"

"It is full of good British subjects who will bow to the laws of King William III."

"Indeed, you are *quite* new to the Carolinas."

Annoyance rippled across his face. "I assure you, the Vice Admiralty court follows English law."

"But the men who sit upon it are Carolinians." She lifted one brow. "Nicholas Trott will be the man whose duty it will be to prosecute me, yes?"

"Your questionable charms cannot blind a man to the law."

"My charms, as you put it, won't be necessary." She shrugged a shoulder and the loose sleeve slipped off and fell against her upper arm. "There has never been a piracy conviction in Charles Town. Never. Despite all of England's attempts to have the Jamaican piracy laws enforced here, the Carolina Assembly has never put those suggestions into law—"

"I'm here to change that."

"And you think that the first pirate conviction from their court will be against a helpless woman?"

She settled her face into a mask of innocent docility and watched the way he breathed through the linen, a slow but furious intake of breath. His free hand curled into a fist by his side.

"Most harlots can play the innocent, when it serves them," he said. "Play if you must, it'll serve my purpose all the same."

"Come, come. You know my friends will see me released before the trial date is ever set."

"Your friends have abandoned you." Leighton turned on one heel and strode toward the door. "You've been shunned like a leper in your own town."

"There is one man who will never abandon me—"

"Your pirate lover?"

Her heart stopped. A strange pressure filled her head. Black spots began to wink before her eyes.

"He left you to rot in this prison." Leighton turned on her at the cell door with a light gleaming in his eye. "He abandoned you and your charms on the day he escaped quarantine."

She heard one word.

Escaped.

Her voice rushed out, "He's alive?"

Leighton's smile dimmed. "Yes, he's alive, from what my men could see by the tails of his shirt flapping."

She fell to her knees to the slimy stone floor with a force that drew blood and would leave bruises.

He's alive.

"Mark me, woman. I haven't lost my prize yet." He bared his teeth as he spoke. "You'd better pray he comes sniffing back for you. If he doesn't, you'll soon swing on a scaffold in his place."

CHAPTER TWENTY-NINE

Roarke would not abandon her.

He would come for her.

She knew he would.

She prepared herself as if, at any moment, he would burst through the cell door. To keep up her strength, she ate every rancid spoonful of watery soup and plucked the weevils out of the stale bread so she could eat it. She kept aside some water to wash her face. She ran her fingers through her hair until she'd combed it free of knots, and then wove it in a tight plait to keep it out of her eyes. She walked in circles in the cell to keep her legs strong. Whether he broke into the prison, or seized her on the way to trial, she needed to be ready to run.

Meanwhile, a little voice whispered in her heart.

Two weeks he's been gone.

A day went by, and then another. Leighton did

not visit, and the guard never spoke. She hovered beneath the window, straining her ears to catch the conversation of the folks who passed beneath, but she heard nothing but whispers. Once, when she sensed a larger group approaching, she dug her fingers into the mortar between the stones and climbed the wall until she could seize the iron bars. Hanging there with her cheek pressed against the damp wall, she held her breath to better hear their conversation, but they marched by as silent as ghosts.

Two weeks and two days he's been gone.

Her thoughts ran wild. She should have asked Leighton more questions. How had Roarke escaped with the house surrounded by soldiers? Had he bribed those men with the fear of Leighton in their eyes? If he had stumbled out the back door covered in sores the men would have shot him dead, and with reason. Was it smallpox that had laid him so low, or was it only the ague or swamp fever? Did he escape only to collapse somewhere? Was he still there now, far from help, ailing amid the reeds, alone? Even now he could be—

No.

Roarke was *not* dead. Her heart still beat, and so his heart must still be beating. Their one night together had bound them as surely as if they were bound by rope. It was a binding as strong as promises or public vows. His presence was like a warm ghost in the room. His voice whispering her name was a lullaby she heard before sleep every night. She still felt his touch like a tingling pressure upon her skin. He was coming for her. She felt his urgency as if she inhabited his thoughts.

She remembered that he had friends in the backcountry, in places too dangerous for Leighton's soldiers to search. Roarke would have gone straight to those pirates for help. He would recover among them, learn of Leighton's intent, and then muster what aide he could to come to her rescue.

That was the reason for this silence, this delay, this torture. Roarke was recovering and making a plan.

Meanwhile, the little voice still whispered in her heart.

Three weeks, and still he's gone.

On the twenty-seventh day of her imprisonment, Adriana woke coughing.

Her throat stung. She struggled out of the haze of sleep. She reached blindly for the water jug she kept by the pallet. She tilted it upside down, but not a drop slipped out to wet her lips. She clattered it to the flagstones, still coughing. She became aware of a haze in the room, a strange taste in her mouth, and as she blinked her eyes open she realized that the room billowed with smoke.

Fire!

She stumbled to her feet. Flickering orange light sifted through the window, casting ominous shadows through the room. She banged on the door and called out for the jail keeper. She peered through the slit but saw nothing but darkness broken by a fire-lit haze. She pushed against the planks but the door was as tightly bolted as it had always been. She pushed harder, praying that the bolt would give. Then she balled her hands into fists and pummeled the surface, ignoring the slivers of wood that pierced her hands.

A coughing fit seized her. She held her hand over her mouth until it passed. She looked at her palm and saw speckles of soot.

She sank low against the door. The room was hot as midday, thought she could tell it was still night. She noticed that the smoke was seeping through the cracks in the city-side wall of the bastion more thickly than anywhere else. She could hear raised voices outside, panicked voices. People were alert. They were trying to put out the fire.

She glimpsed her dirty dinner bowl by the floor. Her jail keeper hadn't come to fetch it yet. He knew that was his duty. He would come. He would release her, maybe with guards, because he knew she was his charge.

He would not leave her here.

Leighton's angry face rose in her mind, but she rejected the idea that Leighton would abandon her to her fate. He was spiteful—he needed her alive as bait to catch Roarke. Leighton craved a public spectacle. He wouldn't let her suffocate or burn...unless during these last weeks he faced resistance from what friends she had in Charles Town, the very same resistance she'd warned him about.

She shook herself. Speculation was useless. She had to make a plan. She lifted the hem of her chemise and pressed the linen against her face to work as a filter, then scrambled to the outer wall opposite the one belching smoke. The haze was growing denser. The temperature in the room was rising.

Think. Think.

Then she heard an eerie whistling and felt a pull of air. By instinct she curled herself into a ball just before the explosion.

The walls of the bastion shuddered. The vibrations rocked her bones. She braced herself for flying shrapnel and piercing slivers of wood but the walls held firm. She buried her face in her hem as one blast followed another. Shock passed through her mind when she realized that—like any military fort—this bastion held barrels full of cannon powder.

She covered her ears and told herself that at least death would come quick. It would be like the crash of the fire ship against the ramparts of Saint-Malo, she told herself, as another explosion made the flagstones rattle out of their mortar. She remembered the brilliance of the inferno as the exploding ship spewed fire into the heavens.

She'd first met Roarke that night, on those cold, windy ramparts. He'd shielded her from the falling debris with his own body. He hadn't even known her then. She was nothing more than a dirty street urchin giving him trouble for his English accent. She was hardly worth his attention, never mind the risk to his own life he took when he chose to protect hers.

He had always been protecting her.

Mortar shuddered and shot up from the floor, but her ears rang so loudly that she hardly heard the explosions anymore. She closed her eyes and lost herself in the memory of Roarke kissing her. She remembered the gentleness of his touch as he ran his fingers over her body. She sank into the lullaby of his voice murmuring her name.

He loved her.

He'd told her as much.

Dust filled the air after another explosion, closer than the rest. Debris rained down upon her and suddenly the room filled with light. When the ash and the glowing hail stopped, she raised her face to see a figure framed in a fiery glow.

CHAPTER THIRTY

At the sight of her, Roarke fell to his knees. *Alive. She's alive.*

Relief sang through him. He said her name, and then grasped her to pull her close. It was like hugging a bag of bones.

Drake ducked in through the broken door. "This place is full of powder kegs. We've got to go *now*."

Roarke lifted her. He was not as strong as he should be, but she weighed nothing in his arms. Violently kicking away debris from the splintered door, he followed Drake through the thick smoke.

Chaos reigned in Charles Town. In the street, women coaxed blindfolded horses in the opposite direction of the fire, while men, rolling up their sleeves, raced toward the blacksmith's shop, from which the fire had spread to the ramparts. Soldiers out of uniform flooded in and out of the far door of the bastion, clutching firearms and rolling barrels of gunpowder into isolated piles. The glow of the fire cast flickering shadows. He and Drake didn't bother using those shadows, as they had as they'd first approached the jail, because now no one paid any attention to two men running, one with a woman limp in his arms.

She started to cough, jerking in spasms against his chest.

"Stop ahead, Drake."

The harsh, ragged sound of her coughing was music to his ears because it meant that she was alive, but it worried him as well. Drake veered off the dirt road between two houses. Roarke settled her against the wooden wall. He pushed her tangled hair off her brow as he spoke to Drake over his shoulder. "There should be a water pump behind one of these houses."

His friend set off. Roarke laid her head back against the house to open her throat as widely as possible. Her breathing wheezed in her chest. He needed to get her away from all this smoke so she could clear her lungs.

Her dark lashes fluttered against her cheeks. She ran her tongue over her parched lips. "You," she said, "have a strange habit of returning from the dead."

Laughter caught in his throat. He seized her face. Soot stained her cheeks and her shift sagged over her shoulders, but to his eyes, this woman had never looked so beautiful. Despite her labored breathing, Roarke kissed those dry, parched lips.

He stopped kissing her only when he heard Drake coming down the alley, sloshing water over the ground.

"Drink," Roarke said. He seized the pail and raised it to her lips.

She needed no encouragement. Water dribbled out of her mouth, over her chin, and in rivulets down her chest. She stopped only to breathe, and then set her lips to the edge of the pail again. She seemed to gain strength with each gulp, sitting up straight and grasping the pail herself.

She coughed suddenly, splattering water. He put the pail down and took some measure of relief from the fact that her hoarseness was abiding. When she finally lay back, he sensed that she'd be all right.

She brushed her fingers over the short bristle of his beard, and whispered, "I knew you would come for me."

Roarke was glad that Drake had wandered to the street end of the alley and did not see the way Roarke tumbled from a crouch to his backside. It would not do to have his second-in-command see his captain knocked off balance by a woman's soft words.

"Always," he mustered, his throat dry from more than just smoke. "Always, my love."

He pulled her into his arms again, close enough so he could feel her heart beating in her chest.

Another explosion shattered the night. His ears popped with the force of it. The sky erupted in a red-orange glow. Smoking pieces of wood clattered on the rooftops and skittered across the street, some landing, still glowing, in the alley where he pressed her against the wall.

"They missed a few kegs of powder," Drake said drily, wincing as a smoking piece of wood struck him in the shoulder. He brushed it off. "Leighton will have to pull his men from the waterfront now."

Roarke understood the unspoken. If Leighton pulled his men from the waterfront, then they wouldn't have to take the long, dark route overland to cross to where the *Neptune* waited, a route that would slow down the healthiest of men, never mind a woman who looked like she hadn't eaten in a week. If they could make it to the waterfront, they could steal a boat and row their way around while Adriana rested inside.

Roarke flexed his hands over her shoulders. "Can you walk?"

"I can do better," she said, pushing away from the wall. "I can run."

Watching her struggle to her feet gave rise to two equally strong emotions within him: A fierce pride for her grit, cut with a grounding humility that such a woman would find him worthy of her.

Later, once they were safe, he would tell her all of this. He gave Drake a nod and they plunged into a street still raining with ash. Townsfolk raced away from the fire, patting embers from their own clothes. Dogs darted through the streets. The scent of burning cypress grew stronger. By the fortification gates, a cluster of townspeople were trying to reform a water brigade, shouting to others to gather the buckets abandoned in the square.

Drake's pace stuttered as they stumbled into that open square. They all came to a sudden stop. Roarke reached back and drew Adriana behind him. He knew she'd seen sights like this on the deck of many a pirate ship, but he would spare her if he could. He didn't much like the British Navy, but it gave him no pleasure to see young soldiers speared by wooden slivers, men sprawled and broken like dolls, and pieces of bodies caught in the eaves.

"They were blown here," Drake said quietly. "From the last explosion."

"Probably trying to save the powder."

Roarke wasn't sure what drew his eye to that one particular body. It was as covered with blood as the rest. No sword hung from the officer's missing belt, and his clothes were torn and charred. Maybe he noticed because the smoky glow of the fire gleamed on one epaulet. Or maybe Roarke just knew all too well the set of that rigid, unmoving, pockmarked jaw.

His old enemy was dead. The man who had imprisoned and half-starved Adriana now lay broken in a colonial square. Adam was avenged. Roarke waited for the surge of triumph he'd always anticipated, but it never came.

Leighton held no power over him anymore.

"There'll be a crowd on the beach," Drake said, eyeing the swarm of people racing out of the fortification gates. "Stealing a boat won't be easy."

"It doesn't matter." Roarke drew Adriana against his side. "We don't have to hurry anymore."

Adriana stood at the stern of the *Neptune,* watching the glow over Charles Town as the ship made its way past Hog Island. With the ship almost at full sail, Roarke left his command. She breathed a sigh of relief as he slipped his arms around her and laid his chin on her head.

She hugged his arms against her midriff. "We're safe."

"Are you feeling any better?"

She felt as if she'd been pounded against rocks like dirty linen, but he didn't need to know that. "I'm hungry," she ventured. "I could eat a horse."

"I've already sent the cook to heat up a meal for both of us."

She closed her eyes and settled into the warm circle of his arms. Every bruise and scrape on her battered body throbbed. Despite the ache, a rippling sense of anticipation seized her when she felt the rocking of the ship shift from the calm waters of the inlet to the rhythmic sway of the open sea.

"I was so worried about you." She watched the glow in the distance dim. "Leighton told me nothing, except that he was using me for bait to catch you."

"You were strong bait. Leighton would have succeeded a dozen times over, if I'd had my way.

Drake put a stop to every reckless effort I made to rescue you. That man has a vicious left hook."

She turned in his arms to look at him more closely, wondering if, because of the smoke and haze and the thrill of seeing him, she'd only imagined the smoothness of his cheek. "Your fever wasn't from smallpox."

"No." He shrugged. "Some kind of swamp fever." He captured the hand she'd laid on his chest and kissed her knuckles. "It passed in less than a week, but left me shaky. By the time I escaped quarantine, Leighton had every entrance to Charles Town guarded and he'd put a phalanx of soldiers around the jail to guard you. He shifted the watches on the ramparts every four hours so they would stay alert."

"But how did you escape from quarantine in the first place? When Leighton dragged me to jail, he left six soldiers picketed around the house."

He blew out a long sigh and found some interest in the horizon beyond her head. "That was someone else's stupid, reckless doing."

Her heart did a little skitter. She said, "Joachim?" though she already suspected she was wrong.

"Joachim escaped later," he said. "To his freedom, I suspect."

Good. The voice in her heart spoke firm. *Good.*

"But that Gaillard boy of yours," he continued, "nearly got all of us killed."

"Etienne." Her heart did a little skip-beat.

"Had I any real strength in me when he proposed the escape, he'd have learned what an uppercut to the jaw felt like. But while half-dead from fever, I could only argue with him over the map of Charles Town he'd found on your table."

She remembered that map. She'd purchased a copy because she'd been looking to buy a warehouse. She needed someplace where she could store all the cargo from the ships coming in and out of the bay.

All those concerns now up in smoke.

"Once I regained some strength, your Frenchman brought me to the map and showed me a route between houses that led to the fortification walls. He knew of a hole dug deep enough under one part of the fortifications for a man with a bag of goods to smuggle through."

"Smuggle?!"

"Apparently your young swain earned some cash slipping goods through the swamp. He knew the lay of the land well enough to warn me that the water was high this season."

Her thoughts tumbled over one another. All those trips to Charles Town... Did his father know, and approve?

"Once I was beyond the fortifications," Roarke continued, "he told me to find my men and my ship. I was sure Leighton had seized both, but your friend knew otherwise."

"How?"

Roarke hesitated. In the dim light of the evening,

starlight gleamed on the planes of his face. "After Etienne left your house that night, he set out to confront me. Itching for a fight, I suspect."

Guilt was a sharp needle plunging deep.

"But as you know, I was not in my lodgings. So he rowed out to the *Neptune* to confront me."

"And found Drake," she said softly. "Who figured out that something was terribly wrong."

"Your boy told me that he saw the *Neptune* raise sail as soon as he rowed back to shore."

She sighed. Poor Etienne. It was one thing for him to know that she loved Roarke. It was another thing for him to come to the disheartening conclusion that Roarke had spent the night in her arms.

"But the soldiers around the house," she said, plowing forward, "how did you get past them? Did you bribe them?"

"Your foolish Frenchman made himself the bait."

She caught her breath.

"He's about my height, he has dark hair, and he was wearing my clothes. The soldiers didn't know he was in the house. He said that if he were to run out the back door in the middle of the night, those soldiers could only assume the escapee was me."

Her mind flashed with the memory of Etienne laughing as he raced her through the woods around the Santee, tearing ahead of her, the dirty bottoms of his feet flashing, his linen shirt billowing around his slim frame, his silhouette weaving through the shadows of trees, his body springing up and soaring over a fallen trunk, his laughter fading as he disappeared, ghostly, deep in the backwoods.

"The soldiers," she stuttered, "had muskets."

"Settled across their legs as they dozed."

"But Etienne only had moments—"

"—seconds—"

"—before they rose up and aimed."

"The damned fool bolted out of the house so fast that the soldiers didn't get a chance to fire off a shot. By the time the soldiers mustered and gave chase, he had a good start. As soon as the soldiers dispersed, Joachim and I slipped out and went our separate ways."

Reckless, brave, gentle Etienne! She'd never known him as well as she thought she did. But he'd proven that his love was so true that he was willing to risk his own life to save the life of the man she loved.

She hoped someday to see him again. She hoped to come upon him living in a whitewashed house in the deep woods with a lovely Huguenot wife and surrounded by a dozen dark-haired, doe-eyed children.

She curled back into Roarke's embrace, pulling his arm around her so they both could see the glow of Charles Town burning.

"Did you set the fire," she asked, "to create a distraction?"

"No, although we considered it. We considered everything, even digging a tunnel."

"Through a swamp?"

"I would have done it with my bare hands. Every day I woke up sure we'd get news from our outposts that Leighton had ordered the trial to begin. But apparently, friends in the city objected to your arrest."

She raised her brows. Leighton had made her think that she had been abandoned by everyone.

She was far more powerful than she'd ever thought.

"When one of our men came to tell us about the fire," Roarke said, "I convinced Drake to take advantage of the chaos to slip into the city."

"And you called Etienne a reckless fool."

"Twenty-seven days you languished in that dirty jail cell. I wouldn't allow it one day more."

His grip tightened around her. She turned her face so her cheek pressed against his warm chest. She heard his heart beating fast as his hands slid up and down her arms, as if he couldn't find a good enough grip.

"It's my fault," he said into her hair, "that you've lost everything you've worked for. I can't even ask you to forgive me."

She thought about her fine garden, the silks folded amid lavender in the chest at the foot of her bed, and the bag of coins hidden under the loose floorboard in the parlor. She thought about the map on her dining room table and the plans she'd left behind.

And, strangely, she thought of Joaquim, his dark

face bright with silent laughter, as he finally ran unfettered through the backwoods.

"Let it all go up in smoke," she whispered, curling her hand around his arm. "My real fortune is with you."

EPILOGUE

From the crow's nest Adriana shaded her eyes as she gazed over the flat green land spread out beyond the bow of the ship.

"So many estuaries," she murmured to Roarke, as the ship tacked its way through one of the winding silver rivers. "We've been wandering this web for hours. Are you sure the pilot knows where he's going?"

"He's native, he knows the land." Roarke placed his forearms against the edge of the crow's nest as he squinted at the unbroken wilderness. "The fact that he speaks French is proof that he knows the backwoodsmen who've settled here."

She gazed over the new country with a flutter of excitement. The gentle wake of the passing of their ship startled a flock of large white birds. Strange trees with exposed roots gripped the shallow shore. Even from the crow's nest she spied ripples beneath the water, proof that it teemed with life.

Adriana breathed in the sultry air. While recovering in the swamplands, Roarke had heard from Carolinian traders returning from the backcountry of how the French were settling at the mouth of a river called the Mississippi. A whole new world stretched beyond the Carolina backcountry, a world far away from the laws that gave no quarter to people struggling to build a better life. What greater refuge for an English pirate who once fought for the French, and a Frenchwoman who had escaped English justice?

"It reminds me of the Santee," she said, seeing in her mind's eye these wetlands turned into rice fields. "Or how Charles Town must have been before the English cleared the island."

"It's a frontier where the natives still rule," he said. "What men have come are the kind who trade with the tribes, marry the native women, use their guns only for game, and don't bother with forts or jails."

"No rules," she murmured, "no unjust law."

"A new start." He pressed his lips against her hair. "Freedom."

Freedom.

The word settled into her heart. Everything she'd done up to this point in her life—dressing as a boy to keep herself safe, signing on to a merchant ship to earn a skill and have coin, taking up with the pirates, moving from the safety of the Santee to Charles Town in order to gather a small fortune—had all been done for one simple reason: So that she could live safely, independently, and *free*.

Now Roarke ran a warm hand down her back, distracting her from her thoughts. He ventured lower, nudging away the waistband of her breeches so he could slide his palm over the curve of her backside. She smiled a secret smile. She knew he loved when she wore breeches, especially now that she was enough of a woman to fill them out.

She tilted her head to meet the brightness of his gaze, more green than gray today because of the reflection of the land around them. The onshore breeze sent tendrils of his dark hair dancing around his face. A smile played around his lips, mischievous and knowing, for they'd only just finished dressing. They had shucked their clothes as soon as they'd climbed to the crow's nest, taking advantage of a moment of intense and delicious privacy in a place where she could cry out her pleasure without worrying that the sailors could hear her.

The suntanned crinkles at the corners of his eyes deepened. Words weren't always necessary between them anymore, especially when it came to this. Her pulse jumped as he lowered his lips toward hers.

A shout of *Captain* rose up from below just as Roarke gently sucked her lower lip into his mouth. He smiled and pulled back from the kiss. Pressing his forehead against hers, he grinned ruefully. They were all too familiar with such interruptions.

He leaned away from her and shouted, "What is it, Drake?"

"A settlement!"

The rail dug into her side as she strained to see what Drake was pointing at. From on high, it looked like nothing but a wet thicket of willows and dwarf palmetto trees, but as the ship tacked closer to shore she glimpsed, camouflaged by the shadows, a cluster of thatched-roof huts amid what looked like a small native village. A few people had started to gather, a motley group of backwoodsmen in breeches and linen shirts, natives in loincloths, and a few bearded trappers dressed head-to-toe in skins.

Roarke clasped her hand.

They were finally home.

*****

ABOUT THE AUTHOR

Lisa Ann Verge is the critically acclaimed RITA-nominated author of eighteen novels that have been published worldwide and translated into as many languages.

She started her career writing sexy, adventurous romance about hot men and dangerous women and now she also writes life-affirming women's fiction under the name **Lisa Verge Higgins.**

Lisa is a five-time finalist in Romantic Times' book awards, her novels have won the Golden Leaf and the Bean Pot, and twice she has cracked Barnes & Noble's General Fiction Forum's top twenty books of the year. She currently lives in New Jersey with her husband and their three daughters, who never fail to make life interesting

To find out more, check out her website at www.lisaannverge.com

www.ingramcontent.com/pod-product-compliance
Lightning Source LLC
Chambersburg PA
CBHW071230190726
48292CB00007B/2222